The Lowering Days

The Lowering Days

A Novel

⌄ ⌄ ⌄ ⌄ ⌄

GREGORY BROWN

HARPER

An Imprint of HarperCollins*Publishers*

THE LOWERING DAYS. Copyright © 2021 by Gregory Brown. All rights reserved. Printed in the United States of America. No part of this book may be used or reproduced in any manner whatsoever without written permission except in the case of brief quotations embodied in critical articles and reviews. For information, address HarperCollins Publishers, 195 Broadway, New York, NY 10007.

Han-shan, "Cold Mountain Poem 16." Copyright © 1958, 1959, 1965 by Gary Snyder, from *Riprap and Cold Mountain Poems*. Reprinted by permission of Counterpoint Press.

HarperCollins books may be purchased for educational, business, or sales promotional use. For information, please email the Special Markets Department at SPsales@harpercollins.com.

FIRST EDITION

Designed by Kyle O'Brien

Library of Congress Cataloging-in-Publication Data has been applied for.

ISBN 978-0-06-299413-4

21 22 23 24 25   LSC   10 9 8 7 6 5 4 3 2 1

For my parents, and in memory of my
grandmothers and grandfathers

Men ask the way to Cold Mountain
Cold Mountain: there's no through trail.
In summer, ice doesn't melt
The rising sun blurs in swirling fog.
How did I make it?
My heart's not the same as yours.
If your heart was like mine
You'd get it and be right here.

—Han-shan

Another time in a lowering and sad evening, being alone in the field, when all things were dead and quiet, a certain want and horror fell upon me, beyond imagination. The unprofitableness and silence of the place dissatisfied me; its wideness terrified me; from the utmost ends of the earth fears surrounded me. How did I know but dangers might suddenly arise from the East, and invade me from the unknown regions beyond the seas? I was a weak and little child, and had forgotten there was a man alive in the earth.

—Thomas Traherne, *Centuries of Meditations*

The Lowering Days

What's the story of this place? This valley? This river? This bay?

The story of this place? The story of this place is simple. The men take the women away, and the sea takes the men away.

But how do the men take the women away?

Love. Fists. Knives. Pregnancies. Money. Guns. Words. Love.

How does the sea take the men away?

Very, very easily. Just a little swoop of wind, the leap of a single mischievous wave. It's like taking a breath. That's all freedom ever is: the ability to breathe. Try it. Open your lips. Press your tongue down against your back teeth. Close your eyes. Yes, sugar, just like that. Now take a breath. Make it small. Think of a newborn's lungs, no bigger than a clementine. Now take that breath. You feel it? Of course you do. There's another man gone by the sea.

And what does the land do through all this?

It cries out for justice.

Part I

One

W E WERE WILD KIDS, ALWAYS covered in river dirt and sweat. In every corner of the house one could see our passing: ochre footprints slapped across the kitchen floorboards, sand spilling from our beds, mud from our hands smeared along cabinets and door handles and the hulls of the miraculous boats our father built. With the windows thrown open in summer to the river and the calling of owls and coyotes and wood frogs, it sometimes felt like the line between the world inside and the world outside vanished. Perhaps that's why my brothers and I never questioned our parents' ability to summon each other back from short and great distances. It wasn't until I was grown that I realized this was unusual at all. Certain cultures believe a song or chant voiced in one place can be heard in another place many miles away. Passamaquoddy people talk of *motewolon*, people with extraordinary spiritual powers who can hear for great distances. All these years later I am still convinced my parents carried some similar summoning magic. And while I don't have the language for such a thing, I know only this: love should always be able to call love back. That seemed simple enough to us as children.

My name is David Almerin Ames. The other day I woke with a sudden need to make sense of old things before more new things came on. I guess this isn't so unusual. By giving myself permission to freely survey the lives I grew up among, moving from one household into another much like the river that surrounded us, I'm hoping to stand in the flow of history without being crushed by its weight. I'm a doctor now, and while one might think I'd seen enough absurdity to throw my hands up to time and chance, the secret curse of being a caregiver is the hunger for control. Every malady has a potential cure if you get to it soon enough. So it is that I've often thought about what could have been stopped had someone gotten between my father and Lyman Creel when I was a teenager. But I'm talking now of mystical things, of surreal places and impossible tasks. To begin the right way, we must start with the Penobscot.

The Penobscot River rises from the mountains and lakes of northern Maine and runs down the state like a spine. It shares its name with the Penobscot people, who were the original inhabitants of the river and ancestors of the waters. The Penobscot Nation, along with the Micmac, Maliseet, and Passamaquoddy tribes were known collectively as the Wabanaki, the people of the dawnland. For thousands of years they'd been the first people here. Until, as prophesized in the visions of elders, ships filled with white faces came from the east, sowing impossible sadness. It was in the east as well that healing was supposed to start. The Penobscots ran their nation from a mile-long island rooted in the river, and their ancestral territory included the entire Penobscot watershed: the river, its water, its banks, its islands, and Penobscot Bay, which, over time, had become my family's home as well.

Thirty miles downriver from the tribe's island reservation, a small tributary took one final detour through the woods and around our house before rushing into the sea. As kids we called this artery the Little River because it felt like ours. Of course it wasn't, but we were children and didn't yet understand the danger of thinking land was something one could own. Down in the woods a narrow peninsula jutted into the waters. My parents, Arnoux and Falon, built a long dirt drive out to the peninsula's end, then cleared just enough timber to frame a small post-and-beam cape. Salt pulled down from the nearby sea permanently colored the dirt, and the drive was as hooked and white as a human rib bone. Dogs we owned spent hours out there licking the earth. During big storms we thought the entire peninsula would wash away, and we thought about retreating to town to stay with friends or relatives. Stubborn, stalwart, deeply rooted to the bottom of the river, the land remained, and so did we.

My father made it through his war by dreaming of boats. He grew up downeast, in Passamaquoddy territory, the orphaned son of a French mother, who ended her life by driving her father's car off a windy cliff hanging out over the Atlantic, and a part Passamaquoddy and part Welsh father he never knew. Unable to save his parents, he enlisted in the navy and went to Vietnam to save others as a combat medevac pilot in Quang Tri. When he wasn't field-cauterizing bullet wounds or pressing his fingers down around severed arteries, he drew sketches of boats and mailed them to American magazines. Gaff-rigged ketch by A. Ames. Catboat by A. Ames. Sailing dinghy by A. Ames. I still have some of those sketches, and when I run my fingers along their lines, I feel as though I am reaching up and tracing the lines of my father's face as I knew them as a child. Established boat designers began to notice those sketches as well—here was a kid who had an eye, who harbored interesting ideas, here was one to watch—but it wasn't until my father found the bay and my mother, falling deeply in love with both, that he began to build.

In the evenings, my father liked to sit outside and tell us how some nights after we fell asleep he closed his eyes, left his body, and slid into the river. Becoming a fish. Becoming a bird. Becoming mist. Becoming driftwood. Transformed, he claimed he would float the final stretch of the Little River, spill into the Atlantic, and cross the sea. Other nights he would go north, moving up the Penobscot, turning into a bird or a flying fish when he came to the four massive, water-blocking dams built at the height of the Maine lumber boom to provide hydroelectric power to the tanneries, saw mills, and paper mills. He would travel until he reached the headwaters and saw the base of Ktahdin, "the greatest mountain," a sacred place where the earth mother reached into the sky and the Great Spirit was not so far away. "Climb the mountain, but never to the top," he would tell us. "Pamola doesn't want you there." According to Penobscot legend, Pamola, a ferocious spirit bird, lived at the summit. It was Pamola who caused the cold winds and blinding snowstorms that swallowed the state. That my father's stories were impossible didn't matter. When he spoke, time seemed to slow, and we all believed he could build alternate realities with his voice. But perhaps all young sons think that about their fathers, whether good or flawed men. Other nights my mother sat beside him listening to the lapping river in the green dark with Skip James or Bessie Smith records playing back in the house. Her stories were about the strange things she and her younger brother, Reggie, had seen out among the country of the lower Penobscot Valley when they were kids, and to say our family, though small in number, was a family of storytellers would be true.

THEIR FIRST SPRING ON THE river, my parents woke each morning to the sound of a pair of bonded tiger owls calling about the forest. Arnoux tried for weeks to spot the owls in the hemlocks but never could. Falon was scared to look up at the trees at all. Suspicious of sentiment in general, she consumed stories and myths without emotion. Show her a great, gushing romantic, and she'd show you a great dummy blind to the real world. The trick, she thought, was balancing one's wonder with one's objectivity. She held little hope for Arnoux in this regard. Some people weren't meant to simultaneously feel a thing and study a thing. Perhaps that was why she loved him so hard. He was so unabashedly filled with magical thinking and pure masculinity. She should have known better. How many women had been killed by that exact combination?

It wasn't the escapist potential of stories that obsessed her, but how a tale united people in meaning-making—if you paid attention, you could see the entire unfolding of human history in a story. The owls, though, were something else. She couldn't find the narrative in them, and because of this she couldn't approach them with any sort of rationality. So their beauty filled her mornings with a combination of curiosity and crippling alarm.

The solution to her unease, Falon realized, was to walk, outpacing and exhausting her dread. The house they were building on the river peninsula was nearly finished. Arnoux would come home from the library or the grocery store or the hardware store to find Falon, edgy with excitement, waiting for him in the yard holding a canvas tote of sandwiches and a dented green thermos filled with coffee. "Now?" he would say, his eyebrows lifting. She would nod. "Now."

More like pilgrimages, these walks would often last the entire day, and I grew up with the idea of my parents having mapped the entire world by foot before I was even born. On a hot morning in July they went deep into the forest. My mother was seven months pregnant then with my older brother Simon and completely uninterested in her doctor's advice about resting. As they set out, the forest air was black and cold against their skin. Horseflies swarmed their bodies. They could no longer hear or see the river. After a while, they came to an overgrown logging road and a clearing backed up against tall cliffs. Despite the long banks of shade, the air felt unnaturally warm.

Massive boulders littered the earth here. At the back of the clearing, a fieldstone foundation was attached to a partially collapsed brick chimney. Inside the foundation, a root cellar tunneled deep into the earth. When Falon got down on her knees, poked her head into the opening, and sang John Prine's "Hello in There," Arnoux grabbed her by the shoulders and yanked her back. She toppled over and then scrambled to her feet, cradling her stomach. The blend of anger and laughter she felt rising ended when she saw the sheer terror on her husband's face. It somehow seemed cruel to tell him it was just a hole in the earth, to scold him for being reckless with her body and their child, so instead she said nothing and hugged him for a long time in the ruins of the foundation.

"I'm right here," she whispered. "I was just playing." She was shocked at how long it took Arnoux to stop shaking.

"Odd to leave the chimney." Arnoux cleared his throat as his body finally stilled.

To the west, green pines cradled the sun like a torch. "You can't in good conscience completely dismantle a story," Falon said.

"Maybe not."

"What about that?" She pointed down the slope from the house, where a barn was backed up against the cliff. Maybe twenty feet high at the ridgeline, she estimated. Twelve-foot square sliding door at the front. Enough room for two horses and a tractor. Yellow paint peeling up off the clapboards.

Arnoux shrugged. "Only one way to know."

Inside they found a single-engine Citabria under an oil-stained canvas. The plane was red and white, the chrome spotless, the curved cockpit window unblemished by a single smudge. A narrow arm of dust topped each propeller vane. The remainder of the barn was empty, but the space smelled of warm hay and long-gone horses.

"This was it," Arnoux said.

"What?"

"The thing whoever owned this place loved."

Arnoux eased open the cockpit door. Eight black gauges filled an immaculate yellow-wood dash. There was a center console with a series of push knobs. Two crimson steering yokes shaped like bow saws. The smell was breathtaking: as intoxicating as an old book and as pure as the cleanest sawdust from the finest mast log he believed he would ever fall and shape. When he closed the aircraft door, his hands were shaking. He pulled the canvas back over the plane so every inch of steel was covered, walked to the opposite side of the barn, and sat down in the dusty light with his legs crossed and his hands in his lap.

"You don't want to get in?" Falon was confused. "Don't all boys want to sit in airplanes? Imagine playing bang-bang shoot 'em up or some other bullshit?" She regretted the words as soon as they hit the air. Arnoux never talked with her about his time in Vietnam, but at the dinner table she sometimes noticed one of his hands off to the side, fingertips systematically touching, palm clenching, wrist angling in different directions. She understood that these complex and involuntary motions were an old tic, the ghost of a former version of her husband. Without him even realizing it, those hands she loved so much were again working the controls of a medevac helicopter.

Arnoux closed his eyes, thought about lying down. He didn't understand how he could feel this dizzy, how the pressure in his ears could be this powerful when he was so low to the ground. "We need to go."

Back outside, Falon ducked under rowan trees. Darted behind a boulder. Circled around and tried to jump on Arnoux's back, even with her belly. She wanted Arnoux to join her and be playful, but he was no longer Arnoux. He had slipped out of the present and turned brooding with the simple opening of a plane door. She was used to this behavior in herself, but not in her husband, who may have been a bit mad, but was solid, almost always present, and unfailingly cheerful.

"It's peaceful here." She was standing beside the chimney now. If she touched it, the soot would never wash away.

"You don't think it's spooky? Some guy probably died right here where we're standing."

Falon put her arms around her husband's waist and held him as hard as she could. "Someone has died just about everywhere, Arnoux. That's not news. You're scared."

He nodded. "That barn is immaculate. And the house is a vanished shitheap. Think about that. These things ruin people, they get obsessed."

Falon thought about the place and the life they were building together. Then thought of what they had been before finding each other. She just a town girl who had run away to California for a while to chase some ideal she could never even define. Arnoux, an orphan kid from downeast who joined a war of all things because he wanted to *save* lives. Her wrists and forearms began to ache with the pressure of holding her husband so tightly, but she didn't let go, would not let go until they were far away from this clearing and could again hear the river that signaled home lapping around them. "Be something else," she whispered into his ear. Then she turned his body and moved his hand over her stomach. "Be with us."

By September, the house was finished. In October, Simon was born. After that, my father started going into the draw alone to visit the plane, which he named Reynard, after the red fox trickster of French folklore. At first he sat on the barn floor thinking. Then he opened the plane's door and sat just outside the craft. Finally, he began sitting in the cockpit. Soon after, the occasional wail of an airplane engine echoed up the river.

THAT WINTER A PENOBSCOT LOBSTERMAN traveled down the river to the bay, looking for a better boat. Arnoux had awoken with a feeling that something was shifting. He sat at the kitchen table drinking a constant stream of coffee and growing increasingly convinced that some new direction was under way. Falon rolled her eyes at her husband's optimism. Then a beat-up Dodge truck curled through the trees into sight. A man stepped out and stood outside the small house, scratching at his neck with one callused hand. He looked around at the trees as if taking stock of something.

"I heard you're a boat builder," the man said when Arnoux finally greeted him. "Wooden ones."

The man introduced himself as Moses Jupiter and asked Arnoux if he could build something sleek and practical and planked in rich oak, all for a reasonable price. Arnoux wanted to ask, *Why me?* But he was too terrified this Jupiter character might walk away and there would never be another boat for him to build in his life. "I didn't grow up with any old ways, just what I've learned on my own," Arnoux said.

"Guess your ways will have to be good enough."

Arnoux unleashed a sudden and conspiratorial grin—the one people would remember years later for its power to both disarm and engender camaraderie. "Mr. Jupiter," he said, "I'll build you the boat to beat all boats or turn my hands to a bloody pulp trying."

Rather than alarming Moses, this intensity of phrase seemed to intrigue him. Arnoux ducked back inside the house and came out carrying a sheaf of yellow legal-paper sketches. He started spreading the drawings of boats around on the ground in the half-frozen mud. "These are nothing," he said. "Your boat will embarrass them all."

Moses laughed and set his hand on the younger man's shoulder. "Let's just start with something that floats."

All through December Arnoux sat at a small red desk in an alcove just off the kitchen drawing plans for the boat and for a workshop on the property. Falon sat beside the woodstove in their bedroom holding Simon, still an infant then, and writing short community notices for the nearest local newspaper, then three towns over. Late each afternoon the snap of an ash log drew my father's attention up from the desk, the sound of fire releasing him from his sketches back into the actual world. He reached up and touched the window. Bits of ice gathered under his nails, and he shuddered. He thought of Falon, imagined his lips pressed to her stomach, his lips kissing the undersides of her breasts, his lips tracing the back of her neck as she pushed his hand between her thighs. Desire, a taste like salt. His hands bathing her at night, lathering her stomach, caressing her feet. Her massaging oil into his tired hands. Only when the ash log snapped again did he allow himself to look toward the bedroom. There, framed in the doorway, he saw his wife's bare legs, crossed beneath the opening of her robe. He rose, and went to her through the heat.

Early in the morning on New Year's Day, Moses Jupiter came up through the cold in his coveralls to help Arnoux finish his shop. Falon's brother Reggie was there as well, and together the three men worked for a week in nearly three feet of snow with their breath smoking in the light. With three axes, a couple of chainsaws, and a borrowed skidder, they logged out a small clearing back on the bank of the river. They framed a shed from rough timber. They roofed the structure with salvaged sheets of tin. Watching the men stand against the horizon, Falon thought of horses, of all things—creatures proud, powerful, seemingly eternal, and perhaps a little dense. Horses could be marvelous. But horses could be blinded too.

The finished boat shop sat back among the river birches exactly two hundred yards from the house. A shed with a plywood floor and a propane-fired space heater. Falon's only request had been a single window built into the shop's south wall so it faced the house. The river froze solid that winter. Full-moon tides washed massive cakes of sea ice up into the woods. Each morning, buzzing with the smell of his wife's hair, her body, their bed, with the scent of his newborn son's skin, Arnoux stepped out into the thin winter sunlight and leapt between the cakes as though they were icy footstools, his outstretched arms wheeling for balance. Watching him dance about the snowy woods, Falon felt as though her husband were slipping impossibly far away. It was the longest two hundred yards she had ever imagined. One morning she almost asked him to tie a rope from the shop door back to the house, but then she realized how foolish it sounded. How and when had her life become watching and worrying about a man all day long, a man, no less, who was only six hundred or so feet away?

By early April, the cold was beginning to release the bay. Arnoux was oblivious and giddy with accomplishment. Falon was realizing she couldn't spend another winter entombed inside their house. As their differing realities set in, a stunning twenty-six-foot-long wooden lobster boat emerged from the woods.

For some bizarre, hard-to-fathom reason, my father refused full payment for that first boat, taking about half what the job was worth. He talked about how it didn't seem right to be paid for something that brought him so much pleasure. He talked about owing Moses a debt that didn't concern money, the debt of one's beginnings. "That feeling you get when building a thing," he said, "that should be enough."

"Well, it isn't," my mother said. My parents had built their life together on the river based on money Arnoux had from the sale of his uncle's small farm where he grew up. My father ground out extra money working maintenance jobs along the harbor and on coastal logging crews. My mother tutored and taught at the schools when there was a substitute opening. They were never rich, and it was never easy. Starting a boatbuilding outfit and later a newspaper pushed them to the edge of financial catastrophe even before my father's reckless approach to money. "My life is not yours to make more difficult," my mother said. "Our children's lives will not be yours to make more difficult." She told him he was cruel, shortsighted, naive, and obstinate, not to mention selfish. Finally she said she had not come into the world to raise a husband, which was a wonderful thing, but only when it had sense enough to make reasonable decisions. "No free rides, Arnoux," she said. "Your time for their money. That's how this works. You do something that doltish again, I go."

I believe that was the only ultimatum my mother ever gave my father. For years after, lumber scraps appeared around the house with love notes written on them in dark pencil. They were always signed "With love, Your Dolt."

From then on my father took cash for his builds, though still not as much as most thought his work was worth. My brothers and I could tell when he'd shorted himself. Days would pass where our mother didn't say a single word. When she didn't even look at our father. When she didn't pull us onto her lap to read to us. Finally something would shift. My mother would start to sing the old ballads of love and bondage she adored ("On the Rock Where Moses Stood," "She Moved Through the Fair," "Samson and Delilah"), and my father, wherever he was—across the house sorting paints, in the woods felling a white pine to shape into a mast, down at the marina underneath a ketch scrapping away barnacles, outside the school waiting to pick us up, sidled up to The Fish House counter in town drinking coffee, gossiping, and looking preposterous in his crimson overalls stained with chainsaw grease—would hear her song, come home to her on the river, and wrap his arms about her waist. My brothers and I would nod to each other, confident that all was well and that our parent's summoning magic was alive in the world.

MY FATHER'S INITIAL FINANCIAL DECISION created a certain buzz in the community. It also generated a second and perhaps greater benefit: enduring gratitude. For years after, random deliveries of seafood and venison and other game showed up at our house as payment. Whenever we needed to be plowed out in the winter, Moses Jupiter would suddenly be there in his laboring truck. When our mother wanted to get a weekly newspaper going in the lower Penobscot Valley and was having trouble securing a loan, Moses rallied the collective lobstering community. Thirty grizzled fishermen visited the bank president's home early one Sunday morning. By noon the loan was approved.

Just as my mother had been pregnant with my brother while she was tearing through the woods making discoveries with my father, she was pregnant with me and then my brother Link while she renovated the salt-blasted brick harbor building into a newspaper office. Once a dormitory for cannery workers and later an emergency hospital never put to use during World War II, my mother filled the space with bookshelves and desk lamps and an archives room down in the basement. My uncle Reggie scoured the state collecting and photocopying back issues of every daily and weekly Maine newspaper dating back to the Civil War. My father tore out old walls and ran new electrical lines through the building with the delicacy of a surgeon repairing arteries. My mother, cradling her stomach, removed the emergency air-raid protocol posters, hoping that the bombs were indeed long gone. She saved the gas masks she found in storage bins in the basement, setting them about the newspaper office on windowsills and bookshelves for decoration.

Back at the house in the evenings, the three of them stood in the yard watching the sun sink behind the river. The renovations were almost done. My mother hoped to print her first issue in a month, and she was already searching for stories. She wanted to write about the Penobscot River, but she wasn't yet sure how. Clean water movements were starting up everywhere. There was hope that the environmental carnage of the lumber era might finally be over. Meanwhile a series of tribal land claim cases was gaining momentum. It seemed they might be headed for Washington, DC. Lawsuits by the Penobscot and Passamaquoddy nations called for a staggering two-thirds of the land in the state of Maine to be returned to the tribes, along with massive financial reparations. Instead of invoking broken treaties—no new news there—lawyers for the tribes were claiming that while the tribes had indeed sold the land in question to the federal government during the 1800s, the sales were illegal because they'd never been approved by Congress, as required by the Indian Non-Intercourse Act of 1790. The deals were therefore nullified, and the land was still owned by the tribes. The strategy was smart. Two-thirds of the state. And they might get it all back. People were panicking. She thought she might start there.

The light was hot and the hills were deep and green and smoky with the scent of pine. Paint speckled her arms, and her bones were heavy. She watched her husband drink two beers out in the setting sun with her brother, the two men standing in the gravel yard rocking back on their boot heels. They never sat. Men were always standing around and never sitting. She wished she could figure out how to tell them to just sit down and enjoy things already.

"The Lowering Days," Falon said, interrupting the silence.

"What?" asked Reggie.

"That's what I'm going to name the newspaper."

"Sounds ominous."

Falon yawned, took a sip from her husband's beer, then grabbed and finished her brother's. "People don't pay for cheer," she said. All things needed their story, and she was already planning the paper's narrative. Over the years she'd sometimes tell people the name came from her great-grandfather, who'd been a doctor up the Penobscot in Prospect and also routinely presided over funerals, gathering the townspeople in mourning on these lowering days, as he called them, when a body was sent into the earth. Other times she said the name came from the birthing day for a boat, the lowering day, when the finished hull was first slipped into the waiting sea.

"The Lowering Days." Reggie repeated the name slowly. He scuffed his boots around in the dust like a kid and grinned at the cloud swirling up around him in the light. He was tall and gaunt with broad shoulders, and his face always seemed to be craning through doorways well before his body. The bond between Reggie and my father had been fairly immediate.

Looking back now, I understand their respect for one another grew from a shared belief in duty. When thousands of American kids were burning their draft cards in protest, Reggie Harper adopted a much quieter track, staying home in Seal Point and caring for his aging, ill parents. Meanwhile the rest of the world turned in full and fiery revolt. His own sister decamped for California two weeks after graduating from high school. She would return three years later but never speak much about those thousand or so days of what all assumed to be a combination of pacific heartbreak, collapsed idealism, and a mysterious unrequited love. She spent another year downeast near the Canadian border at a farm where she devoted three hours a day to meditating in a cedar-framed zendo with a group of like-minded and amiable Buddhists and eight hours a day growing potatoes, squash, and kale. She claimed it was the simplest year of her life but stopped short of implying she should have stayed at the zendo farm, knowing, I suppose, that she would then be claiming a life without us.

"I like it," Reggie said. "The name. It has a weight to it. It means business."

"I should hope so," said Falon. "I'm not interested in running some community rag people use for toilet paper in a bind."

The only Penobscot Bay lobsterman who didn't show up at the bank president's house that long-ago Sunday was Lyman Creel. Lyman was president of the lobster co-op and a highliner with a talent for filling traps. He had organized area lobstermen to work together, not against each other, bringing in a collaborative model that existed atop a powder keg of hard personalities and old territorial thinking. Lobstermen still fished grounds handed down from grandparent to parent to child, packed sawed-off shotguns in their cabins to deal with interlopers, and refused to acknowledge life jackets as sane ideas, but they no longer just sold their catches from the backs of their trucks on the side of the road. Now their hauls were cataloged, divided, packaged, and shipped wholesale all over the country. There was even a gear trade, a supply depot, a commissary store, and a communal fuel pump down on the harborfront. Lyman believed supplying lobsters all over the world was the real goal. He'd been looking into selling in Japan and China. He knew every ocean shelf, reef, and trench out as deep as Georges Bank, and despite his collaborative spirit, which may have been grounded in communal profit more than communal unity, he was ruthless around his fishing grounds—once he'd nearly cut another fisherman's hand off by spiking him through the wrist with a harpoon when he caught him around his traps. He and his family were also our nearest neighbors. Lyman's wife, Grace, was a social worker and community organizer. She was also my mother's oldest friend, their bond dating back to grade school, and it was no accident that they had built their lives beside each other in the woods, despite the lingering divide between their husbands. Lyman and Grace had two children. Their son, Galen, was a year younger than Simon. Their daughter, Wren, was the same age as Link and me.

A mile of thick state forest separated our houses, and a well-worn path through the trees connected us. Stacks of lobster traps cluttered the Creels' yard, while the detritus of boatbuilding littered ours. We were a boatbuilding family, and they were a fishing family. We should have existed in a sort of natural harmony, one industry being dependent on the other, but that wasn't the case.

My father had made it through his war, in truth, not just by dreaming of boats but also by deserting. In 1970 he traveled from Vietnam to the Azores islands on a two-week furlough. He planned to live in a rough seaside shack and study Portuguese wooden boatbuilding traditions and how boatbuilders had to conform to the fisheries they served. Everyone on base told him it was a crazy thing to do on a combat break. *Go get drunk, man. Go get some rest. Go get laid and then go get laid again.* Hungry to start a new life, Arnoux wanted none of that. At night, in the Azores, as the Atlantic winds crashed about his cabin, he began to be haunted by dreams of body parts. Severed appendages slowly filled the waters surrounding the islands. By his tenth night away from the war, there wasn't a single wave left in the sea, only hands and feet and wrecked torsos and severed digits fed on by schools of ravenous fish. The war, my father realized, was over for him. He took what he knew about building boats and fled.

Lyman's path had been far different. His family had owned lumber and paper mills along the Penobscot River for generations. When Lyman realized that his own family and their mills were killing the planet, he decided he could no longer be a part of it. He dropped out of college, where he was slowly being groomed to take over the family empire, enlisted in the army, and served four tours in Vietnam, earning a silver star for rescuing a platoon of men during an ambush in Da Nang. After he returned home, Lyman married Grace Creel, took her name as his own, denounced his family, and dedicated his life to struggling out a living as a fisherman. He hoped never again to have anything to do with a mill.

Though many still saw Lyman as a spoiled rich kid, his fishing prowess had earned him respect over the years. And he wasn't an entirely unsympathetic figure in the bay either. As a teenager he'd watched his best friend, a Penobscot boy named Billy Jupiter, a distant relative of Moses Jupiter, fall from a bluff during a night of drunken foolishness. Lyman and Billy were both in love with a girl named Falon Harper. Later she would become Falon Ames, and then my mother. Between Billy's death and the awful toll his family's mills had taken on the Penobscot Nation, a nickname emerged that would follow Lyman the rest of his life: Indian Killer. "There goes that Indian Killer," people said, some with disgust, others, sadly, with reverence and a bit of awe.

As a child in a small community you can feel the fault lines running beneath your family and other families. These invisible tension wires tie one adult to another. You tiptoe around them. You step over them. You don't know why they are there, only that they are there, and that they are terribly dangerous things. You realize it only takes a few wrong steps to crack open the earth. Then what's to keep it from swallowing everyone you love?

Compared to my father's wild stories of bailing on the war and being chased across Europe by the navy, Lyman's wartime heroics seemed banal and predictable. I believe it infuriated Lyman that his community could love my father, a deserter, while he, the war hero, the lobster diviner, the visionary advocate who had organized an entire fishery, was still simply known as the Indian Killer.

Two

SIX WEEKS AFTER A DELEGATION of Japanese investors made their Valentine's Day visit to the shuttered Penobscot Narrows Paper Company mill to explore purchasing and reopening the operation, flames engulfed the sprawling property. I was fourteen years old then, and had no idea how that fire was also about to engulf our lives as well.

Years later nighttime walkers, motorists, and stargazers as far north as Kenduskeag would still describe the horrible red wall of dancing heat they claimed they saw devouring the southern horizon that night.

By morning, as the sun crested above the land, a charred palace hung on the banks of the Penobscot River. The caravan of Japanese saviors seemed a vanished dream. A palpable sense of both loss (that mill, the sprawling, environmental monstrosity that it was, had sustained generations of people in the Penobscot Valley) and joy (all vile things have their end too) ran along the police scanners, breakfast counters, harbor front, and general gossiping and gathering spots of Eastport, the small mill town known for its paper production and its dark history. Some five thousand years earlier, the Red Paint People had inhabited the area. Named for their elaborate funeral practice of covering their bodies in red ochre before burial, they settled on Indian Point, a slip of land jutting out into the

Penobscot River. The same slip of land was later called T'kope'suk by the Penobscots, and revered as a camping ground because of a spring there. When Colonel Jonathan East and his Massachusetts land grantees arrived in 1762 to survey Indian Point, they were reportedly driven mad. Some thought their lunacy came from Penobscot curses, others, from their own greed, lit by the towering white pines, fish-brimming river, and resource-rich valley that wound all the way down to the deep waters of the bay. When East returned a decade later to colonize the land, building a saw mill, a general store, a massive plantation house, and log homes for twenty more ambitious, land-hungry families, his madness returned as well. East burned his lover in the town square for being a witch. In an awful but predictable American twist, history forgot the name of the murdered woman, while East had a town named after him. Six months after setting his lover on fire, East died alone in the woods in a gruesome logging accident, the first victim of the curse his lover had supposedly laid over Eastport. Now Indian Point cupped the smoking remains of a paper mill, and town residents claimed that the mill was the latest casualty of the curse.

A woman out walking her dog the night of the fire told authorities she had seen a figure pass through a break in the fence around the mill site. Trespass happened fairly often. Shattered glass and cigarette butts littered the ground. New graffiti, phrases ranging from the profound to the imbecilic—"Still Cursed," "Suck It Eastport," "What Will Our Sad Fathers Do Now?"—constantly appeared on the buildings, silos, and smokestacks looking down the river. The woman thought something in this intruder's posture seemed different, though. The figure hid nothing. Standing upright, it boldly walked into the dark collection of industrial buildings. The dog walker stopped and watched. Twenty minutes later, the same short and skinny figure, wearing an oversize green hoodie, came out of the mill, moved through the fence, and turned up the street under the silver light of a clear, full moon. When the woman yelled, the figure turned, just long enough for the woman to determine a few key details. This bold interloper was a girl. And she was young, no more than fourteen, essentially the same age as me and Link and Wren and Galen.

Then the girl in the green hoodie turned and disappeared down an alley that connected to an ATV trail through the town woods.

The ringing phone woke us in the middle of the night.

Moses Jupiter was on the line. "Falon," he said, "get up here. This is bad." Not *This is going to be bad*, or *This will be bad*, but *This is bad*.

Our mother had turned on every light downstairs. From outside, in the woods, deep in the night, our little house must have looked like it was on fire as well. My mother was throwing clothes on and scribbling notes down at the same time.

Then she was out the door, driving through the dark in her beat-up Volvo station wagon, following the river north, craning her head at every bend for the sight of flames. Back home, my father, Link, Simon, and I sat at the table, catching our breath and wondering why it felt like a death had hit us.

Though we lived twenty-five miles away, my mother was the first reporter on-site. Truckers and midnight motorists heading upstate had pulled their rigs over on the rickety green bridge spanning the river. They stood along the swaying stretch of asphalt and steel, gawking. Some of them were crying. A pilot coming in to land at Bangor International Airport was so distracted by the intensity of the blaze that he almost missed his descent angle.

Reggie met my mother in Eastport to help take pictures. What Wren and I saw the next day in the darkroom at *The Lowering Days* was shocking. Flames towering into the night like a column of fire dropped from the sky. Flames dancing with a hundred shades of crimson heat. I didn't understand how one girl could cause such a thing. The photos that began to circulate on the news in the days after were just as strange. Heaping piles of charred debris. Warehouses torn down to black studs. Windows melted. And in the background: all the green wonder of the narrows as the river funneled through the chute of high, ancient cliffs and tall pines toward the sea.

It took twelve hours to put out the fire. Later, when asked why it hadn't spread or caused a greater environmental impact—the mill, while closed, was still filled with stores of chemicals—the state fire marshal was honest. Instead of the heroics of the firefighters who had responded, he credited the intentionality of whoever set the fire. The arsonist knew the mill—the facilities, the machinery, the layout, the operation—and had managed to start several fires in specific locations that would damage key buildings and machinery without igniting chemical or flash fuels. According to the marshal, the fire starter had used the river on one side as a control line and the machinery as a dozer line, essentially boxing the fire in to various areas. Furthermore, the state police had received an anonymous call about a mill fire in Eastport at 1:35 that morning. His investigation put the fire's official ignition time between 1:45 and 2:15 a.m. "The warning helped," he said.

In the days after the fire, speculation about the girl's whereabouts began to consume us. We thought she must not be alone. "How does some kid disappear when a whole state is hunting for her?" Link asked one night.

"Hunting," my mother repeated the phrase. "That's exactly what this is. A hunt."

I pointed out that, officially, she was "wanted for questioning." My father shook his head, but then stopped short of saying anything.

"Don't be as callous as the rest of them," my mother snapped. "Look in the mirror some morning and think about how little you actually have to lose in this world."

Shame and anger turned about the room with silence, and that silence seemed to go on and on. I vaguely understood that her "them" covered two categories, men in general, and more specifically European men, many of whom were my ancestors, who had overrun places like Indian Point, taking this river valley as their own and turning it into something very different from what it had once been.

"Those mills have been using the Penobscot as a sewer for a hundred years," my mother said. "Maybe this is how it starts to stop."

ˇ ˇ ˇ

A WEEK AFTER THE FIRE, a letter arrived in the mail at the *The Lowering Days*. It was written on a brown paper bag, instead of dioxin-bleached white paper.

Dear Readers,

This paper is run by a white lady, but she's a white lady who cares. Her heart is in the right place. She gives us the space to be seen and heard. Wəliwəni.

This paper has also shown it cares about truth for everyone, whether human, white, Penobscot, mountain, tree, river, or air. So this paper gets the truth.

Kənótamən? Wiseləmo sìpo, wiseləmolətəwak ahč nətalənɑpemak pɑnawɑhpskewəyak. Kis ɑpɑčihle ɑkələpemo. Apčiláwehle. Wekalohke. Nlátəpo pɑnawɑhpskewəya. Ata sésəmihle, nič kəwičintohətinena, nič kolitəhɑsolətinena. Nič ničkin kki. Nič wəničkisolətinɑ awenohčak nɑkɑ pɑnawɑhpskewəyak.

The fire I started was meant for the mill only. Not to hurt anyone else. I acted alone. To the mill: this is for the river who you harmed, my people who you poisoned, and all the men and women who had to make themselves into machines to keep you alive. I think it's good you're gone. Some things have to stay dead so others can come back to life.

To my people: nənotélətamən àhči nəpɑlítəhɑtamən. The river is us. We are the river. I couldn't listen to your crying anymore.

My mother hid the letter in her coat, closed the office, and came home that afternoon. With shaking hands, she set the letter on our kitchen table, where it sat like a bomb. None of us dared touch it.

I suppose she showed us the letter because she had to show it to someone. I was amazed it had come to *The Lowering Days*, not the big daily paper in Bangor. But it made sense as well. Over the years my mother had become something of an ally to the Penobscot Nation, the river, and the land. Furthermore, she was tenacious, arguably reckless even, with the truth, believing that it deserved to be heard at all costs. She had often run articles and editorials by tribal leaders and sought to give white issues and indigenous issues equal space.

So it had been arson in the name of a river under centuries of assault. The weight of that truth began to settle over our household as we all stood in the dimming April light eyeing the letter and listening for cars we knew were not out there and footsteps we irrationally feared might be coming. That night my father locked our door for the first time I could remember.

And what of the arsonist? If she was indeed a teenager, she was a precocious one, and chillingly direct. Yet she seemed unsure as well. *I think it's good you're gone.* I wanted to know how she had done it. Had the decision been quick and rash? Or had she agonized over the choice? What I was sure of was that the mill was not an innocent victim. The Penobscot Nation had long claimed that the narrows mill knowingly discharged toxic chemicals and wastewater products from the pulp and papermaking process into the river, poisoning its fish and plants. They had data to back their claims. My mother wrote about it all, of course, from all angles, and the environmental debate had filled my childhood. Now, on the eve of its potential reopening, the mill had been burned flat. The girl had directly addressed the paper mill, animating it in the process. From then on it would forever be a living, breathing entity in everyone's eyes. Of course it had always been alive, filled with the lives of those who lived and worked within it, a moving, evolving system, not unlike a body. An ecosystem, Wren had pointed out to me when we looked at Reggie's photos a week earlier.

Three

OUR MOTHER HAD BEEN SITTING on the letter for two days, unsure whether to publish it or not, when Grace called. She wanted us to come to her house to talk.

"Let's get this over with," my mother said to Link and me. "I'm not an idiot, Almy," she added when she saw my face. "Grace is mad because she knows about the letter, and she knows about the letter because of you."

I was certain my father hadn't told anyone about the letter. I was sure my mother hadn't either. She'd refused to notify the state police or the state fire marshal's office. She'd refused to even tell Cal Hayes, the Walineyayo County sheriff, and a family friend. I, on the other hand, had immediately told Wren. Suffering too under the weight of the letter, Wren undoubtedly had confided in her mother.

"You're using us," I said.

"You're coming."

"You think Grace will go easier if we're there."

"I don't need Grace to go easy," she said. "I've known Grace and how to handle her my whole life. And I gave birth to you, which means I get to use you, especially when you act like an idiot."

"Which is often," my brother added with a grin. Link, in his defense, had done nothing. Still, he went across the room and grabbed his coat. Then he stood watching our mother in the same way he looked at Simon or me or our father when he didn't think we were paying attention, as if he were memorizing everything about us. Though I thought Link obsessively collected all this information out of boredom, a kind of analytical game to pass the time, as I got older, I realized it was something much deeper. When we were little kids and our parents went somewhere without us, Link would spend hours drawing pictures of where they were and what he thought they were up to. The inside of the grocery store. The inside of the movie theater. The inside of the car as it moved down the highway between Portland or Bangor and home. Whenever Simon asked him why he was drawing these pictures, he would look up and coolly say, "Because I need to be there too. To protect them."

We made the long walk through the forest in silence. Eventually we reached a stone wall nearly five feet high. An acre or so of land had been cleared, and the wall formed a perfect circle around the clearing. A driveway ran up to the circle's edge and then stopped. The most curious thing was that there was no break, opening, or gate anywhere in the wall. There was just a spot where the stones had been tapered into steps so you could climb over and back down the other side. The impracticality of a wall without a door had always puzzled and excited me.

Stacks of lobster traps and coils of rope and crudely built sawhorses were stacked outside the stone wall. Homemade lean-tos had been raised to protect fishing gear and engine parts. Inside the wall, however, there was only the Creel family's small house and a neat grid of vegetable gardens, mulched with straw. The effect was one of overpowering refuge: in here, inside this wall, we will not abide grease and grime and disorder. In here, we will be clean and pure. Where the Creels' space was neat and ordered, ours was often a disaster. Just that morning I'd come downstairs and found Link lying on the floor in front of the TV in the living room, watching an old black-and-white zombie movie. Our father had dragged the TV home after the other one, a big wooden console that had belonged to my grandparents, stopped working. Now the working one was stacked on top of the broken one, and I wondered if we'd put another one on top when this one quit. That's how things seemed to go at our house on the river. An old rusting car with a hood that wouldn't fully close, parked beside a new and running car. A spent barbecue grill, a moldy cover still fixed over it with a bungee cord, resting beside a new grill, which was never really new, but bought used off some friend. Sheds were filled with broken rakes waiting for mending leaned up beside whole rakes. Shelves held working lawn mower parts and burned-up ones as well. Things could be fixed, reused. Worst case: even scrap metal was worth a few cents. I thought clean yards were for people with time and money. The Creels had no more of either than us, yet somehow it seemed they'd cheated the system.

Link stopped at the wall and said, "I'll stay."

"What for?" our mother asked.

"I'll just stay," he said.

The trees about us were too dark, black almost. They kept shifting as if alive. Then I remembered the ravens that Lyman raised, and slowly, magically, I began to see wings in the branches. "It's cold," I said, looking up for the birds.

Link shrugged, lifted his hand into the air, and extended his fingers.

"What's that about?" I asked.

"Quiet. I'm concentrating. Gotta find the wind."

After a moment, Link lowered his hand and licked his finger. "Tastes off," he muttered.

I shook my head, embarrassed for my brother, who was full of strange tips and tricks about feeling the world out. Our mother, who somehow seemed secretly proud of his principled stance, turned and climbed the stone steps as I followed.

GRACE, GALEN, AND WREN WERE all waiting for us in the kitchen.

"Let's start the bullshit, then," my mother immediately announced.

"It isn't like that, Falon," Grace said. "I know you're going to print that letter. Fine. I can't stop you. What I want to talk about is the aftermath."

My mother seemed genuinely surprised Grace wasn't putting up a fight. "When the truth is out there," she said.

"Something like that."

Notebooks, pens, and vinyl records were stacked on the kitchen table. Dark feathers peeked out from books of poems and cooking magazines. Piles of laundry were neatly folded in chairs. Heavy hemlock beams spanned the house's ceilings. Bundles of pungent drying herbs hung all around the room, tied and looped over rough nails driven into the timbers. Grace Creel was wearing a red bandanna knotted around her wrist, and a black bandanna tied over her head. I had always loved her voice, which seemed to arrive in a hiss or a whisper, but never with anger. It forced you to really listen for the words, which were often tough like my mother's, but usually infused with a soft love I often found lacking in our own house. "When *everything* is out there." Grace crossed her arms. "You know this place, Falon. Someone is going to find her eventually. It's going to be ugly."

My mother started to respond and then stopped. Her face reddened, and she dropped her gaze to the floor. She didn't seem to know what to say.

Wren and Galen were across the room, watching things unfold. Wren flashed a peace sign in the air. She was wearing one of her father's old green army jackets, the sleeves folded over at the cuffs. A piece of black duct tape was stuck on the chest, underlining her father's name. It made the name stand out more clearly, and I thought about how other kids might put the tape over their parents' names to hide or erase them. I had never seen a single photo, garment, memento, or scrap of evidence from my father's military years. Galen was sitting at the table, thumbing crumbs around the surface. He was tall, at least six feet already, and possessed a stunning wideness. Everything about him was broad, from his shoulders to his chest to his face. He even had unnaturally wide spaces between his teeth, and I remembered Wren telling me how she used to try to slip quarters between them when he was sleeping.

"This wasn't some accident," Grace said. "After that letter comes out, whoever finds that girl might kill her."

"Or hug her." My mother's voice was as soft as I'd ever heard it. "Or hold her up."

"That isn't this world, Falon."

Wren and I looked at each other. We both knew we were at the heart of this exchange in some way. Together we slipped out of the kitchen. Wren led me around the house, displaying various curiosities: a marble-size knot of shrapnel that had been inside her great grandfather's thigh for fifty years. Six round blue rocks her father had given her from the sea. A fox skull she found in the woods, which she and Galen had sent back and forth between each other's rooms when they were younger, the fox living with her in the winter and summer and with him in the spring and fall. A journal about palmistry that had been her grandmother's. I moved back over to the rocks. They were perfectly round, not a blemish on them. In their color I felt like I could see the ocean moving.

"They'd be bluebird eggs and hatch for us if the world were a better place," Wren said, and rested her chin on my shoulder. I could feel her breath against my neck.

I sighed. "But all we have are blue rocks."

"And the curse of living goes on." She moved away from my body, finishing our pointless comedy act as all the weight of what was brewing in the bay pushed back in from the next room, where we could still hear our mothers' voices.

I looked around. Though the house was a little dank around its corners, overpowering signs of love filled it as well. Every shelf and windowsill held a sepia photo of either a person or a homestead or a pasture, and to read the stories stitched together by the frames was to see a stunning act of preservation, to understand the lives and landscapes of at least three generations. Boots and slippers were neatly lined up along one wall. Names and dates marking people's heights over the years were penciled on a doorjamb in a vertical totem.

Outside I heard the crunch of tires on gravel and then saw a truck bending through the woods. Lyman Creel was coming home from his day at sea. The sky had turned dark and green, the air taking on the heavy electricity of a storm. I could see my brother still holding his position along the wall.

"He can't make up his mind," Wren said.

"About what?"

"Which is more dangerous. Us or the storm coming in."

In the kitchen, the voices had paused, and I imagined them watching Lyman's homecoming as well. I jerked my head toward the kitchen. "We should go back to them, shouldn't we?"

Wren shrugged. "Probably. The thing about parents is, they need you more than they let on."

My mother and Grace Creel were still standing across from each other, neither willing to sit. Galen, with all his stunning wideness, was nonchalantly reading a comic book. Link had come inside and was standing beside our mother.

"I'm interested in the truth, too," Grace was saying. "But not at the expense of people's lives. So we need to figure out what we can do to help her, not just use her."

"Use her? *She* sent in a letter. *She* asked to be heard. I'm not going to swallow it and censor another marginalized kid."

"She's a child, Falon. You're not."

I glanced up at the window. Lyman was sitting on the rock wall with his legs dangling over, as carefree as a child, pulling off his yellow hip waders, which he set in a pile with the rest of his gear. No one else seemed to notice him out there. I, however, could not stop looking. Just then the wind ceased. Rain started falling in thick sheets, kissing the trees, sizzling against the roof. The pine canopies swelled and thrashed, and five ravens filled the sky. Within seconds the birds had surrounded Lyman, turning him into a pocket of rippling darkness, and I thought it strange and a bit lonely, to see a man greeted by his birds before his family.

Grace turned to watch the ravens joyously dance about her husband as well. She smiled for a moment, and then her face darkened. "There's too much history stacked on this for it to go softly."

"That's the social worker in you talking," my mother said. "Maybe not everything is supposed to be soft, Grace." My mother was looking out at the rain as well. She seemed for the first time to register Lyman's presence. "I should go," she whispered.

"Don't be like that," Grace started, though I could see in her face that she was hurt.

Our mother was already across the room, pulling the door open on the storm. "Stay," she called back to us as we hesitated. "Wait for the rain to break. What Grace has to say is important. But I'm not the one to hear it." She seemed so small, framed in the open doorway with the rain cutting down around her as she turned to her friend. "What I do isn't easy. And it's even harder to do as a woman. So the truth is, I'm the thing that can't be soft, Grace."

Grace was looking down at the floor. "I know, Falon."

In the yard my mother and Lyman didn't acknowledge each other. I'd never seen two adults trying so hard to act like the other didn't exist. Lyman reached into a little canvas sack and drew out chunks of fish and began tearing them into pieces for the ravens. He stroked their heads as they snapped up the bits of meat. I couldn't make sense of this man. Here was a father who had built a wall around his family. Here was a man who loved his family. Here was a man who loved those magical black birds. And here was a man who had once loved our mother. He didn't seem at all capable of the ugly things I'd been told he had done. The largest of the birds spread its wings and rose high into the air then. I had to duck to follow its flight through the window. When I'd almost lost it in the storm clouds, the bird paused, pinned its wings to its side, rolled over, and fell in a free dive. I gasped, and Wren, who was watching as well, shrugged like the performance was normal. When the plummeting raven was only feet from the earth, it suddenly shot its wings back out, loosed a playful series of croaks, and rose powerfully into the air. Lyman was smiling at the aerial display, and I felt something passing between us. The back of my neck began to sizzle. I felt a sudden urge to flee. Lyman raised his head just a bit and cocked his ear, as if he too had felt the bizarre exchange.

"Why does he hate us?" I said to Grace, relieved to get away from the grip of the window.

"He doesn't hate you. He's bitter. Thinks something was taken from him."

"I'll bite," Link said. "What?"

Grace took her time with the question. "I don't know exactly." She seemed genuinely perplexed. "The idea of a life, I guess. Lyman saw a life with your mom when he was a kid. Losing something like that can haunt you for a long time. I love Lyman, but I also know he never really got over that night with your mother and Billy."

I watched Grace smile at the shock on all our faces. That night was not something anyone ever talked about. "Hide the truth," she said, "and watch the same mistakes get made."

Link nodded. I did as well. It sounded like something our mother would have said.

"Like rotten mills getting reopened," said Wren.

"Maybe," Grace said. "But people need rotten mills too. Rotten mills pay for houses and food. Rotten mills make hard lives a little less hard." Grace crossed the room and hugged Wren. Then she went to the table and kissed Galen on the forehead before turning to us. "Lyman isn't what you think. You see him and see just one thing. But you can't be human and be just one thing."

BETWEEN OUR HOUSE AND THE Creels' house a network of deer trails wound up to a bluff overlooking the spot where the river emptied into the sea. Here the outrushing waters gathered in a black whirlpool. My brothers and I would often stand atop the bluff and toss driftwood and cans and firecrackers down into the dark water. Sometimes the debris emerged back up the river; other times, we imagined it surfacing far out at sea. Often-times, though, the water never released its grip, and we wondered where the disappeared things went. A single apple tree that seemed impervious to time sat atop the bluff. Its trunk was a soft pink all year long, and crisp red fruit hung from its branches even in February, when ice encased the apples.

Ghost apples, my father called them. Fruit that will not die. That stays eternally lit like a beacon all year long. That tree became a talisman to us. Passing each other in the halls at school we whispered, "Meet me at the ghost apples." We told our friends. We told our teenage lovers. But never our enemies. No mention of that tree was ever made to any who carried threat. Though we made regular pilgrimages to the bluff, we never touched the tree or its apples.

Link and I waited out the rain and then began the walk home. When we didn't find our mother at the house, we backtracked through the woods, out to the bluff overlooking the ocean. We found her there beside the ghost apples, staring at the sea. She was soaking wet and shaking with cold as dark came swiftly on.

"Let's go home, Mom," Link said. "It's been a weird afternoon."

"Speak for yourselves," she said, all toughness still. "I've had a fine day." Then she sighed. "But, yes, home. I think I'm ready."

My father and Simon were working down at the harbor still, and the house was empty. My mother sat at the table and folded her hands, twisted with cold, in her lap. Link put a kettle of water on to boil, and we all turned to watch the pines become black notches against the graying sky.

"I think that all went quite well," our mother tried to joke, "with Grace." When we said nothing, she shrugged.

I took my mother's hands and began slowly rubbing them between my own. At first she pulled away, and then she relented. "Why were you out on the bluff, Mom?"

"I needed advice," she said.

When the kettle began to hiss, Link rose and poured the steaming water into a large clay mug. He set the warm crock before our mother. "From the apples?" he asked.

"From her," she corrected.

The *her* was Nigawes, and while her story, a creation tale of sorts that I was never really sure whether my parents invented or stole, had been a constant of our youths, it was years since our mother had talked about Nigawes or Sanoba or their story.

"You're going to print the letter," I said.

"I have to," she said.

Suddenly I remembered being seven or eight years old, and my mother coming home from working as a volunteer escort for Planned Parenthood in Bangor. She would walk into the house and drop the bulletproof vest they made her wear under her coat on the kitchen table. It sounded like hate, and fear, that Kevlar striking our table. I remembered my mother sitting on the living room floor and holding the swollen face of a woman who one summer lived with us after escaping her abusive husband, a man who would have killed her had she stayed. I must have been ten or eleven. I remembered my mother holding that woman's hand and quietly singing to her for what seemed like days. *Trouble in mind, I'm blue, but I won't be blue always, cause the sun's gonna shine in my backdoor someday.* When I asked my father why my mother volunteered at a place where she had to wear a bulletproof vest, he said, "Because other people won't." When I asked my uncle why my mother wore the vest, he said, in typical grand Reggie style, "Because your mother is a hero, because your mother is a lioness."

All the anger had faded from Link's eyes. He smiled at her and shrugged a little. "We know, Mom," he said. "We'll stand with you."

"My noble, foolish boys," she said and reached out to touch both of our faces as we sat down with her at the table.

I tried to push from my mind all that had happened that day. I was tired and simply wanted the day to be done. "Sanoba and Nigawes," I said. "It's been a long time since you told us about them."

"Too long," our mother said. As we drew near to her in the wood heat of the kitchen and darkness fell over the river woods, she began.

∨ ∨ ∨

THE TWO HUMANS WERE STRANGE figures. Their bodies seemed made of clay and stone. They were rigid and cold and full of icy reflected light during the winters. Then slowly they filled up with warmth and color in the spring. Over time, they found they could move. Then they found they could think and feel. Still they didn't know what they *were*. Years earlier they had risen from the earth at two separate spots along the granite banks of the great river that rose in the northern mountains and emptied into the sea. For a time each was happy, living alone, moving through the world, becoming less like stone and river water and sea wind and more like a man and a woman. They lived along the mouth of a great river. There they had searched the coastline and found many plants and animals to care for and admire, but never anything quite like themselves. Over time, they grew lonely.

The man was called Sanoba. The woman, Nigawes. One winter, both Sanoba and Nigawes became possessed by the same belief: if they traveled to the river's heart in the mountains to the north and told the waters their troubles, the waters might soothe them. So, traveling separately, unaware still of each other's existence, the man and the woman left the coast and went up the river in search of something they could only vaguely define: relief, purpose, joy.

In the mountains, each stood atop a separate snow-capped peak and sang to the river of their sadness at being alone. Slowly, the river answered. The waters intensified and grew, rushing through the land more forcefully. Over time the river carved a valley between the two mountains. It was then that the two figures saw each other.

Together Sanoba and Nigawes traveled back down the river to the sea, where they made a life. What began was a great love that filled the land with children. Eventually Sanoba grew tired. He couldn't keep all his people straight. He couldn't provide for all their needs. He longed for that old freedom of standing atop a mountain and being angry or sad or relieved to be alone. What bothered him most was that he felt deceived. He had wanted love, not servitude. Had he known it would fall to them alone to fill the entire earth, he might have chosen a different life.

"If you don't stop making these children," he told Nigawes. "I will go."

"Stop *making* them?" she said. "You can't put a life on one person, Sanoba."

The two lovers were standing on a bluff high above the sea. Sanoba walked to the edge and hung his feet out into the wind.

"I will do it," he growled.

Years had passed since they first saw each other across the sky. Nigawes knew her husband, knew his contradictions, too. She knew he was full of bitterness and fear and courage but that he was a cowardly man as well, and there, standing at the edge of the sea, she called his bluff. "You may *leave* us," she said. "But you will never fully go away from us."

Sanoba was furious at her stubbornness. He had unleashed an actual threat, and what did she have to say in return? Some self-righteous warning that meant nothing. He believed it had finally come to this: she no longer respected him enough to even say anything of actual substance.

Of course it was not that at all. Nigawes was scared of the change she had observed in her husband. She alone seemed able to see it—their children approached Sanoba just as they always had—and that frightened her even more. Sanoba sounded the same. When he went through the woods, he left the same footprints. Walking the hills, he reached out to touch the same birches. The change had to do with color. She noticed it first in his eyes, where every so often a scarlet tendril would flicker for a moment. Then, slowly, he began to redden. His fingertips turned hot and crimson. At night she uncovered her husband and watched his chest. When it rose, a faint scarlet blush lifted to the surface of his skin. To her Sanoba had always seemed blue and green, built from the sky and grasses. Now it was as if he had swallowed the sun and it was battling to get free. What madness could steal a man's color, fill a body with fire? The scarlet glow beneath his skin grew so fierce that when he turned to look at her or reached to hold her, she had to look away. No one else seemed to see it as he went about putting a pot of water on the fire to boil or returned from the river with a carved stone toy for the children, and that scared her even more. Listening now to Sanoba's rage, Nigawes understood that her husband had been infected by something truly cunning that would go to great efforts to keep itself hidden: resentment.

One morning Sanoba was gone. For a year after that, Nigawes lived alone with her children. Sanoba returned the next spring, after the last snows had melted and the trees were beginning to bud green. He believed he had made a point. He imagined that his family would not be able to survive another winter without him. He wanted to know that he was needed. More than that, he was lonely and ashamed of his abandonment.

But what he returned to was a land that had been neatly harvested in the fall, maintained through the winter, and replanted in the spring. Sanoba watched his wife and children continue to live the way they had in his absence. They harvested and replanted the earth and filled the valleys with trees and swept the meadows with grasses and wildflowers. They called down rain. They brought ravens to the skies. Deer and bear to the woods. During the day Nigawes ignored him. At night their lovemaking was ferocious, desperate. They crashed against the land, rage-filled and weeping. When Nigawes didn't take with another child, Sanoba grew suspicious. When she didn't let him help clear and turn and tend and grow the world with her and their children, he grew despondent. His punishment was not unjustified, nor was her lack of trust in his dependability. He had vanished, but he had come back, and he thought that should mean something. Although she kept using his body for her pleasure, howling and clawing against his chest and back deep into the night, she never looked into his eyes or touched his face. Sanoba understood he was on the outside of something now—that perhaps he was no longer needed at all. Of course this rejection was his fault. Unable to face that truth, he took to the easy responses of blame and fury.

For one thousand days Sanoba tried to kill his wife. Every night Nigawes evaded, outsmarted, and thwarted her husband's murderous impulses. When he went to the mountains to confess his guilt, he found they had grown so tall with old secrets and slights that they could hold no more.

Nigawes grew tired. Trying to survive would eventually kill you, she knew. The red that had overtaken her husband years ago had turned black. This, as much as her sadness over his abandonment, was why she couldn't look at him at night. It wasn't even blackness, so much as a void of light. When he passed in front of a tree or a boulder, an absence of color overtook the world, and Nigawes gasped, gripping her hands so her children wouldn't see them shaking. Satisfied that what she had once loved no longer existed, she acted.

When Nigawes had cracked the trunk that was her husband's spine and torn out the rocks that were his eyes and shaved the grasses that were his hair and let run the rivers that were his blood, when she had carved his body into a hundred pieces, hoping that whatever small bits of blue and green he still held might slip free and live on in the world, she stood atop the bluff where he had made his threat and she had taken her stand and cast her husband, piece by piece, into the whirlpool at the mouth of the river. Fate would decide whether to take his bones out to sea or up the river. She blamed the waters for his death. An accident while he was fishing. Her children did not challenge her story. They pretended to forget the thousand days prior, to forget the great, quarrelsome love that had brought them into the world. It was easy to accept the danger of the sea. But Nigawes understood that her lie was an awful one. Whether justified or not, she had killed her husband, killed the father of her children, killed her lover. And she had blamed her deed on the world.

After that the waters began to return pieces of Sanoba. Every year a new bit washed ashore: the stones that had been his eyes, the sea grasses that had been his hair, the gnarled driftwood trunks that had been his legs. Unable to bear touching the wreckage herself, Nigawes sent her children up and down the coast to recover their father as she watched up on the bluff above the ocean. She grew old waiting. At night she dreamed of her husband's hands—sliding around her waist, cradling their youngest son to his chest, stroking the back of her neck, gripping her thighs. When she woke, she found she could not move. Her feet had rooted into the earth. Fruit had begun to grow from the branches that had once been her arms. She closed her eyes. She lit the hanging fruit like red lanterns. She hoped her children would someday find their father and together come home.

Four

THE NEXT WEEK, MY MOTHER printed the girl's letter in *The Lowering Days* alongside this short editorial of her own:

Around here, people talk about stolen land and people roll their eyes. They say there was no Trail of Tears. No Little Big Horn. No Sand Creek Massacre. That doesn't mean we weren't complicit in genocide as well. We maimed and killed Native people, took Native lands, outlawed acts of Native cultural expression, forced Native assimilation, and hoped for Native extinction.

In 1790, the First Congress of the United States passed the first Non-Intercourse Act, declaring that any transfer of land from Native people to settlers had to be approved by Congress. Between 1794 and 1833, the state of Maine transferred the title to ninety-five percent of the Penobscot and Passamaquoddy people's land to itself without congressional approval. It also began selling Penobscot islands in the river.

We used that land. We logged it. We cleared it. We farmed it. We dammed it. We exploited it.

Some who believe the soul is the animator of the body believe there is a source point from which it begins. Here in Penobscot territory, that source point is the Penobscot River.

When I was a kid and went upriver to visit family, I used to see a thick foam everywhere along the shore. We'd spend all day in the water and come out covered in this stuff. We had no idea what it was. Boils and lesions appeared on our skin. Headaches tried to force us inside. It was all from the mills. This poisoned water ran straight through Penobscot lands. The fish they ate started to kill them.

It seems a child could no longer stand by and watch that harm continue. This fire may cost us future jobs. It may cost us comfort. It may cost us what we feel we are entitled to: money earned from taken land.

But think for a second about what it might save us.

The phones at the newspaper went dead under a flood of angry calls and strange tips—the strangest perhaps a man claiming to have seen a young girl step off the Passagassawakeag Bridge, spread her arms into an arc of flaming wings, and soar off up the river into the mist. The county sheriff's office issued a public warning, also printed in *The Lowering Days*, about the dangers of public vigilantism. They assured people they were searching for the letter writer's identity and whereabouts, and that it was their search to carry out.

In the aftermath of the letter, Grace Creel called a community meeting down on the harbor at The Fish House. All were welcome. Grace was there representing social services in the area. Cal Hayes came, both to keep order and to speak about the efforts of law enforcement. My mother was planning to speak as well. We found notes and scraps of paper all over the house. She talked things over with my father. She went up the river to sit with Moses Jupiter and talk to the Penobscot Nation. I imagine now that she must have felt very alone through it all.

One hundred years ago the rafters of The Fish House had hung with the huge carcasses of four-hundred-pound drying cod. Now the place was a shack diner nestled atop the harbor's seawall. The kitchen and the back storage room hung out over the bay. Ten cedar logs, pinned at one end to the bottom of the seawall, extended into the sky at a sixty-degree angle to support the structure's underside. The whole building, which was painted four different shades of blue and capped by a mottled green asphalt roof, looked as though it were set up on a small, trembling tea saucer. Locals took bets on when the establishment would catch a wind stiff enough to dump it into the sea. "Going down to The Fish House to place another catastrophe wager," they'd say.

The diner was often something of a ghost town, empty except for a few stoop-shouldered men who sat about considering a second cup of oily coffee and filling the air with blue cigarette smoke. In the afternoon the lobstermen would come ashore, replacing the harbor workers and retired morning gossips to drink a dollar beer before heading home. Most days it seemed like Ruston Garvey, the owner, would be lucky to make a hundred dollars in profit.

Now it was noon on an unseasonably warm Saturday in late April, and every chair at The Fish House was filled. The breakfast counter was packed two deep. People were even sitting on the edges of the fold-out card tables Grace had set up with coffee carafes and platters of dough-nuts and cinnamon rolls that she, my mother, and Garvey had begun baking at sunrise.

Wren and Galen were across the room, sitting behind their mother. Me, Link, and Simon stood near our father in the opposite corner. While we listened to my mother defend both the girl's action and her own de-cision to print the girl's letter, I could tell my father was proud. So was I. Link was worried about the danger our mother might be inviting. Simon was simply scared. He was about to turn eighteen. I imagined him lost in his own life, clinging to his dreams of leaving the bay for college and setting about becoming what he wanted to be in this world. Now it seemed a web was forming around us all.

"That letter was a manifesto," someone said. "She's a terrorist."

The word bent the air with hate and fear.

"No," Grace cautioned. "It was a clarification, maybe even a call for understanding."

Most of the room balked at the idea.

"What about the parts in Indian?" someone else asked. "How do we know they weren't a threat?"

"A threat." My mother narrowed her eyes.

The question asker looked a little embarrassed now. "Y-yes, ma'am," she stuttered.

"Telling choice," my mother said. Her tone had shifted to take over the conversation, moving Grace and Cal aside. "Smarten up."

I felt Simon cringe beside me. Looking around the diner, I saw fear. I wondered why my mother had to play coy with a whole room full of hurt and scared people. She'd had Moses translate the Penobscot parts of the letter when she went to sit with him. She knew exactly what it said. So why couldn't she just deliver the truth, if it mattered so much to her? What felt like an act of radical terrorism to many was, for this girl, simply an attempt to defend an ancestor—the river—and a plea to be seen and heard again after being made invisible for generations.

"You bomb a mill, you're a terrorist," someone was saying now.

"No," Grace Creel answered. My mother seemed surprised and a little disappointed, as if perhaps she had forgotten she might have allies here. "It wasn't a bomb. We're not starting that."

"And it wasn't a mill," said my father. "It was an empty building."

"Come on, Ames."

"She's wanted for questioning, is what she is," Cal Hayes interrupted. "People need to stay home and listen to their scanners. Stop searching all over the countryside with a rifle and a homemade badge pinned to their hats. Let us do our jobs."

"She should turn herself in, then," someone said from the back of the room. "Stop wasting our time and money." It was a woman's voice, gruff and tired. Several people around the diner nodded in agreement.

"Don't be simpletons," my mother hissed.

I felt the room recoil, rear up, and open its jaws as if to snap.

"Falon . . . ," my father started. There was an attempt at peace in his voice. Despite his desertion, the topic of which still trailed him like a dark shroud even at The Fish House, my father's boats and his dedication to the fishery kept him respected and perhaps loved around the harbor. Though he kept his small workshop in the woods near our house, by now he had established a larger boatbuilding yard down on the harbor front. Around the bay he built boats for local fishermen for next to nothing, while he charged the summer people outlandish amounts of money that left us bewildered and fearful that our father would be laughed to ruin by these rich men and women. As his renown grew, my father tossed out the sums—$40,000, $70,000, $90,000—without the slightest hesitation, and each winter the phone continued to ring with the voices of New York stockbrokers and Boston lawyers and Toronto architects looking for an Arnoux Ames–built wooden sloop or ketch. For my father, boatbuilding was a form of prayer. "When I'm working on a boat, I'm not even here," he often said. "I'm somewhere totally else. I'm talking with my ancestors. You could shoot me in the heart and I wouldn't die." War records didn't pay bills here. Fair fishing regulations, occasional dope deals, flush-with-cash tourists, and affordable, well-made boats did.

"Don't you dare, Arnoux," my mother said. "This isn't about you."

My father raised his hands and backed away. A man to his left grumbled, and someone in the back whispered "Coward" under their breath.

"The soapbox is getting tired, Falon," Garvey said from the front of the room. He looked small and frightened behind his white chef's apron. I noticed he didn't meet my mother's eyes. "Might be time to let it rest."

"You don't know me very well then, Rus. If this girl walks into any white newspaper, police station, or lawyer's office and says, 'I did it. Here I am,' it could cost her her life."

"That's not what I'm asking for," Grace said.

"Maybe not," my mother said. "But what about the rest of us? When did our heads get too thick to mistake wanting justice for wanting blood?"

I think it was the use of the word *us* that saved my mother from the mob in that moment. That, and a new voice cutting through the anger.

Lyman Creel had come in off the wharf after a morning out on his boat. He walked into the diner like it was any normal Saturday. Bits of ice clung to his red beard, and his cheeks were raw and wind-hardened. He took a safety pin off his sleeve and began to dig black chips of grease out from under his nails. The room had gone silent. My mother was watching Lyman, along with everyone else. He slowly poured a cup of coffee into a small blue mug and then walked over to Grace and hugged her.

"Hi, sugar," she said, leaning in and kissing him.

"Hey, baby," Lyman answered with a sigh. "It's been a long day."

"Sure has."

There was something touching and startling in this moment of intimacy. Somehow it seemed that Lyman, by ignoring us all, had reminded us of how to be human. He had a copy of the most recent issue of *The Lowering Days* under his arm as he moved across the room. Two men stood up from the corner table they'd claimed and let Lyman sit down with his paper and his coffee. In the soft, watery sunlight pouring down over him through the window, he appeared as content as I had ever seen him. Outside, gulls dove through the orange air, disappearing into the sea after the bloody chum fishermen were emptying into the ocean.

"I think it's good you gave that girl a voice like she asked, Falon," Lyman finally said, shocking us all. His words moved through the crowded tension of the diner, and when he paused to take a breath, the slow, steady clicking of the ancient steam heating system was the only sound. "Maybe the mill was the original crime," he said, "not the fire. Maybe we all failed to see it for too long."

Lyman's eyes briefly found my mother before they both looked away. I felt my father tense at my side. "I don't know what else to say." He placed his hands in his lap and opened them, looking down at the callused welts worn into his thick fingers. Then he shrugged and bent back into his coffee. I watched Wren and Galen cross the room to be with their father.

Galen passed Lyman a doughnut. Wren took her coat, comically small in this context, and draped it over her father's heavy, rounded shoulders, damp still from another day battling the sea for a few dollars, just enough to keep the lights on, the mortgage paid, and food in their refrigerator.

None of us knew what else to say.

Part II

Five

THE MAN LISTENED FOR THE dawn birds returning to the trees and added more wood to the fire. The logs were small and snapped in the soft gray light. There was an art to keeping a fire low enough to avoid notice but warm enough to survive the night. While a bright, high sun blistered the days now in April, the temperature often struggled to escape the forties still, and heavy snows drifted through their campsite. The man pushed up the coals in the fire, where a flat stone was heating. He laid two gutted and filleted fish on the stones and listened to the fat sizzle.

The campsite was surrounded by thick woods and set in the shadows of Bald Hill. Though they'd put leaves and branches over the tent to better disguise it and packed in bales of straw for insulation, it wasn't a home or a place for staying. Adam Greenwind was Penobscot and found it insanely strange that he was sitting over an early spring fire in the deep woods, essentially hugging an old migratory route, trying to figure out what to make of his life now.

Two weeks before, he had stepped into the hallway of their little ranch house in the middle of the night and found his fourteen-year-old daughter, Molly, frantically packing a bag. She was terrified when she looked up at him. Out the hallway window he could see the silhouette of the birch-bark wigwam he and Molly had started building that fall for a tribal project about exploring family heritage. They'd raised the sapling frame and sheathed the structure in birch bark, but they'd been unable to finish the wigwam before winter. While he'd spent all February and March talking excitedly at breakfast about getting back out to finish the wigwam, Molly's enthusiasm waned. Instead, in the mornings, her eyes continually fell on the unopened stack of bills and delinquency notices piling up on the table. When he moved the stack onto his dresser so she wouldn't have to see it each morning, she'd retrieved the bills and put them right back at the center of the table. That was Molly. Not one to let things be pushed into the dark. He had started getting dressed in his work clothes again as soon as he woke, even though there'd been no work but odd jobs for almost two years, since the mill closed. It just made her more upset. "You can't fool me into thinking things are okay, Dad," she said. "I leave you behind and go to school. Every day you're just here alone. I hate it."

The old grandfather clock working time over in the living room was the only sound in the house. He thought he heard deer or raccoons scurrying around outside under the moon. He imagined Molly's horse, Cricket, curled up in her corral shelter, picking out the same night sounds. He thought he caught the whine of sirens in the distance and began to really worry. Dawn was two hours away, and he understood that light would be no help to whatever was happening here. He grabbed his own duffel bag and began stuffing supplies into it, packing light, but packing smart.

Molly stopped. "You can't come."

"See if you can stop me."

He thought she might start crying, but then her face changed, shaking a little, pushing something far down. "I messed up."

"We all do, sweetie."

"Stop acting easy, Dad. Stop acting cool. It isn't you."

"Okay," he said. "Then tell me what happened."

She had been honest with him. Now it seemed nothing would ever be the same.

A fire that practically took an entire mill to the ground in an evening. How had Molly done such a thing on her own? He hadn't raised his daughter to keep her head down and stay invisible. "Too easy to be an invisible Indian," he often told her. "Too easy to give 'em exactly what they want." He'd raised her to have a backbone and act in defense of those who needed defending. But not this: destruction, violence—those were angry ways, easy ways. He wondered now if it was his fault. Most of her life Molly had watched him come home from the mill too tired to hardly think. While he'd tried to be careful, he had a big mouth, and it was just the two of them at home. Molly listening to him complain about how the paper company treated its workers, constantly putting more on them, skimping on safety supplies, slashing overtime, even canning free coffee in the employee lounge near the end. Listening to him rant about the chemicals and the waste and awfulness of a mechanized world. Listening to him talk about how hard it was to *know* your birthright was to caretake the earth, all while *doing* work that injured the river and traumatized the land. Of course causal relationships were complex, yet here they were.

In the distance Adam could almost make out the high, sandy hill from which this place took its name. His grandmother used to tell him about Penobscot warriors who would race up the hill's treacherous shifting sands. It was a hard run, and dangerous—a broken leg or ankle, a stumble and fall down the hill, a landslide coming down behind you, these were all real risks. So the challenge took great strength and endurance, but also intelligence and strategy. His grandmother had told him how Penobscot women made the sand run too, often winning the contest. He had first shown Bald Hill to Molly when she was five or six, and told her the same stories. He remembered how her eyes had focused and hardened at the idea of a female warrior besting the hill climb. There had been no shock, no surprise there, and he thought it interesting that when they left their house for the woods after the fire, they had almost instinctively traveled here, to the shadows of the proving hill.

Now Adam listened to the woods around the camp, heard nothing, and grinned at the lie. Several peeled and cut ash saplings were stacked near the edge of the fire's light. Molly had spent all yesterday gathering and cutting the sticks to the right length for a fish weir. She was still asleep in the tent, and he knew that when she woke she'd start measuring and fitting the weir together and wrapping the sticks with netting. He almost rose, but stopped himself. He could hardly go twenty minutes without checking to make sure she was safe. It reminded him of their early days together, when she was an infant and he lived for her first year of life in conflicting states of wonder and panic, amazed that such a tiny thing could exist in the world and terrified that those tiny lungs and that tiny heart might at any minute stop doing exactly what they were designed to do and take her away from him.

Somewhere to the west, a twig snapped. "No need to make it easy on me," Adam said without looking up. "*kkʷey*, Moses."

A figure stepped out from the woods. He was tall, with a stone turtle pendant around his neck and his gray hair braided back in a ponytail. He moved softly despite his age and the heavy pack on his shoulders. "The stick was a stumble, not a courtesy."

"How long have you been out there?"

"Probably just as long as you think." The other man returned the greeting. "*kkʷey*, Adam."

Adam blew into his hands, trying to take the cold from his palms. Then he pointed to the pack. "I didn't ask for any of that."

"You're not the only one who needs to eat."

Adam didn't think to question how Moses had found them. He had known someone would come, had known too it would be Moses, who he had known all his life.

"This is a pickle, isn't it?" Moses finally said.

Adam laughed. Of all the phrases to spill out of his friend, who spoke at least four languages. "I don't know." He nodded to the fish cooking on a rock at the center of the fire. "We've got food, heat. No holes in the tent."

"No handcuffs yet, either."

Adam grinned. "I'd like to keep it that way."

"Me too," Moses said. "Molly?"

"Still sleeping."

The older man moved to the weir sticks and lifted one, turning the tan wood in his hands. "Where's she going to put it in?"

"Beats me. Somewhere with fish."

"It's a good weir."

"Should be. You taught her." Adam felt the unexpected edge in his voice, crackling the air. "You pick a lot up hanging out with an old Indian revolutionary while your dad has to make a living."

"I see," Moses said.

Adam paused, turned the fish on the warm rock, tried to calm his anger. "*Wəliwəni*," he finally said, embarrassed at his disrespect. "For the supplies, for coming."

"It's nothing." The man waved his hand through the dim light. "What other things can I do for you?"

The precision of the phrasing was not lost on Adam. Not *What do you need?* or *How can I help?* but "What other things can I do for you?" *What's your plan?* was the first thing most people would have asked. Adam appreciated that Moses had not.

"This isn't your mess to get caught up in."

"When did I ever ask you to be afraid for me, Adam? *Mòsa sakeləkéski-hkač* Pride has no place here. Stop being messy."

Adam took a deep breath and released it. The directness of the rebuke felt good. He'd grown up on the reservation fixing things on the island and tinkering at every turn: fishing poles, radios, canoes, neighbors' air conditioners. Back then Moses and the other elders had called Adam "Many Solutions," partly as a joke and partly out of wonder, for the child seemed able to figure out how almost anything worked. When he wasn't fixing things, Adam was gardening. Working his hands through the earth, studying how it could take sun and water and make food and medicine for its children, how it could heal and adapt and sustain and persevere— that was his greatest joy. But life takes you elsewhere. He remembered the worst years: he and Nonie and Molly, just a baby then, shivering in a rented room on the island. No heat half the time, no car any of the time. Young and broke and hungry and angry at each other because the world never seemed to have enough for them. And there was that mill, just down the river, with its doors peeled open like a waiting mouth, promising money, promising the balm of the white man's world: *resource, opportunity*. Adam looked into his palms now as Moses sat down beside him. He feared this mess was beyond the power of his hands to fix, heal, wrangle, or resurrect.

"Can you meet us at the house near dark?" Adam asked after a while. "One week from now."

"You're going back."

"There is no back."

Moses put his hand on Adam's shoulder. "But there's family still."

Adam nodded. "Bring your truck, and the hitch that fits Cricket's horse trailer. I need you to find a place for her."

"I know someone," Moses said. "Good people. Discreet people. What else?"

But what was his actual plan? At the mill, he'd been immediately respected because of his ability to figure problems out. So come on, Adam. You were a carpenter and a nut for working on tape recorders, cars, and radios since you could practically walk. A draftsman and a welder. A foreman and a safety supervisor. Sure, you got driven out of a job, but you've got a lifetime of practical knowledge in that thick head of yours. So what's your plan? Stay out of sight as long as possible. Wait for the initial rage to calm down. Protect Molly. Find a way back to a normal life again, no matter how long that might take. If he was honest, he hoped for something he couldn't quite articulate. For the anger to pass. For the land to protect them. To find forgiveness on the other side of it all.

"It's not just Cricket," he said. "We need somewhere to go for a while too." He didn't want to take this trouble up the river any closer to the reservation, he explained. So it had to be downriver, toward the bay, where the waters widened, and where their ancestors had for centuries traveled during the warm season, leaving their river villages to harvest fish and shellfish on the coast and get ready for winter.

"We can't come in, Moses," Adam said. He would do anything to keep

Molly out of jail or the foster system, which to Native people were the same damn thing. "What if we did, and I never got her back?" He felt his face going hot at the idea, and he looked away.

Moses Jupiter reached out and brushed the wetness from his friend's cheeks, then hugged him. "I know, Adam. It will get better. *Ménakač peči-kati-sakámkʷihaso.* Don't forget to light a fire near the water. Don't forget to dance, to sing. Did you bring a drum?"

Adam nodded at the tent, where his grandmother's drum was swaddled in a wool and horsehair blanket.

"Hug Molly for me," Moses said. "Tell her I'll bring waffles next time. Rock-sizzled fish only goes so far when you're fourteen. *Minač kənamihol.*"

IT WAS SNOWING A WEEK later when Molly and her father came out of the woods and returned to their home. Molly was glad for the awful weather. It kept the roads and trails clear, at least. She'd resisted leaving the woods, yelling about how dangerous it was. Her father didn't budge, and under different circumstances she would have respected his conviction. Out in the yard the wind was throwing screens of snow up in great howling gusts, and while she could hear the sound of a truck coming up the long dirt road to the ranch house, she couldn't see Moses until he was out of the vehicle and almost right in front of her.

Her father nodded to the older man and then turned to her. "Do you want to go inside?" he asked, pointing back to the house, which sat in a small clearing on the wooded hill.

"Not anymore," she said. It wasn't a lie, either. The night she had come back home through the woods with the smell of smoke trailing her like something she might never escape, she had understood when she pushed open the thin front door and looked around the kitchen, with its brown veneer cabinets and boot-worn blue-and-yellow linoleum floors, its old pea-green refrigerator sputtering in the corner, and its odd assortment of knickknack salt-and-pepper shakers—two highly racist Indians in full headdresses and dance regalia, the king and queen of hearts from Alice and Wonderland, two dancing puffins dressed in colorful clown outfits—that her father kept arranged on the windowsill as a reminder and a way to honor her great-grandmother, who had collected the curiosities, that she might never again get to turn that doorknob and walk inside carefree.

"I'm okay, Dad," she said.

Adam nodded, tightened his coat, and disappeared back into the whorls of snow to wait. A moment later she heard the truck door slam. When the wind dropped, she saw her father sitting in the cab, rubbing his hands together and looking off through the trees. She was the one who favored the cold.

Moses Jupiter did not love the cold either, but he was happy to see Molly, the closest thing he had to a daughter or granddaughter, standing in the snowy yard. While she didn't show it, she must have been freezing as she stood rooted to the snowy earth. She had wrapped her sneakers in plastic bags and duct-taped them at the ankles to keep the snow out. Overall she didn't look much different. Maybe a few pounds lighter. Tall for her age, and rangy. Limbs like braided rope, baggy jeans, and a hooded sweatshirt that hung from her like a sail. It was hard to find a way in to hug her, always had been, as she seemed composed of only edges. Yet her face betrayed a certain kindness, a belief in the good of people, he thought.

"Molly," he said.

"Seskahsen," the girl corrected.

"I didn't forget. I helped choose that name. Do you remember what it means?"

"Light or something."

"No," Moses said. "A brilliant, uninterrupted light. The unrelenting light."

Molly wanted to hide, but the only place to go would have been into the house, or into the truck cab with her dad. "I don't feel like a brilliant anything anymore," she said. Then she relented, moved across the snow, and hugged Moses.

Moses didn't want to let her go. "Don't be a shit about your name," he whispered into her ear. "It's not a gift to question."

Her eye roll was subtle, but not lost on him as he reluctantly dropped his embrace and raised his hands. "I know. I'm just an old man full of folksy sayings."

"No," Molly said. "I'm glad you're here. I'm just upset and scared."

"*čkǝwi*. Walk with me." Moses started toward the paddock. He'd been checking on Cricket for two weeks now, since the fire broke out and Molly and Adam vanished without a word. He'd even called the middle school, pretending to be Molly's grandfather, and told them that he was ill and his granddaughter was caring for him. It was a small enough place that the lie wasn't questioned at first, but big lies never last too long in small towns. He knew others would start asking about Molly and Adam soon. The connection between their disappearance and the fire would follow.

Behind him, Molly hadn't moved. "If you skip this part, you'll never forgive yourself," he called back.

In the paddock Molly pressed her face to Cricket's neck and sank into the smell, hide and hair and a quiet, unflinching love she had never found outside of animals. The horse trailer was parked beside the little pink ranch house. Molly studied the land. Through the snow to the west was the valley and the center of town. Beyond that, the river. And just beyond that, in the shadows of exposed hematite cliffs, rolling green mountains, and a steep, sand-layered hill, a small tent sat covered with ferns and brush. Old home, new home, she thought, and shook her head at the absurdity of their life now. The ranch house was a faded fuchsia color with a sky-blue metal roof. She loved the quirkiness of it, and so had her father. It might have been the ugliest house in the state of Maine. "A pink house was good enough for Bob Dylan and the Band," her father used to say. "Seems like it should be good enough for us." She knew the real reason they never repainted the house was because it was the same color now as when her mother first fell in love with it and lived with them there, before she went off to have a different life somewhere else. While Molly had long since stopped asking why her mother left, she still imagined her as *skʷéwtəmohs*, a swamp woman. Moses had first told her of the swamp woman when she was a little kid. They were legendary female spirits who lived alone in the wilderness and helped hunters and travelers who were in trouble. Molly knew her story was just a child's tale erected to survive a certain unforgivable pain, but since their hidden life in the woods had begun, she swore she could feel her mother out there watching them, perhaps guiding them.

Her dreams had been strange as well. Each night she was visited by a snowy, cliff-carved world filled with thick pines taller than any she had ever seen. Their canopies split the sky, wild green branches churning with snow. Ravens danced about the trees. They seemed the only inhabitants of the high, deep woods. Each morning she checked her head for a fever, worried about what an illness would mean now for her and her father. There was no hospital. There was no grocery store. There was always medicine, in the earth, in the woods, all around, but would it be enough? Finding her skin cool to the touch, she would spend the rest of the day trying to assemble the collection of strange images into some whole, as if building a puzzle. The frozen pines constantly swayed and cracked in the cold. The sound seemed to call the ravens into more of a frenzy. It was dangerously cold in the dreams, well below zero. And when the heavy snows ebbed for a moment, she was able, far in the distance, up a great mountain, to see a small golden chair sitting on a rocky ledge, backed by blue light. The chair appeared to be made of twisted wood. Sometimes there was a small boy sitting on it, other times a tall, hulking man. His physical presence was so dark that it seemed to swallow all the light about him. He had a bald head and was dressed in black furs, and when he grinned, his teeth were so white that her eyes stung. Other times the chair was gone, and a bright-red apple tree held the summit.

She was starting to *see*, she thought. It was not a place for people. In the dream world the rivers were undammed and the trees colossal. If it hadn't been winter, she was sure clouds of insects would have clogged the air. It was the world before every tree had been cut, every tract of earth mined, every river harnessed, everything put to use.

There was also music, a constant quiet melody on the wind. She had been gathering bits of the dream song together now for days, and she wished badly that she could walk out of the woods to the Catholic church to play the piano her fingers had loved since she was a small child. Her father had once read her a passage by a Jewish philosopher about how one's life, the entire span of it, should be treated like a singular work of art. She saw the fire as a necessary brushstroke. She thought she had understood how much it would cost her. She had been a fool. So many things were gone now. She wondered what her friends were doing. She wondered if she'd ever see them again. She missed the crappy cafeteria food at school, and the awful fluorescent lights. The loud banging of lockers that made her anxious. The musty smell around the nozzles on the water fountains. The look of all the cars speeding out of the parking lot after the bell rang.

Last night the dream had changed. The landscape was the same, remote and snow-ravaged, but she was near the sea. She could make out the familiar rocky coast of her childhood and the Penobscot River, moving through the land to the north. There were two white eagles, one small and one much larger. They were falling from the sky. They seemed to fall forever, and for some reason she screamed to warn them. They made no sound in return, continuing their plummet in silence. When Molly woke, her father was holding her. She thought about how it looked as if he had aged twenty years in the last two weeks. She couldn't tell him about the dreams. For him, everything had been reduced to staying hidden, staying safe, staying alive, and she hated that all the stress of her action was falling on him, and now on Moses too. Even Cricket looked older as she traced the fresh gray hairs around the horse's flaring nostrils and stroked her ears.

"Where will you take her?" Molly asked.

"Somewhere safe," said Moses, "loving."

"You won't tell me."

"*Mèhsəma*. In time."

"When I'm less of a danger," she said, and sighed. "My dad won't let me turn myself in, but people deserve to know what happened. That's why I sent the letter."

Moses glanced across the yard. Adam had not left the cab of the truck, where he was watching them through the windshield and blowing into his hands. "I'm not sad about the letter." Anger rose in his voice as he slid into Penobscot. "*Sákewəso awəpálihle. Ni wəči-ahtɑ wəlitəhasiwi.*"

The words cut deeper than the biting snow. She was hurt at the insinuation that she had sinned against herself by betraying their values. The truth was, she was still stunned each morning when she woke up at the campsite, so far away from her old bed. She remembered the Abenaki corn hanging all over the house, blue kernels reflecting the light. Jarred dry beans and different-shaped squash arranged on the counters. Pumpkins sitting on each stair like toddling members of the family. Her father lifting the black ash seed box that had been his grandmother's and smiling as he said, "This is an act of resistance. Growing our own food from our ancestors' seeds instead of going to McDonald's." But as those moments receded further, memories of the day a year ago that had ultimately led them here returned more often. A group of white kids had started talking about the old mill while standing around in the April slush, waiting for the bus after school.

"Someone needs to do something for the earth," one kid said.

"Or the trees," said another.

Molly wished they would all shut up. Youthful zealotry, rage, environmental defense driven by a bunch of hokum teenage angst—she was almost embarrassed at how cliché they all sounded. And she was mad at how historically blind they were.

"Someone is," she said quietly.

"Yeah, yeah," a tall, disinterested boy spoke up. He was a senior, and Molly had no idea why he was waiting for a bus with a bunch of freshmen and sophomores. "Scientists, conservationists. I know."

But you don't. She couldn't find the words to tell the boy, who seemed in his cool skepticism to have grabbed all the authority in the world, no matter how false she would later realize his expertise was. You don't at all, she thought. Whole cultures. Whole tribes. Whole indigenous communities you barely, if at all, even know exist. We've always been doing things for the world. Caring for it, supporting it. Seeing it for what it actually is: a living being, a home.

"It's Molly, right?" the boy said.

She narrowed her eyes, imagined slapping him in the face. She knew he knew her name. At the same time she tried not to puke out an enthusiastic, head-nodding little dance of joy at the thrill of being noticed. She took a breath to keep from embarrassing herself. *Seskahsen*, she thought. *It's Penobscot. I'm a keeper of the world your world is completely ruining. I'm one of the ones who wasn't supposed to survive.* "That's me," she quipped.

The boy nodded into the distance. "The question I have, Molly, is: Is it enough? All these studies and reports and things. All the bullshit no one even hears. Is it enough?"

She didn't know how to answer that.

"Sometimes you have to go after the thing that's hurting other things. Look at these people out in California who are blowing up bulldozers and sabotaging cut sites."

"You're talking about violent crime."

"No," said the boy. "I'm talking about acts of mercy for things other than us."

Mercy. The word coming from a white boy. That angle on things coming from a white boy. The audacity sickened her. What if he was right, though? How far was too far? How little was too little?

"Sometimes change is violent," the boy said. "It's a shitty mess."

Molly barely heard him. She was looking over his head to the shadowy outline of the distant mill as she realized she'd been quietly telling herself the same thing her whole life.

She spent the summer and fall sneaking into the mill, exploring the layout, learning its topography, figuring out what would burn and how, devising a plan. Her goal was not just fire, but rebirth. At night she peppered her father with questions about plants and gardening, and he gleefully went on and on like a man who'd rediscovered an old friend. Pushing deeper inside the abandoned mill site, she planted fire-loving seeds and seedlings wherever she thought the land would support life. She delighted in the small guerrilla act of slipping a living pocket of complex DNA beneath the earth of a hulking paper mill whose days, she was convinced, were numbered. While most of the world watched the news or dozed off, dreading getting up for work tomorrow, here she was digging holes for shagbark hickory trees in green spaces between maintenance sheds and loading docks. Even with all her planning, most days the fire seemed impossibly foolish. But when she thought about stopping, she saw that tall, aloof boy and his white face, theorizing about change. As winter set in, she began picturing the world she was trying to build after the fire. Who knew what seeds would germinate, activated by fire as plants had been for millennia, and what would pass on with the burn? Pitch pine and scrub oak and larch and willow. Blazing star and wild lupine and fireweed. If they came, they would come as a tapestry of new life emerging from the ashes.

Now, in the aftermath of it all, she could tell none of this to the man beside her, who she loved as much as anyone in her life.

Moses cleared his throat. "Your dad might have had a job there again, at the mill."

"Exactly," she said. "I'm already down one parent, and working at that place kills people." She had been convinced the minute the mill reopened its doors, her father would slide directly back in.

"So does being poor."

Molly winced. "My dad left the island and took that job because of me. He wanted to make things, to garden. Not be a mill worker."

"Stop feeling sorry for yourself," Moses said. "Your dad wanted you."

Of course that was the real truth. But childhoods run on bitterness and resentment just as much as imagination and love. She rested her head back against Cricket's neck. "Do you remember what you used to call me, Moses?"

"Of course I do."

"Little Fast One. I still smile when I think about that. After my mom left, I used to ride Cricket all around, thinking, 'I am the Little Fast One. I cannot be sad.'"

"Some things can't be outrun."

"I'm learning that. When I started the fire, I stopped feeling angry for the first time in forever. Now I just feel sad."

"The fire," Moses said. "You're not the first person to want to do something like that."

Molly thought of Moses's stories of resistance, stories she'd heard her whole life: the fight for Penobscot voting rights in the state, how he'd traveled to California and been part of the Native occupation of Alcatraz, the seizure of the replica of the *Mayflower* in Boston, the spiritual walk across the country to support tribal sovereignty, him and a bunch of other tribal members occupying Baxter State Park for a week because they wanted Ktahdin returned to them, and the victory of the Maine Indian Claims Settlement Act, when Jimmy Carter put his pen to a sheet of paper, and the Penobscot Nation was suddenly all over the national news.

"Was it too much?" she asked.

"That's not for me to say," Moses answered. "You need to go be with your dad now, Little Fast One. Cricket will be okay."

Molly slipped a carrot from her pocket. "*kkàseləməl,*" she said, and Cricket's small, square teeth accepted the gift, which of course was a goodbye with gratitude and, she was certain, love. Across the yard, watching his daughter from the cab of the truck, Adam Greenwind looked away, convinced his heart would shatter.

Six

LYMAN CREEL DRIFTED UP THE inlet cautiously. The eastern channel of the river opened before him, the golden waters breaking around the bottom of Verona Island. He turned the throttle down and hesitated. The boat softly rocked from side to side on the swells, and the feeling of being on the sea lifted his spirits. It was a world of contradiction. Being on the ground but afloat at the same time. Being rocked and soothed and just as suddenly pushed and tossed if the waves picked up.

And here was yet another contradiction, a Penobscot Bay lobsterman going up to check on his traps in the river. Not unheard of, no. But not common. Not loved, for sure. It was only a few traps, he'd told himself. Just a test.

Lyman stretched and rubbed at his eyes. The sun, low and rich on the horizon, had only been up for an hour, and this too was part of what he loved. Being out in the world as the world came back to life. There was a simple pleasure in having the light and the heat and the sounds and smells of the dawn come to him as opposed to going to them. So daybreak found him having coffee with Grace each morning, then feeding the ravens, before heading for the water.

Grace knew about his experiment. He'd never been one to keep much of anything from her. "It's not being fished," he'd told her when he first started thinking of setting a few traps in the channel.

"Doesn't mean you should," she told him.

These lines were often vague: where river ended and sea began, where sea ended and river started. It was the same water, rushing down from the north to mix with the ocean, and then rising back up the river on the tides. The same water. A weak excuse. Of course Grace was right. This wasn't where he normally fished, and territory meant everything. You didn't go to places that weren't yours. Yet, here he was.

That morning Grace had looked at him strangely over her coffee before kissing him goodbye. "Be safe out there," she said. "Don't be greedy."

He dumped four aspirin into his palm and chewed them slowly between his back molars, gagging at the bitterness. His knees screamed this morning, and lately his right shoulder had started to grind and lock sometimes when he lifted a trap. There was too much tension in the job, but what job wasn't a battle? Coming out of the winter, he'd started thinking about fishing up near the river as opposed to pushing deeper out to sea. He wondered now if he was just being lazy. Still, a couple weeks ago, he'd run a half dozen traps up the river. He'd been waiting for some backlash from the Eastport fishery, but it had yet to come, and a certain sense of being in the right had slowly supplanted his doubt and his guilt.

Lyman washed the aspirin down with the bottom of a cup of black, silty coffee. Flinched at the acidity of it, wondered if it was really worth it. Bad body parts, bad medicine, bad coffee, and bad meals, these days at sea that ran together like an unbroken line. But then you'd see the sky in a certain awe-punching light, or a seal pup playfully following your wake, or pull a jackpot trap, and hope would suddenly be there again, not dancing just a few miles out of reach like it loved to do, but right there with you. Lyman shrugged off his feeling of unease and powered the boat forward. The familiar lift of the hull, the stink of gasoline, the aiding push of the rising tides, all soothed him.

He saw something in the water then, a few dozen yards from his first trap. A homemade circular carved-stick fishing weir had been set up near the mouth of the channel. The sun was bright and directly in front of him, making it hard to see clearly. He slowed at the weir, studying it, and as the boat drifted around the structure, Lyman caught a glint of something else in the distance. Out near his first buoy, a person was leaning out of a canoe and pulling up one of his traps.

Like an answer to a dark insult, the anger came on instantly. "Hey!" he yelled. Of course the words wouldn't make it across the water. "You. What the hell are you doing?"

Then he was throwing the outboard into a full, whining roar and spinning the boat forward into the sun. Fury rising through his body like gasoline.

He squinted into the glare and winced, the ache in his knees and shoulder splitting up to his skull. The person had noticed him. They were moving faster now. He couldn't tell if they were emptying the trap into the canoe or just trying to get it loose of the gunwale and back into the water. Closing the distance, he realized the person was young, and a girl. He remembered the weir, noted the canoe, the dark skin, thought of the cooked remains of the mill just up the river. He couldn't believe the bravado. Setting up a fish weir and poaching his traps just a few miles away from the scene of the fire. He was almost on the canoe now, and he kept waiting for the girl to cut the warp line and just take the trap. It would have been faster. But she didn't.

He was just feet away now, and he realized he'd kill the girl if he hit the canoe. He threw the throttle down to nothing and cut the steering wheel hard. The big lobster boat spun sideways and tipped almost ninety degrees to the water, riding up on the crests. Lyman had to hang on with all his strength to keep from sliding overboard. The wake of the breaking boat barreled forward. In an instant the canoe was flipped, girl and trap gone overboard.

"Shit," Lyman muttered, working to steady the boat. He grabbed the gaff hook and scrambled to the side. Black waters churned and folded all about. He saw the girl thrashing, bobbing up and down, and wondered if she could swim. He caught hold of her sweatshirt with the hook. She was screaming and swearing at him as he pulled her in.

Hauling the girl to the edge of the hull, he yelled, "What were you doing to it, the trap?" He tried to grab hold of her, but she pulled away and slashed at his hands with a pocketknife she'd brought up from somewhere in her soaked clothes. "Are you fucking kidding me?" he swore. "I'm trying to save you."

She laughed then, coughing water, managed to say something he couldn't make out. Her eyes were all rage, and blood covered her chin. She slashed again, and Lyman danced back, narrowly avoiding the blade. This time the girl's momentum carried her under the water, and he grabbed hold of her again with the gaff before she could drown or flee. Tired of the game, he violently hauled her up the side of the boat, flailing and screaming in panic, and knocked the knife out of her hands. Lyman reached out and grabbed the girl by the throat. She stilled instantly. Then he pinned her down against the deck, felt her neck flattening against his palm. It was like crushing a plastic bottle, so easy, just a gentle squeeze. He felt her breath moving under his hand. Saw her nostrils flaring like an animal's. She arched her throat up against his palm and he could feel her daring him to do it. For years after he would be shocked by how badly he had for the briefest awful moment wanted to crush the windpipe of a child.

"Not yours," he managed to say, gasping for breath himself and loosening his grip.

"Or yours," she hissed back at him.

The whine of a second engine suddenly filled the air. Another fishing boat was coming down the other end of the channel. He recognized Moses Jupiter's boat in the shape of the hull. A blast rang out, deep and full, and it took Lyman a second to realize that it was a shotgun firing. Moses Jupiter had shot at him. The other lobsterman had a shotgun lain over the helm windowsill as he steered with the other hand. A second shot rang out, and Lyman ducked, felt the shot sing through the air above him, thought he heard a crack somewhere but wasn't sure. "Fuck," he swore, and got even lower, forgetting the girl for a moment. As he tried to get to the cabin, where he kept the little sawed-off, a third shot caught the water right in front of the boat. This was madness, all of it. Moses Jupiter had him pinned to the deck of his own boat.

The girl was unfazed. She stood tall and carefree at the bow. When her eyes caught Lyman's, he swore she was enjoying this. He watched helplessly then as the girl turned and raced across the deck. Without slowing at all, she launched off the side of the boat in a full dive, split the water with astonishing force, and disappeared. Ten seconds passed before she broke the surface, swimming as smoothly and quickly as anyone he had ever seen. She dove again and came up under the drifting canoe, somehow managing to flip the boat over and swing her body into it in one powerful, continuous motion. He'd never seen anything like it. A fourth shot broke his trance. Moses had slowed and pulled his boat around between Lyman and the girl, effectively shielding her. The girl and canoe were gliding to the shore. It was only when Lyman grabbed his radio that he realized that one of Jupiter's seemingly random warning shots had taken off his antennae. Radio static and the hard racing of his own heart surrounded him as he turned and powered back toward the bay, the hand that had momentarily gripped the girl's neck shaking with a combination of adrenaline and fear that he thought might never still.

ALL SPRING, RUMORS TRICKLED IN to the newspaper office. Sightings of a man and a girl out among the woods, here and then there. Deer killed out of season. Snare traps and fishing weirs set around brooks and marshes. Poaching itself wasn't odd. Hunger, survival, want, never having enough food, or money, or time—these were influences many of us understood. It didn't take long for a connection to be drawn between the fire and the sightings. What was abnormal about the man and the girl was their ghostliness. There was only one credible report of actual contact. A state game biologist studying bat colonies along the lower neck of the river had come out of a cave with a bag of guano samples and seen a girl and a man standing before her. The man's eyes had widened in surprise, and then the girl had stepped in front of him as if she, just a child, might protect him. The woman set her sample kit down on the ground and raised her hands. Before she could speak, they were gone, faded or vanished back into the woods. The report added a second layer to the story we had all been caught up in: the girl who had started the fire, if this girl was indeed the same one, was not alone after all.

What the game wardens, local hunting guides, and newspaper people like our mother couldn't unearth—the location and nature of the man and the girl—Link and I took it upon ourselves to discover.

By June I had become convinced that the two were forest creatures who grew hungry, turned human, and stepped out of the woods each night to take food. As far-fetched as that was, it seemed to me the best explanation. Only something made of the earth could ingest the bones and gristle and hide of an animal and return to the earth without leaving more evidence. Part of me knew better—there's the magical, and there's the impossible—but it was into summer then, that season of possibility and wonder. I stared out at the woods beyond my bedroom window every morning, imagining a man and a girl stepping out of the trunk of a red oak or a northern white cedar, my two favorite trees.

Link believed the two had holed up like outlaws in one of the caves notched into Hatchet Mountain, where bear denned and raptors nested. Years earlier we'd discovered a nesting pair of gyrfalcons on Hatchet. Reggie claimed we were full of shit, said gyrs didn't nest this far south. When we tried to take him up the mountain to prove our claim, he just shook his head. "I'd rather sit right here and beam with pride that my nephews are already starting to spin tall, shit-stuffed tales," he said. As for the gyrfalcons, I'd never seen an animal so stunning. We went up the mountain every clear afternoon after school to sit with them, to watch them. They were bright white and dappled by hundreds of small, dark-brown teardrop-shaped spots. In flight their wings opened as wide as a car. And when they took off from the cliffs, air blasted down off their wings like the exhaust from a furnace. Somehow they'd wandered down from the northern reaches of the Maritimes, and we watched in amazement as the majestic couple returned to their cliff nest each spring for three years before they suddenly disappeared, and we knew they'd been shot by a fisherman or poisoned by a farmer. Over time the nest had grown massive: five feet deep and nearly ten feet wide. It didn't seem right to let it be taken over by anything when it had once housed something so rare and stunning, so Link and I climbed all the way up the cliff and dismantled the nest stick by stick. Reggie met us at the bottom of the mountain after all and helped us pile the sticks into the back of his truck. "I won't tell you I'm sorry," he said. "Every fool knows a falcon keeps moving, even in death." Then we drove ten miles up to Prospect, where the river narrows around Verona Island, and we floated the nest, piece by piece, down the Penobscot as an offering to the departed falcons. "Why the narrows?" Link asked. Something I couldn't quite voice about the spot had made sense to me: the thick, thundering river bending into the narrowed gorge, squeezed on its banks by towering spruce and pines, the massive green and blue glacial boulders that heaved their river-rounded backs up through the cold trickling water, the way fish leapt into being after mayfly hatches, spinning just above the surface in the long orange afternoon light. "Some places are like portals to eternity," Reggie said after a few moments of silence. "You stand in them and look around, and you feel how long and unending the world is. You become a part of something beyond time. Maybe this is one of those places."

It was the type of answer we expected from our uncle: a bit profound and a bit baffling. Reggie lived in a small house stacked floor to ceiling with books and was a constant source of warmth, obscure knowledge, delightful bursts of profanity, and at times disturbing peculiarity. After his parents died, he had flirted with law school, then attended divinity school for a year, developing a fascination with eschatology that ultimately led him to drop out, start farming apples, and embark on a long and semi-dignified career in eccentricity.

While my uncle wasn't some doomsday prophet wildly predicting the end times, the ending of things did fascinate him. He didn't believe the end of a life could be as simple and cruel as Christianity claimed, where one's final experience in the physical world was one of judgment—death, followed by an odd, divine verdict: heaven for you, hell for you. Instead he was convinced every ending was followed by some kind of reunion with the divine, whether that was a simple return to the earth or a wild celestial journey to some other plane of existence ruled by a grand, theistic being we'd yet to prove existed. In his eyes the end of the world, or the end of living, as we understood it, was not a terrifying premise at all but the first tilt toward reunion.

This isn't to say his eccentricities didn't become problematic at times. He once shot out an unplugged television with a Winchester deer rifle because he was afraid the droning voices of advertising had found a way to transmit their signal even when the machine was powered down. And after his parents' death, he became increasingly obsessed with the doomsday clock created by the Atomic Scientists of Chicago after World War II. The clock tracked the level of continuous danger humans were creating for themselves with their preposterously large, inventive, violent, and misguided brains by monitoring the world's proximity to midnight, a metaphorical number-time representing the tipping point of global catastrophe from which the species would not be able to return.

He became known in town for randomly giving those around him periodic updates on how close the world was to its end. I remember a year in the 1980s when I was just a child, and my uncle was red-eyed and jittery from too little sleep and too much gin. The Cold War was devouring the news cycle. Both the United States and Russia were stockpiling nuclear warheads. Reggie showed up unannounced on a Saturday in June, started a bonfire in our backyard without asking, and burned a truckload of garbage and apple waste. Then he sat down in our living room in a great, grandstanding whirl of trash-fire reek and announced that the world was "three minutes from midnight, according to the Atomic Scientists, and we best get our goddamned affairs in order." I was only seven years old or so, and while I was scared, I was secretly grateful. If the world was ending, I believed I deserved a warning. Knowing the potential of death was present, that summer I set about memorizing every moment I could. I sat against the garden shed facing the woods, the hot cedar shingles rough against my back. The air smelled of river earth and sawdust. When I pushed my hands into the ground, the spongy carpet of moss sank just enough that my fingernails disappeared. Purple lilacs rose around the shed, hiding me from view, and it was here I sat reading books and imagining prehistory and the mammoths and giant beavers that once walked the land. The air filled with moisture as the tide moved in, and turned dry with heat as the sea went back out. I fell asleep and woke with the sun warming my feet and fell asleep again. I heard my father's table saw buzzing and my mother's heart singing. My brothers playing with a cap gun in the yard. They were all with me, and under the lilacs I closed my eyes tightly and knew I would never need anything else. And I never really have. My parents felt differently. They forbade Reggie from coming over until he got help. It remained the only time in my life that our door was ever closed to my uncle. A year later Reggie had gotten sober. He sold his apple farm and bought a hotel and attached bar downtown, near the newspaper office and our father's boatyard. It was time to come in from the woods, he said, and be a little less alone.

That summer I spent as much time as possible at the hotel or the boatyard or the newspaper. I knew that at any of these locations, my mother would never be far from sight. The truth was, she was falling away from us, disappearing down into the story.

When she said "I'm going in to town," we knew she meant she was going to visit the paper, and no one was to follow. Even when we were welcome, after school or during holiday breaks, we existed at the paper in a probationary limbo. The shelves of old books and ancient linotypes and tarnished printing equipment, the weight of dust and paper, the squares of hot orange light falling through the antique windows—all of them joined together to remind us we were intruders. She had never been a gentle woman, but here she was barely our mother at all. Once I picked up a water glass and crushed it in my fist to see if she'd react, and she sat right at her desk with her glasses slipping down her nose and went on editing a story as the blood oozed up between my fingers. At times like this, when some story came along and displaced the rest of the world, I believed it was up to us to sustain her.

As the rumors spread and our mother's obsession grew, the land around the fire, somewhat stunningly, began to come to life. Willow shoots broke the charred earth around the mill. Fireweed shot up thick and flaming purple. Small families of hickory trees sprouted. Lupine emerged along ashy paths for forklifts and delivery trucks. Other plants came, too, rising into the summer. What had for more than a hundred years been a lifeless gray industrial landscape turned verdant. As people chased the arsonist and her father, looking for answers, for justice, the plants and trees ignored the noise and simply grew. Locals began to notice, then the news people as well. After that people began coming from all over the state. "We needed to see it," visitors said of the mill site. "There's something happening here," a couple who came all the way from New Brunswick told my mother during an interview. "Don't look away," they said. "This is a work of life. Whoever did this had a plan."

These people used the word *pilgrimage*, not knowing what else to call their journeys. "We just felt called." Over and over a similar refrain was repeated in the diners, convenience stores, gas stations, coffee shops, hair salons, barbershops, beaches, river parks, and flea markets around Eastport as people came to see the land after the fire.

My mother had pointed out how rare the act really was. "White men blow things up," she said. "Native American women don't." And she was right. If a Penobscot kid was going to perform an act that perhaps went against everything she'd ever been taught, there would have to be more to the story. Link and I sat at the newspaper office on a hot day in late June, reading more about willow trees, trees that just happened to clean and remove dioxin, heavy metals, and other toxins from the earth in which they grew.

"Imagine a tree doing that," I said to Link. "Healing the ground around it."

Link was about to respond when Cal Hayes walked in, carrying a deer skull under his arm. The sun had bleached the skull mostly white, but a few bloody strings of white fat and red gristle still clung to the jawbone.

"Those two have done it again, Falon," Cal yelled on his way across the office. As Cal walked by, he turned the deer skull so it watched us the whole time. He was the smallest man we knew, so short in fact that from a distance it was easy to mistake him for a child.

Our mother had been working all morning on a story about pollution killing bald eagles along the river. "This game bores me, Cal," she said, sighing. "I have better things to worry about than a deer skull. You could have at least cleaned the thing. It smells awful."

"I was thinking you'd get mad if I did. Now you're mad I didn't."

"Mad?"

"Pictures. I figured bloody pictures sell more papers. So I didn't want to mess with it too much. If you've got a red marker, we could gore it up even more."

Cal was joking, of course, but now our mother was actually mad. "That yellow-journalism garbage isn't what I do."

"I didn't mean anything, Falon."

After that our mother threw Cal out of the office, but only after angrily taking the skull from him and snapping a few pictures of it posed on the back deck, with the light and the ocean behind it. Cal looked at us knowingly and left with a satisfied bounce to his walk. It was hard to provoke a reaction from Falon Ames more potent than a dismissive sideways look over her glasses, and Cal had succeeded royally with the fleshy skull of a jacked deer.

"Where was it?" I asked.

"They found it along the river. Below Snub Point."

Link went over to a desk in the corner of the room where USGS maps of the bay and the lower section of the river were spread out among a scattering of tacks, string, and sticky notes. The maps were marked and annotated with supposed sightings and call-ins.

"That's fifteen miles up the river," I said.

"Calls about sightings aren't coming in from there anymore," our mother said.

"You think they're working their way downriver to the bay, don't you?" Link said.

Our mother suddenly seemed far away and distracted. "I'm busy," she snapped. "On a deadline. Go do something. Go be kids." Then she disappeared into her office and closed the door, leaving Link and me alone with the maps and the musty smell of the deer skull.

Link left, but I stayed at the newspaper office for another hour, staring at the maps until the world around me had dissolved into visions of the river. According to the Penobscot people, years ago a giant frog monster descended on the river's headwaters and selfishly gathered up all the water for himself. Dark, starving times gripped the land. People began to die in great numbers. The world became all shadow. The great Penobscot hero Gluskabe saw his people dying out and felled a tree on Akəlópemo, the frog monster, killing him. Then Gluskabe watched in awe as the crown and branches of the fallen tree slowly morphed into water, becoming the main stem of the river and its many streams and tributaries. Driven by thirst, some of the people jumped into the water, becoming fish, turtles, frogs, other sea creatures, and ensuring that the Penobscots would forever be related to the river and its animals.

Thousands of years later, white people began building dams across the Penobscot to generate power, again choking off the waters. Then something unprecedented in US history happened: the Maine Indian Claims Settlement Act returned three hundred thousand acres of land to the tribes, awarded them $81.5 million for development, and extended federal recognition, moving the tribes out from under state agencies and closer to actual self-governance, though, many argued, not nearly close enough, as the state continued to try to govern the tribes like municipalities, instead of recognizing them as sovereign entities. It returned the ancestral waters and islands of the Penobscot, and acknowledged the tribe's right to fish and hunt their lands as they saw fit. Small, bitter victories, but victories still.

Now these two were moving through the land, hunting and fishing when and where they wanted. No one here ever had enough, so the French hated the Irish and the Irish hated the English and the English hated the Penobscot, and everyone hated anyone they thought got better breaks. My mother argued that the man and the girl shouldn't be considered poachers. As much as a person could claim ownership of earth, the river and the lands around it were theirs. Some agreed, seeing two people of a sovereign nation entitled to subsistence hunting and fishing rights throughout their ancestral grounds. Others saw two fugitives exploiting a loophole.

I sat with both opinions for a long time and let my mind go back through the history. Don't be mistaken: the goal was always destruction of a whole people. In 1755 Spencer Phips, then lieutenant governor of the province of Massachusetts Bay, issued a proclamation declaring the Penobscot people enemies of the crown. Phips called on all "his Majesty's Subjects of this Province to Embrace all opportunities of pursuing, captivating, killing, and Destroying all and every of the aforesaid Indians." That goal was quietly alive still in the minds of far too many here, I worried.

You drive through these small towns now and see gas stations and schools and idyllic waterfronts and nicely lit art galleries and stately libraries. Most people never know the truth, our true history: for instance, how there was once a small scalp station on the Sheepscot River near Wiscasset where British merchants paid colonists forty pounds for the scalp of a Penobscot man, twenty-five pounds for the scalp of a Penobscot woman, and twenty pounds for the scalp of any Penobscot child under the age of twelve years old. This was at a time when the average settler made less than a hundred pounds a year. And so the choice gradually set in: watch your children starve to death or rip away, maim, mutilate, and kill the babes of others.

MOSES JUPITER WAS WAITING IN our yard with a horse when my mother and I got home. A tall gray-dappled mare. From the car, my mother and I watched in puzzlement. We were not horse people.

Moses had unloaded the horse from a trailer and was walking around alongside the animal. He led the horse into a trot, slowed, and made four big loops around the property. "Getting her ready for you all," he called back to us.

The animal paused along the woods and nosed into a stand of witch-hazel trees to eat the berries, apparently taking a liking to their ancient, restorative qualities, and I grew a little fonder of the beast for her good taste in flora. Behind us, down the road back in the woods, my father's saws buzzed and sang. Simon's car was not in the yard, and Link wasn't home either.

Moses brought the horse back into the dusty drive and produced a carrot from his pocket. "Think she's getting there. I've been here for hours, letting her acclimate."

My mother ignored Moses and started unloading groceries and boxes of files she'd brought home.

"You've just been hanging out in our yard?" I asked.

Moses shrugged. "No one came to greet me, and no one came to tell me to leave."

Somehow I knew my father was aware of the scene playing out up at the house. "That's pretty weird."

Moses shrugged again. "Her name's Cricket because she's faster than the wind and quiet as a bug." He turned to me with the carrot. "Hardly ever speaks."

"Please tell me this isn't actually happening." My mother was scowling over the roof of the car. "That you didn't actually bring us a horse."

Moses stopped and collected himself. I could see him carefully work-ing his way through his vocabulary, looking for another way to frame things. "I never was big on lying," he finally said. "You want this carrot or not?"

"Just don't." My mother took the vegetable and threw it across the yard into the trees. The horse didn't move from our side. "Where's Arnoux?"

"Not here," Moses said.

I pictured my father peeking out the northwest window of the shop, glimpsing Moses's truck banging down the road, towing a horse trailer. He would have grinned and gone back to whatever he was working on. He wouldn't have been foolish enough to immediately come out of the shop when he heard my mother's car, either. It was one thing to pull in to see a horse in our yard. Another thing to pull in to see him standing beside a horse in the yard.

"That horse is a girl?" my mother asked.

"Yes, ma'am."

"Thank Christ. I'll keep her then. This place is overrun with dicks and idiots."

"Wait," I said. "You're serious?"

"Don't worry. I've got more carrots." I was amazed Moses could toy around like this and get away with it, but my mother had long been fond of him. "*Wàlamto áhahso,*" Moses said. "She's a good horse, Falon. *Pálsk*ʷ *awo.* Proud. Just the right amount of rascally, too. She'll eat all your tomatoes, but she'll shit off to the side of the doorstep instead of right in front of it. She's an Indian horse, though. If she doesn't do something you ask, don't get mad at her. It's just the language barrier."

"Why are you getting rid of her?" I asked.

"I didn't say she was my good horse. Belongs to a friend who can't afford to keep her."

I tried to remember if any of the reports called in to the newspaper about sightings had mentioned a horse. "Where's this friend now?" I asked.

"Look at the little journalist," Moses said. "He's taking after you, Falon." His gaze slid through the tall green hemlocks standing in the yard. He raised his hand and fanned his fingers in the air. "Hard telling. In the trees, in the wind, here and there, I suppose."

The sun had come west around behind the largest of the trees, a hundred-and-twenty-footer which towered over our house. I reached out, and Cricket nuzzled my palm. In the light my hand was green and the horse was green and her neck was warm with thumping blood. I felt the line between many worlds, animal and human, natural and man-made, collapsing. Her blood thumped louder, harder, under my hand, and mine beat back as well. She was full of unseen rivers. She was majestic.

"Falon," Moses said. "We need to talk." His tone had changed, and I felt suddenly afraid. Under my hand Cricket seemed to feel it as well, a long shiver quaking through her body.

"Moses," my mother said, "I believe we truly do."

My mother sat at the table while Moses moved about the kitchen, making coffee. The hard, dark smell of it filled the room. In the distance the saws had gone silent, and I figured my father had gone to pick Link up in town.

Moses stopped moving and turned to fully face us. "Lyman caught a Penobscot girl nosing around one of his traps two days ago," he said. "She'd built a weir out there to fish with. Guess she got curious about why there was a Penobscot Bay lobster trap up in the throat of the Penobscot River."

My mother looked over at me and was about to speak when Moses interrupted her. "He should stay."

"Fine," my mother said. "Keep going."

"The kid was in a canoe. Lyman caught up to her before she could paddle back to shore. He had her around the throat when someone came down the river and started firing warning shots."

"Where exactly was this?"

"In the narrows above Odom Ledge. Out around Verona Island, the eastern channel."

"The narrows." I could see my mother mapping the altercation out in her head. Picturing who fished where, what buoys were traditionally set in what spots. "Why's he way up there?"

"Hard to say. Greed's a long tradition for them, though."

"That bastard." My mother stood and slammed her fist down on the table.

"Don't jump to outrage just because you don't like him," Moses said.

"I like him fine."

"I get it's complicated."

"And not your business."

"*Ačélihoso*," Moses said. "Lyman can't control himself, Falon. I fear he's going deeper into a bad place."

My mother looked through the woods. "Around in the eastern channel. That means the trap was in the river's estuary, not the bay, and a Penobscot kid might have every right to what was in it."

Moses grimaced. "That may be true," he said. "But I didn't come out here looking to stir things up that way. I came out here to tell you something wrong happened to a child. Word's getting around, and I wanted someone with a reasonable head to have the facts. Lyman shouldn't be setting traps in the river. But the kid shouldn't be sticking her hands in them either. That's dangerous business. Dumb business. And I don't think this is a dumb kid. A scared kid. A pissed-off kid. But not a dumb one."

"What you do is cut the warp line and sink it." My brother's voice was full of all the collected, honed, and misguided bravado an American boyhood could manage. Arnoux and Link were standing in the hallway off the kitchen. Reggie was with them as well. I hadn't heard any of them come inside.

"Not if you're starving," Arnoux said. He was looking down at the floor.

"It's illegal to set a lobster trap within three hundred feet of the mouth of a fish weir," Reggie said, surprising us. "So the question might be what came first, the weir or the trap?"

"Who cares?" Link interrupted. "She should have sunk the thing. No more trap, no more fishing on your turf."

"And a good way to get shot," our father said and walked out of the house, trailing an anger behind him I didn't fully understand.

Reggie gripped my shoulder. When my mother nodded, my uncle led me outside. My father was stomping around the yard with his fists balled at his sides. He stopped when he saw Cricket. Reggie and I watched as the horse leaned her heavy head into my father's neck, nuzzling him, comforting him. I moved to join him, and Reggie pulled back against me, "Not just yet," he said.

After a few moments pressed near the horse, my father laughed loudly, kissed Cricket's neck, and walked her over to the woods to retrieve the discarded carrot from earlier.

"Ignore your brother," Reggie whispered and let go of my shoulder.

I HAD ALWAYS THOUGHT THAT land was land. Water was water. An island was an island. None were human-owned, up for occupying, raiding, or abusing. When the wind tore through the trees, I turned to the sky and tried to map the shapes it wrote into the branches. I put my hand to the damp grass in the morning and lifted it when I no longer felt thirsty. Smells were not just smells, but layers of smells, lovingly built like a painting. Twigs on top of leaves on top of moss on top of loam on top of dirt on top of root on top of rock on top of bone on top of basalt. On the forest floor I ran through time. Old leaves under new leaves. Dry needles at the bases of pines. When I scratched the needles up with the toe of a shoe, gnats would whip through the light, flock to fresh scent. I slipped pine cones between my lips. Pressed my ear to the bellies of ancient cedars, heard blood that I believed in beneath the bark. It was in the aliveness of the world that I knew I was alive.

Now I was again reminded of how little I knew about the world's actual workings. Everything had been taken by someone at some point, and those old hurts and wayward entitlements raged on, generation to generation, feeding sadness and violence.

Scared, I began staying closer to my mother at the paper. Two days after Moses brought Cricket to our house, I was there late in the afternoon. I'd just come back from The Fish House with dinner, a Styrofoam container of golden-brown biscuits and thick, spicy sausage gravy, when I saw Lyman Creel, wind-reddened and stumbling a bit. He moved across the harbor front, plunged into the road without looking, narrowly missing a passing car, and walked into the newspaper office.

"I want this printed," he said, and set a sheet of paper down on my mother's desk.

It was obvious that Lyman hadn't slept in the days since the incident. He stunk of whiskey and sweat. Of camp smoke, pine needles, and dirt. Moses had been right. Word of Lyman's act had spread quickly about the bay, and the community's disgust at one of their own attacking a child had displaced their anger over the fire. Faced with all this, the defensiveness sank from my mother's face. "Lyman," she said. "Are you okay?"

"I just want this printed." He tapped a finger on the crumpled sheet of paper. "It's an apology. To that kid I roughed up. No," he corrected himself, "to everyone."

"Lyman," she whispered. "It doesn't work like that. This isn't a confessional. It's a newspaper."

He squeezed the bridge of his nose with his red hands. "Just take it, Falon. Read it. Please."

"I won't."

"I defended you at The Fish House."

"You're here because of guilt and ego. Those are *you* problems. Nothing about that piece of paper interests me."

Lyman swayed on his feet for a moment, turned his face up to the overhead lights, squinting. "You got cruel," he said.

"Maybe I always was."

"People need to know what really happened, and no one will listen to me. But you know how it was. Back then. You *know* me."

Back then. Falon did know. She had been on the bluff the night Billy died. Seventeen years old, senior year. The middle of March on a Wednesday night, and she was at the edge of the world with two boys and a bottle of wine. She could see the hell the summer was going to bring. They both wanted her, worshipped her, and there was such a buzz in that, in knowing she had so much over them. The wine kicked that buzz up a notch, and she got full of herself, thought: This must be close to how it feels to be a man. A few days earlier they'd both bought her a bouquet of Easter lilies from the grocery store. Billy giving her the flowers on one day, and then Lyman showing up with the exact same flowers the next morning, holding them out in the yard, awkwardly nodding to the windows, where her brother Reggie and her mother were watching, and then getting back into his father's big Cadillac and backing around, all of his performance, the formality of his pressed jeans and button-up shirt, the showiness of that rich man's car, the statement of bringing the flowers, really quite hokey and yet endearing as well. It was obvious that he was nervous, had gone about gathering together this performance to give his brain something to fixate on other than what he might say and what she might say. She put Lyman's flowers on the counter beside Billy's flowers and went on with her life, wondering suddenly: What else would they do? Though she hated Easter, hollow gifts, and store flowers more than just about anything, she'd been seeing them both since, riding around, drinking their wine, and marveling at how strange her life had become, to be wanted so badly by two people who you were convinced you'd barely remember in ten years, when you were long gone from here and your real life had started. She watched Billy horsing around with Lyman on the rocks now. The two of them had been stacking up deadfall for a fire before they got tired and started singing Grateful Dead songs to each other. Now they were dancing with each other, a big old foolish drunken waltz like two pseudo-lovers at a bad wedding. She thought about being wanted, the danger in that sort of buzz, then she got angry at the thought that they only wanted her for her body, not everything, and angry that they both assumed they could drink themselves to waste tonight and she'd take care of them after, mother them. She lifted the bottle and drank until her tongue burned, wondered if she could steer them toward each other instead. When she looked back to the cliff, Billy was gone. Seconds before, he had been swaying in Lyman's arms. Lyman was screaming. Running along the ledge, looking down into the waters. Two hours later, at first light, a team of volunteer firefighters hauled Billy Jupiter's shattered body from the rocks. Three months later Falon was in California, trying to forget, and Lyman was headed to Vietnam with dreams of someday taking over a fishery.

"I don't like to think about that night," Falon said.

"They hate me because of it and because of my family."

"You're not a target."

"And you're not the one everyone called Indian Killer for the rest of their life. I got a history here with them."

"You're being paranoid, Lyman. I can't stand it when you get this way."

"My great-great-grandfather was one of the first people who dammed the river. Billy once told me that a lot of his people saw that as the beginning of the end. The frog monster returned, blocking the river, the fish passages, eating all the water up. All this fairy-tale shit. I didn't even know that kid was Penobscot. I just saw someone around my traps and lost it."

"That's the thing, Lyman. She wasn't just someone. She was a *kid*. Tell me you wouldn't have killed her if Moses hadn't shown up."

Lyman blushed, eyed the floor. He didn't answer, couldn't figure out how to even begin to answer. He wanted to say, *No, Falon, no it wasn't like that*. He wanted to tell her Billy's death was an accident. He'd tried to have a good life here. Now old memories of violence and mishap swam up around him. For years he'd pushed the past down and moved forward by working his body to exhaustion. But when his hand curled around that kid's neck, the wall he'd built over the years buckled. Then when he saw the kid's eyes, filled with not fear but challenge, eyes saying, *I've survived worse, and you've done worse, will do worse*, that wall collapsed. Moses Jupiter came around the bend shooting. Might have saved his life. Might have saved everyone's life. Lyman had gone home shaking with rage. Pulled away when Grace put her arms around him and asked what was wrong. When she pressed her hands down flat against his stomach, slid them beneath his belt, squeezed the head of his cock, bit his neck, tried to coax him back to the bedroom to lick and fuck the terror out of him, he fled. Said nothing to Galen and Wren, couldn't even meet their eyes in the yard, where they stood kicking a soccer ball around. Headed out into the state forest, deep into the woods. Whirling sky spinning too fast and heavy with stars overhead. He kept coming in and out of time, wandering the woods, catching the dusk sound of whippoorwills, which terrified him because there weren't supposed to be many left in the world here, and they sounded everywhere. Ate nothing, camped on the mossy earth deep in the light-swallowing hemlocks and spruces. He was closer to the free side of madness than he'd ever been. Too close. He wondered what type of breakdown he was having when on the second day, the long sling of heat and humidity snapped and rain fell like nails, painfully cold and gray. He found a bottle of whiskey some kids had left in the knothole of a tree years ago. Tried not to drink. Stared at the bottle for hours. But whatever resolve he once owned seemed to have slid out with the wall the girl had knocked down. The rain lasted the night, unrelenting, broken only by rips of lightning and echoes of thunder tumbling up and down the coast. Somewhere in the night he came to a decision, a moment of clarity, the only answer he saw to this mess: he would apologize. It was a simple solution, probably too simple, but its buzz cooked up in his head with a desperate certainty until he felt that old boyhood elation of knowing that things could be okay, would be okay, that the world was still good and safe. It drove him from the woods and back home, where he grabbed one of his daughter's notebooks, wrote his amends, tore out the sheet, and walked into town, where he now stood inside the dusty office of *The Lowering Days*, shaking and red-eyed and realizing what a fool he was.

Falon had been watching Lyman through his long silence. She was trying to remember the boy she had known so long ago. "What are you really trying to apologize for, Lyman?" she said finally. "Because I'm guessing it's a little more complicated than terrorizing some Penobscot kid. Just because you rejected your family's money, that doesn't make you clean from the damage they did."

"It doesn't make me culpable either." Lyman's voice was cold, measured.

"Maybe not."

"That was twenty years ago."

My mother pushed a stack of paper over on her desk in rage. "You piece of shit." She laughed. "Talking to me about the past and being innocent, being misunderstood. If I was interested in empty words, I'd be down at The Fish House pissing the day away. We all lost, Lyman. We're still losing."

Lyman started to speak, but my mother turned to me. I had been quietly watching the exchange with the uncomfortable sense that I was looking into worlds that were not mine to see. "Don't you ever become like him," she said to me. "Don't you dare. There's nothing worse than a desperate man. Go home, Lyman."

Lyman reached into his pocket and came up holding a small yellow ball. It took us a moment to realize it was a lemon. Lyman flipped open a pocketknife and pressed the blade into the fruit, deftly cutting it in half. Then he dug in with the blade again, carving off a thin slice. He slipped the bitter disc between his lips and began to chew. He lifted his apology from the desk and wrapped the remaining halves of the lemon in the paper. The entire time his eyes had not left my mother's.

"You used to whisper my name awful sweet," he said, talking around the lemon slice, his tongue working the rind. "I bet you still would."

My mother glared at him, refused to look at the lemon in his hand, refused to look away from his face. "Just sweet enough to make you forget that little blade of yours. Just long enough to get my fingers around it."

"You've got it all planned out."

"I do, Lyman. It wouldn't take more than a slice, a twist, and a little tug to cut your tongue clean out."

"Billy said you were a whore," Lyman said. "Too bad he had to die for everyone else to realize it."

Then Lyman set the lemon, wrapped in the crumpled note, down on the desk and walked out the door, sinking back into the dusk and the gulls wheeling above the harbor. Enraged, I leapt up to follow him out the open door.

Falon knew she'd started something awful, could feel it stalking around the room, vengeful and angry. Knew too she had to stop it before her son went out that door and she never saw him again. "David Almerin Ames," she snapped. "You will sit back down this singular instant. We have sausage gravy to finish, and news to print."

It was my mother's language that pulled me up just enough to forget chasing after Lyman. *This singular instant*—the phrase was pure Mom,

both the grandiosity and the redundancy of it. I came back and picked up
the Styrofoam containers.

But the office door was still open, and the hate leaching down the
walls was making its way across the room now. Falon noticed it too late,
watched it slide around her son, watched it rear up, and before she could
rise to stop it, she watched as that old hate leapt through the doorway.
She gasped, and when her son said "What is it, Mom?" she didn't seem to
know how to answer. It was out in the open then, free. She watched it lift
like a faint red mist, grinning as it pushed up into the wind that went back
and forth along the river, the wind that breathed life into their world.

Part III

Seven

MOLLY HAD BEEN SHARP AND jittery since the altercation in the channel. Moses had come to them at their encampment in the woods twice since, first to check up on her under the excuse of bringing more supplies no one had asked for, and then to tell them he had found a place for them to go. Both times Molly, full of stubborn pride, had barely spoken to him. Barely even looked at him. He couldn't tell which the girl resented more: being caught by Lyman Creel or rescued by him.

Though the wound to her chin had mostly healed, a dark scab still showed where she had struck the canoe when it flipped. After escaping the water, she'd spent the better part of two days vomiting. Her father's anger was matched only by his worry. Sometimes at night she woke gasping for air, then moved through the day feeling that man's hands around her throat like an invisible collar.

During the second visit, Moses told them to get ready to leave. The finality of his sentences seemed to move Molly out of silence.

"You could have shot me on the water," she said.

"I don't shoot things I'm not aiming for. They were warning shots."

"You were driving a boat."

"And you were causing a scene." Moses's own anger caught him off guard.

"He was going to kill me."

Moses shrugged in a way that said *Maybe, maybe not.* "That's why I started shooting."

"And you could have shot me."

"That would have been unfortunate," Moses said, and turned away from her.

Three days later he drove his truck in as close to their camp as he could and parked on a service road near a power company substation. A few moments later Adam and Molly slipped out of the trees, each carrying a pack on their shoulders. Moses pulled a green tarp back. He had filled the truck bed with leaves and pine boughs.

"That's your genius plan?" Molly almost spat.

"Molly," cautioned Adam.

Without another word, he tossed his pack into the bed and climbed in himself. Molly grudgingly followed. Moses arranged the branches and boughs over them as well as he could. Then he pulled the tarp, punctured with a few rips and holes for ventilation, back across the truck bed. It was not a burial, he reminded himself as he secured the ties. Their story was not over yet.

"You have to be joking," Molly said a few hours later when she first saw the abandoned house high in the wooded hills rising over Penobscot Bay. "We're trading the woods for this wreck?"

Moses had parked his truck several miles away, down in a logging cut on the land of a white family he knew. Moses and Adam followed him blindly through the woods as the older man silently and steadily picked his way along old game trails. It was obvious that he knew exactly where he was going. Still he took his time, measuring the surroundings, listening, doubling back to make a secondary trail every so often. Thrushes whistled. Currents of wind moaned life into the pines. No one else was around for miles. Molly loved the adventure, and for a few hours at least she felt all the fear and anger of the last few weeks lift.

Now they stood in the trees, eyeing the massive house. A sprawling white colonial with a wraparound porch and a mansard-style roof, it sat in a hilltop clearing that was slowly being retaken by the woods. The driveway was a long grown-in dirt road, and there wasn't another house for miles. Woods completely surrounded them. The house itself twisted and undulated and sank and swelled along every surface.

She was furious when she saw there was a long, curling driveway, severely overgrown, but passable still. "We could have just driven here," she said, incredulous.

"Could do a lot of things that might end in a jail cell," Moses quipped, and Molly glared at him.

"It isn't ours," Molly said. She looked around at the land. Imagined the awful act of clearing so many trees for this, a forgotten monument to vanity. She thought she might puke.

"No," her father said as he breached the tree line and took a step into the long golden clearing. "It also *isn't* anyone's at this point."

"It's a rich white person house," Molly said finally. "*Awenóhčəwahki.*"

"And maybe the last place they'd think to look for a couple Indian outlaws," said Moses. Indian outlaws. Molly liked the phrase and the idea. She wanted to smile, but bit her lip to keep from doing so.

"It's going to keep you safe," Moses added. He was tired of the anger between him and his goddaughter. Rabid dogs were kinder to each other.

"It's going to be a home," Adam said with a forcefulness that dared anyone to question him.

"For how long?" asked Molly.

"As long as it'll have us," said her father. "Through the winter at least, I hope."

As long as it'll have us. Molly was comforted by the phrasing. Her father had a constant habit of imbuing things with living traits. Molly had not thought it unusual until she went to school and found that other fathers didn't do this. She had been sullen, angry, ashamed for weeks, until her father forced the truth out of her. "Why do you do it?" she had asked. "I don't know," her father admitted. "I just always have. I think it makes me pay closer attention. I think it's taught me to be gentle." This was not what she wanted to hear—she did not want her father to be uncertain or gentle,

she wanted him to be tough and confident and direct and as brave as the
legendary chiefs and warriors in the bedtime tales she'd grown up on—
but she understood that he was being honest. Slowly, she learned to accept
his vulnerability. It would be a long time still before acceptance turned to
pride, and she finally understood all the dimensions of bravery.

"Lots of people have had it a lot harder than this," Adam said.

Moses nervously rubbed his hands against his thighs and turned back
into the woods. "I can't come out here the same way once the snow starts,"
he said. "Too many tracks. But I'll come as long as I can. Only if you want."

"You're welcome any time, Moses," Adam said. Molly grudgingly
nodded.

That night father and daughter camped at the edge of the clearing. In
the morning they'd begin exploring the house itself. Adam gave Molly two
books. One was a survival narrative about a group of unlucky settlers going
through Donner Pass in the mountains of California. Molly read the back
cover and the first two pages and then understood what having it harder
could mean. The second book was a pocket dictionary. A page about two-
thirds of the way through was dog-eared, and the girl scanned through the
entries until she came across the word *squatter*. At her elbow in the semi-
darkness, her father said, "You've been called a lot of awful shit in your life
already, Molly. That's so you know what else people are going to call us. It's
also so you have time to think about what you are and what you aren't."

"Will we become thieves?" There were abandoned summer homes and
cottages, remote fishing cabins, and shuttered lake camps throughout the
county. So far they had not had to resort to breaking into any of them for
supplies.

"Not if I can help it," Adam said.

In the morning they cautiously left the woods. The house had a stone
foundation and a dugout dirt cellar. The entire house had begun to sag and
slide into the earth. There wasn't a single straight line in it anywhere anymore. Molly pictured a huge, proud animal that had had its spine broken
and yet somehow still limped through the days. A backhouse for wood
and storage, long and empty, was built off the kitchen.

Out back was a cavernous detached horse barn with gaping holes in its roof. It was as if the shingles were gradually being sucked down through the openings.

"They had horses here once," Adam said, and Molly went quiet, remembering Cricket and another life.

When they pushed the massive door open and stepped inside, instead of swallowed shingles and splintered rafters, they found an old tractor that wouldn't start, a 1932 Packard with only the rusty frame remaining, and an array of odd junk and farm machinery that seemed shoulder deep. Every step through the property was like wading through an ocean of dead, forgotten things.

Inside the house the floorboards had been removed, leaving just the joists spanning the cellar, a chasm of dense brown earth. Remarkably, despite the lack of light, the forest surrounding the house had managed to start growing inside as well. Tall vines and clematis and pokeweed and lupines and patches of Solomon's seal sprouted from the dirt floor and rose through the rooms.

Molly didn't understand how the land had survived here, how it had been left to start returning to its natural state, why some rich person hadn't bought it up and cut it all down and made it their own again.

"Moses told me a descendant of the original owner, some ship captain, still owns the house and land," her father said, as if able to read her thoughts. "He lives somewhere in Europe. Pays a fortune in taxes he mails across the Atlantic each year to keep things just the way they are."

"Trashed?" Molly asked.

"More or less," her father smiled.

In the main parlor, under a mildewed sheet, the girl found a dusty upright piano, hand-stained a dark coffee brown. She looked at her father, and he nodded. She pulled the sheet all the way back and gasped. There was a smell to the wood, even among all the swirling dirt and dust falling through the room. It was the smell of music. Her hands were shaking as she carefully lifted the keyboard cover, afraid that the entire thing might fall apart in her hands, this dream of dust and old wood. She traced her fingers along the gold letters, MEHLIN & SONS, NEW YORK, until she could picture them with her eyes closed. She sat at the worn keys for the rest of the afternoon, imagining notes, arranging and rearranging the sounds in her head, not yet daring to try to play, too afraid of the disappointment should the piano fail to still produce sound.

THEY SLEPT IN THE ATTIC, wrapped in horse blankets from the barn. Through a porthole window, Molly could barely see a blue sliver of ocean through the trees. Sometimes her father hummed old cowboy songs he knew. Molly made vomiting noises and reminded him he was supposed to sing the Indian songs. Her father blushed and agreed, said he wished the television had played more of those when he was a kid. During the day she practiced strange public school word problems from a book her father had brought, recited animal names and traits, and wrote long lists of what plants around the property were medicinal or edible—coltsfoot and bloodroot for a cough; five-finger grass and mugwort for a fever; goldenseal for wounds; horseradish for torpor; milkweed, dock, mustard, plantain, chicory, cattail, burdock, and fireweed for food and other medicine. At night they listened to the wind rustling in the plants below the floorboards. Molly began to think of them as family members quietly asleep downstairs. On these nights the world seemed to exist outside of time. She didn't think she ever wanted to go back.

Adam was not so sure. They were living a subsistence life of the most extreme order. Some of that was circumstance, but some was choice. There were easier places to go, but he wasn't sure about going to them. He remembered the fervent tales of monastics pushed by the Catholic schools of his youth. When he cut through all the doctrinal bullshit, he realized that the point of the stories was that some people had to detach from the world to find the clarity to live rightly in the world. He thought of Saint Benedict. Of all the peddled religious figures, Benedict was the only one he had ever liked. Benedict wasn't a fanatic. He wasn't a firebrand rabbi like Jesus of

Nazareth, or a zealous woodland preacher like John the Baptist. He was simply a man who couldn't bear how hideous the world had become. The gluttony, the hedonism, the debauchery that infected human life after the fall of Rome—it was all too much. Unable to cope with his heartbreak, Benedict left for the hills. He lived alone in a cave for three years. He studied, and he prayed for a return to a moral world. After he left the woods, Benedict's work slowly gained traction. Over time people started to love their neighbors. They planted gardens. They took care of the poor and the suffering in their communities. Adam thought now about the redemption of his own world. When he and Molly left this place, what would they find? Would the anger and desire for punishment over the vanished mill jobs have been magically replaced by something else? Would her crime be any less of a crime? What about the crimes of the mill owners who had decamped overnight to foreign markets and devastated entire communities without warning? What about those who had first built the monstrosities, and tied generations of family livelihood to the work they created? Despite the hardship, there was clarity here in the abandoned house. To catch something to eat, you did this, not that. To stay warm, you did this, not that. To stay out of sight, you did this, not that. To live, you did this, not that. But how did you make a place accept you again, and how did you make a people see you as human, not simply a monster lurking in the woods?

In the morning Adam woke to the sound of music. It was soft, barely registering in the attic, but it was there. He closed his eyes and fell back asleep, smiling, among the old horse blankets.

"What was that?" he asked Molly later in the day. "This morning."

"I'm calling it 'The Winter King.'"

"It's yours?" He was stunned and proud. "I was afraid I was dreaming. The sound, it was so beautiful."

"It's been coming for a while now," she said. "Since the fire, I guess. Pieces and pieces come to me here and there. I guess I'm just gathering them up."

Adam took a moment before answering, let the word sit between them. They almost never talked about the fire now, even though it surrounded everything they did.

"How?"

"In my head. Between digging for roots to gnaw on and escaping angry white lobstermen." She smiled. "Can we keep it?" she asked. "The piano."

"What else would we do with it?"

"You told me about this family on the island that took the doors and the trim boards off the inside rooms of their house and burned them to stay warm one really bad winter. You said they even burned the kitchen cabinets."

Adam tried to remember the story, found it eventually. It seemed it had been about someone his grandmother had known, in the years before there was a bridge from the mainland to the island reservation, in the years where a Penobscot family risked starving to death or breaking through the ice and drowning while trying to cross the river to the grocery store.

"Yes," he said, letting the old stories come back over him. "Of course," he said, thinking about music and the idea of what happiness could mean. Sometimes even the sad notes, if played properly, could be joyful.

THE WET SEASON PASSED INTO the warmth of the growing season. Eagles began to nest in the tallest pines. And the mountains slowly took on a deep purple hue at sunset. Molly came downstairs one morning and found her great-grandmother's seed box sitting on the makeshift kitchen table. She thought for a moment she was dreaming. Then she began to cry. Of course her father had brought it with them from the house.

"It's time to plant," a voice said behind her. Her father was standing in the doorway, leaning against the jamb. He was wearing jeans and a white T-shirt. Dirt caked his hands, and his cheeks were red from the morning cold. His eyes were as damp as his daughter's.

"The seed box," Molly said, wiping at her face. "I thought I'd never see it again."

"And now you have." Her father smiled. "Some things are meant forever."

They spent weeks bushwhacking the land and breaking the earth in a large, sun-filled clearing deep in the woods. When it was done, their garden was fifty feet wide and nearly a hundred feet long. It was also well hidden. They planted it half full with greens and corn and squash and beans. They filled the other half with storage crops. Beets. Potatoes. Turnips. Carrots. Onions.

Molly and Adam worked into the heat, which came early, cruel and smoking, the air in June bending with steam and heat vapor as if it were late August. They tended the garden. Collected rainwater in troughs and barrels. Watched the heat as it moved from tepid to ravenous, until they seemed to be able to see the sun cooking the air right in front of their faces. They did not slow. They did not relent.

Adam built a simple ramp pump from materials he salvaged around the property. They set the pump on the edge of a small wooded pond and built a box to cover it. Moses brought out four hundred feet of coiled hoses. Molly helped him unkink and lay the water line through the saplings and stumps and underbrush from the pump to the garden. When they were done, Moses recited a prayer of thanks: "*Kchi-niweskw: Wǝliwǝni nǝbi. W ǝliwǝni wskitkamikw. Wǝliwǝni wǝjawsǝn. Wǝliwǝni skwǝde. Wǝliwǝni mǝ zitte nǝdalǝgomak.* Great Spirit: Thank you water. Thank you earth. Thank you wind. Thank you fire. Thank you all my relatives." Then they danced together in the garden and sang old songs to the plants.

The pump had no motor and worked without electricity or any power source at all. A simple hydraulic system, it used gravity and two valves to create a hammer effect that pushed water into a pressure tank and then drove it up the hill and through the hoses to the garden. The pump held a steady twenty-eight pounds per square inch of pressure, and they found they could pull up to one thousand gallons of water a day without doing a thing. Molly took the five-gallon pails she'd envisioned having to lug back and forth from the pond to water with, turned them over, and set about playing them like drums. Her father grinned. Secretly she was disappointed. She had envisioned laboring under the weight of the water buckets, growing muscled, growing stronger, growing even faster.

Eight

THE BATEAU PEELED OUT THROUGH the water as I watched our path for obstacles and Link worked the steering handle on the outboard. It was September, and the air was heavy still, so humid it felt like a damp net stretched against our skin. With the new moon overhead, heat humming in the dark, and water all about us, Link dropped the outboard to a soft purr. I could hear the waves lapping against the hull, but the petrol stink of exhaust and the low vibrations in the seats raised a mechanical wall between the natural world and us.

"Kill the engine all the way," I told him. Stealth was paramount, and I wanted to better feel the night, note all its sounds around us. Anything could be out there.

"His buoys are orange-and-blue striped," Link said, deadening the motor.

"You think I don't know that? I've lived here all my life."

"Don't act tough, Almy. Just watch for buoys and rocks."

Each buoy was tied to a string of lobster traps, and those traps—steel cages dripping with the sea and slick with rockweed and ocean moss— weighed eighty pounds apiece. Coming alongside a buoy, I watched Link reach out with the gaff hook and snag the warp line. He strained against the line, and the bloated trap bubbled to the surface, pouring seawater back into the night. He pulled the cage up onto the gunwale, and I leaned the other way, counterweighting the bateau. If you got tangled in the line and the cage slipped, if it fell back overboard, it would take you with it, all the way to the black bottom of the breathless sea. Five dark lobsters crawled over each other inside the trap. One by one Link tossed them back into the ocean. I thought it was over then. We had made our point. Link was about to push the trap back overboard when he paused. The blade of his pocketknife glinted in the dark, and then I heard the rapid sawing of sharpened steel on rope.

"Link," I hissed. "That's too far."

"He's earned it" was all my brother said.

Then the warp line split and my brother kicked the cage overboard and we sat in the gently rocking boat watching Lyman Creel's livelihood sink to the bottom of the sea. Poaching a trap and emptying it was bad enough. We'd delighted in thinking about the anger Lyman would feel each time he strained his back hauling a cage from the sea, only to find it empty. But cutting a line, sinking a trap—Link knew better. I knew better. Yet Link had cut the line, and I had not moved to stop him. And the feeling of watching Link's feat was one of joy.

Since Lyman's altercation with our mother, our rage had festered and grown. We tried to outpace our anger. I read and walked the woods and swam and ran every morning. Link tried working on Simon's car with him. He buried his hands in grease and swapped out fan belts and bolted brake calipers to rotors. He spent a day in town following our father around the boatyard, sorting tools and measuring and marking out the saw lines for hull staves. He spent an entire morning building a wood-bending jig for a catboat project, but when the jig was done, his anger returned. He spent two days running between stores in town, looking for story leads for our mother. She'd thought people might be more likely to open up to a child. They told him only dozens of dirty jokes, asked him if he wanted some beer, asked him how many people his father had shot in the war. None of it worked, and Link's brain, unwilling to be placated, set itself to solving the question of revenge.

The little green bateau we used was the first boat our father had ever built for us. We must have been six or seven years old then. Now Link had stashed it in the weeds off Shrike Cove. Each night for a week we had snuck out of the house and onto the water. The moon grew brighter as the days passed. The air stayed hot, clogged with mosquitoes even at night. Sometimes when we peered back at the shore, we saw things we knew couldn't be there: lit windows floating high in the tops of trees and trails of chimney smoke curling about where there were no houses; spectral, rib-starved horses lowering their heads to forage along the banks; men and women, naked and weeping, holding each other in shafts of moonlight down by the water. We understood we were seeing different histories that had lived along this bay. On the bluff high above us, the ghost apples watched in quiet judgment. We knew we would be caught, we must have known that, but we didn't care. Our fear made us more aware. Our awareness made us feel invincible.

Chains of small islands dotted the waters of the bay, and we picked our way between them. The throttle shook against our palms. Swells rocked us in the dark fist of the sea. The light on the water was often a rich yellow from all the floating pollen. Sometimes it shone bright red, as if a painter had brushed it across the water.

We were brutal, merciless. We stopped at every orange-and-blue buoy we saw. We dumped lobsters by the dozens back into the ocean. Held the sopping wet warp lines tight as we sawed them clean through. With each triumphant snap, we felt the smallest fraction of our rage release. Another cage belonging to Lyman Creel gone to rust at the bottom of the world.

We whooped. We hollered. We howled and embraced each other once we were clear of the fishing grounds. Along the shore we struggled, wrestled. Tried to choke each other out, tried executing complicated scissor holds we'd seen in dumb action movies. Fell flat on our backs, gasping and laughing. We dove into the water and only came up when our lungs felt about to split, kicking and somersaulting to the surface. We ran and we danced. We were two young kings, and while nothing we were doing was royal, and none of it was good, like all the young kings in history, we told ourselves our dark work was right.

IT SEEMED THE MOST OBVIOUS thing, but we had not thought of it. After several days of watching his catch ruined and his gear destroyed, Lyman was bound to lie in wait. The problem was finding us. He had traps all over the bay and up into the mouth of the river. Link took a nautical chart and unfurled it on the floor in his room.

"Here, but not here." He had meticulously marked the location of all Lyman's buoys he knew about. On the map, the red dots nestled between the depth contour lines. Looking down at them, I could think only of bloody constellations.

"We cut that one last night," I said.

Solemn, intense, he crossed his arms, stood, backed away from the map. He circled the room, checked that the door was tightly closed. At the window he stared out into the woods. When he returned to the map, squatting down over its contents, I was shocked at how grown-up he looked. What I was seeing on my brother's face was a new concentration. He was no longer the boy I used to squat down with in the dirt in the yard, separating out lines of leaves by color. In our games one side was good and one side was evil. We laid sticks between the two lines in the dirt for fortifications. Rocks and pebbles became bivouacked armies. Bits of moss became hospitals and safe havens and places of hope. We would play deep into the afternoons, gathering up small piles of pine needles and setting them on fire around the edges of our battlefield as I told stories about the signal fires the Han dynasty used to light across the Great Wall of China during times of peril.

"You're too quiet," Link said. "I need your help, Almy. You've got a head for strategy."

That was all it took to turn me back to our misguided task: an infinitesimal nod of validation from someone I loved deeply.

"Tonight we stay in," I said. "Regroup, rest. If it's clear weather tomorrow, we go here." I put my finger down on the map at Shadrach's Neck, a slim peninsula of land that reached into the sea like a long neck. The landform had no curve, so neither side of the neck was sheltered by a cove. Still, the seas there tended to be unusually calm. A half a mile beyond the end of the peninsula was a small island. Lyman had four traps in the channel between the neck and the island.

"It's exposed on both sides," Link said.

"Exactly. It's not sheltered like other spots, but it's a straight line on those traps. We can come in the long way, put in up the coast, swing out behind the island. From the island we can get a good look back at the shoreline and the waters around us. The neck being straight lets us see both sides for miles. If it's clear, we go like hell, slice all four traps, come back around the island for cover, and head home."

Link was grinning. He slapped me across the back and whooped. "My brother. My man. That's what I'm talking about."

"Only if it's clear and calm."

His face went serious. "Only if it's clear and calm." That was our credo, our agreement. We would honor whatever gods might be out patrolling the night. We were not about to challenge the sea. We knew its demands, its tolls, its appetite for human life, how swiftly it would take a body if a body didn't properly guard itself.

IT WAS HOMER WHO SUGGESTED that we stand in the confusion of time with our backs to the future, our hungry faces to the past. I wondered sometimes on those nights of delinquency if our parents were aware of our absence at the house. If so, did they ever go outside and watch the sea, or listen for the snapping branches and scuffing shoes announcing our safe return down the driveway? If they had known, surely they would have confronted us, but our parents had their own deeply absorbing worlds and problems. I imagined my mother standing on the back porch, looking down the river, sluggish in the late heat. She would have been able to smell the ocean, and that alone would have bound us to her as we moved through the waters of the bay, opening and closing the throttle on the outboard, angling the oars in the dark water like knives. I was amazed that our dogs, Sam and Daphne, two Irish wolfhounds who paced the river woods like mammoth gray sentinels, kept quiet, turning complicit in our trespasses.

Our father had rescued Sam years earlier, and Daphne joined us later. We were at a January bonfire beside a small ridgetop kettle pond not far from our house. Parties like this, with their particular magic, happened regularly under the full winter moons. Massive pyres of wood were built on the shores of frozen lakes and touched off in twenty-foot-tall blazes. Guitars and mandolins and banjos and singers came out. Chainsaws were set down and flannel coats shucked off. While the players sawed their joyous noise through the night, people danced and spun, reveled and dipped, slid and embraced. Kids and adults threw snowballs, and others spilled onto the ice to slide and skate. Maple syrup was poured over snow, and whiskey and beer passed from hand to hand.

It seemed as if the dog had come out of the woods and simply shown up at the bonfire. Frightened by the intensity of the blaze, it lurked around the edges of the pond, where the vegetation was thickest and the ice thinnest, watching us. The ice had been measured at twelve inches all across the pond. It should have held. Someone tossed a snowball out into the sky, and the massive dog shed all its hesitation and launched into pursuit across the ice. The dog was there, and then, with a sharp crack, it was gone. My father let go of my mother, with whom he'd been dancing, and strode across the ice while his entire community yelled at him to stop. My father didn't seem scared at all. He centered his weight and walked out into the night, convinced that whatever fragility might haunt the glassy surface would not harm him. It was brave and it was noble, but beyond anything else it was a foolish thing to do alone and without any safety equipment. He knelt at the icy lip of the hole, rolled back his coat sleeve (such a peculiar gesture that even to this day when I see a man pushing back his sleeves I fall through the years and see my father, ice pebbling his mustache, his breath smoking out around his scarf), and plunged his arm into the frigid water, holding a flashlight. The dog had been running when it broke through, which meant its momentum might have carried it under the ice past the point where it entered. My father was hoping the small spot of light might give the animal something to locate. Eyes blasted with fear, the wolfhound came up through the opening after a few moments, and Arnoux somehow pulled the great beast free.

When we hiked home, the dog followed us. My father yelled at him. My mother told him to scram. Simon, Link, and I said nothing. When my father threw a stone at the dog, it paused for a moment and sat down in the snow. My father hung his head, ashamed of his cruelty, and told us to go on ahead. In the morning I woke to the sharp crack of the splitting awl. My father was out in the yard in the dawn light, splitting ash logs. There at the edge of the gravel was the wolfhound, watching, divorced from whatever prior ownership it had known, forever loyal now to us.

A year later an old woman came down our road in a truck. She was on oxygen and barely able to drive. She had a wolfhound with her, smaller than Sam, the name we had given the rescued dog, but a deeper gray. She opened the passenger door, and the dog leaped out. "Her name is Daphne," she said to our mother. "I can't take care of her anymore, and I was hoping you could. I heard what your husband did at that pond last winter."

"It was a stupid thing to do."

"It was. But it told me where to go with her when it was time." The woman lifted her eyes to her dog, Daphne, and watched as Sam trotted out to meet her.

IT WAS A STILL AND calm night, colder than it had been any other night on the water, and fall felt everywhere. We put in at Shrike Cove as usual. Then we trawled slowly out into the sea. It was two miles down the coast to reach the neck. Overhead the stars were but endless in their sweep across the sky. We took our time motoring out to the island. Seeing nothing along the neck, I nodded, and Link engaged the outboard.

We reached the first buoy and had the trap on the side of the bateau when a sudden yellow lance of light exploded across the water. The light hit the second buoy, fifty feet away from us, cutting a bright canyon across the dark water, then danced back toward our boat.

"Turn away," I managed to yell just as the beam found us, and I could only hope that all it illuminated were the hunkered-down backs of two unidentifiable figures. When I turned back, I saw Link standing at the gunwale in a daze, fully encased in the bright yellow glow of a spotlight. "Shit," I hissed. "Link."

My brother snapped back into motion. He kicked the cage overboard and slammed the outboard to life. I almost went over the edge as we jerked into motion. Link pulled open the throttle and whaled on the steering bar, launching us into a huge, roaring curve. Water pounded back into the boat, cold and shocking. I slipped then recovered my spot at the bow, do- ing my best to yell out directions and landmarks. I was too afraid to look back. I was certain I could hear another motor, a vast and powerful engine swallowing gasoline in fury.

We carved through the water, disappeared behind the island. Link threaded his way along the shoreline, skirting boulders and crags, ducking into coves and then darting back out when the light didn't follow. Still, in the distance, a second engine droned. I was sure we would run aground out here. But Link was so intense, so focused, his eyes cold and dark and unwavering. I'd never seen anything like it, and I understood then that my brother had inherited from our father that rare and dangerous and poten- tially lifesaving ability to control fear in all circumstances.

The light broke to our left, and it broke to our right. Rocks shot up in a golden wash and then went dark again. On the north side of the island we doubled back on our route, watching the light continue flashing in front of us, and made a hard sprint across the open waters for Shrike Cove.

This time there was no joy, no whooping. Only fear in our freedom, fear that began to overflow as we reached the shore. Link's hand was shaking when he took it off the outboard. He snatched it with his other hand. I leaned over the gunwale and vomited into the sea.

"Lovely." Wren Creel was standing on the shore, watching us struggle in the shallows. "Toss me that rope. Now," she snapped. "Pick it up off the bottom of that boat and throw it to me so I can pull you in."

The force of being told exactly what to do broke our paralysis. I flung the rope to Wren, and she pulled it taut. Then she gently drew us from the water.

She pointed to a spot fifteen feet up the shoreline. She placed my hands at the bow and Link's at the stern and got on the other side of the boat, making us lift our ends and then lower the boat into her hands, where she guided it up the shore to the spot she'd chosen. She'd cut a stash of heavy white pine boughs and gathered up a small mound of twigs and massive oak leaves, and she began spreading them over the hull until the woods had swallowed the boat.

"Idiots," she said. "Boys always move too slowly. They never have enough to lose."

Emboldened and embarrassed, Link growled, "Thanks, now get lost."

"Hardly. We need to get into the woods. Keep watch on this spot for a while. Then if it's still clear, we need to get it out of here."

On the water the light was gone, the only sound the steady crashing of surf against shore. "Why are you helping us?" I asked.

"Shut up. Did he see you?"

"No," I said. Link was avoiding my eyes. "I don't think he got a good look."

"He was out there, though," Link said.

"Of course he was out there. I saw him leave the house tonight, and I knew he'd finally catch you idiots."

"How did you know where we keep the boat?" I asked.

"Not important. I'm not going to tell anyone anything."

"What do you want, then?" Link said.

"I want to go with you next time."

I was shocked. "There isn't going to be a next time," I said. "This is done."

"He's your father," Link said.

Wren shook her head. "Obviously."

"You get that this hurts you too," I said.

"Fifteen minutes ago I rescued you. Don't start treating me like I'm stupid." Wren's stare stopped me from arguing with her. She lowered her head and took a deep breath. "I can't stand what he did to that kid in the river," she whispered.

"Does he know where we stash the boat?" Link asked.

Wren shook her head.

"Then we're going to leave it right here." Wren's wish to hurt her father had gotten its hooks into Link. I could see it in his face as his decisiveness returned. "We'll go out one more time. One week from tonight. When things settle."

Nine

T HREE DAYS AFTER ALMOST GETTING caught, Lyman Creel came to our house, holding a Winchester deer rifle across his chest. There are things you remember in vivid bursts from your childhood, things you shouldn't be able to recall but that still linger with exacting detail. They can haunt you, and they can comfort you. Sometimes they can do both at the same time.

Our house was an indistinct left turn off the paved state road onto a gravel two-track, nearly overgrown by ostrich ferns, goldenrod, asters, and staghorn sumac. Speeding by the turn on the paved road, you might glance suddenly to the left for no real reason and see a shaft of hazy sunlight exploding from the woods. It simply beckoned. The two-track wound down through the woods for a mile before it reached the river, and because it beckoned, my father put a cattle gate up at the half-mile point and nailed a painted sign to it: NO TRESPASSING. WATER MOCCASIN FARM. Though the gate was never locked and often left open, few people came down the road. When some curious stranger risked trespass, my father, brimming with jocularity, would show them around, have a beer with them, and then tell them to get out. Others—Reggie, Moses, friends of my mother—lifted the gate and came and went as they pleased, and I thought my parents were a very strange breed of hermit.

Great oaks and hemlocks curled over the road. The canopy was so dense and green that sunlight was completely absent as we drove back and forth from town. At the river the two-track became more of a path, until it met the drive my parents had skidded out along the peninsula.

It was a Saturday when Lyman came. Link and I were upstairs, Simon and our father downstairs. Our mother was out on the back porch, reading. Unless you came up the river by boat, it was virtually impossible to reach our house without being seen. Sam and Daphne started to bark furiously. Simon rose from the table, nodding at our father. It was as if they already knew what was happening. Lyman was coming down the road. Why he moved in a slow saunter up that road in that false posture of joviality, whistling slightly, spinning his head about to follow the darting birds, all the while cradling a rifle as lovingly and innocently as though it were a loaf of bread he'd come to bestow upon us, escaped me in the moment, but later I came to understand that Lyman was a great actor, a master of artifice who could manipulate camaraderie and threat with chilling ease.

Our father took his time, watching until Lyman was just yards away from the house. He finished his mug of coffee. Went to the sink and washed the cup and turned it over on a dish towel to dry. Then he put on the heavy charcoal sweater he liked to wear out in his shop in the mornings before he took us to school and went into the boatyard office. He pushed his heels into his boots, bent down and tightly tied the laces. Then he opened the front door.

"Arnoux," Lyman said.

"Lyman," my father replied.

Lyman was standing in the light in the yard with his rifle, my father standing unarmed. There was such absurdity in the cordiality of their greeting. From upstairs, frozen, mesmerized, I studied the way Lyman was holding that rifle, up under his arm, not over his shoulder or down at his side, as if at any moment he meant to raise the barrel on my father.

"Your boys ought to be the ones out here. They've been cutting my traps."

The only crack I saw in my father's composure came not from any rising fear at standing before an armed man, but from the sudden shame he felt over our behavior. "It's over now, Lyman," he said. "Let it go and turn around."

"Did you know?" Lyman asked.

"No."

"Get them kids down here, then."

"That's not going to happen," my father calmly said. I thought of how in the woods you had to squat down and deaden your breathing to keep from startling a deer, how you had to work to make yourself small and calm. The smaller you become, the easier it became to *think*, our father often told us. "I'll do a year of work for you for just the cost of materials," he said. "As compensation."

"What kind of work?"

"Building. Boat maintenance. Winterizing. Engine work. Whatever you need to erase the debt. All the debts."

Lyman lifted the rifle over his shoulder and then seemed to think better of it, lowering the gun again. My father stepped closer to him. "You can't tell me that doesn't sound like a fair deal."

Lyman was staring off at the trees. He seemed preoccupied, as if he were reading something in the woods only he could see. I was surprised he hadn't looked up at the windows. "It's an offer with merit," he finally said.

"Then here's the part of the conversation where you turn around and don't come down my driveway ever again."

Whatever peace had materialized cracked again, as it always did between our father and Lyman.

"You would be foolish enough to threaten an armed man."

"The only threat here is you, Lyman. I'm just trying to enjoy a Saturday morning at home with my wife and my kids."

SOMETIMES I STILL DREAM OF that day Lyman came to us. I see myself at fourteen years old, on a crisp September morning. Beyond my windows I see the things I then loved most: the woods and the river going out to meet the ocean, and the pale silhouettes of the mountains. I have my room arranged with the bed's pillows level with the window, so I can simply roll over in the morning and open my eyes and slide from sleep into the sight of those other worlds. With me in the house are other things I love but are easier to take for granted: my mother and my father, my brothers, Sam and Daphne. Outside there's a sound, the scraping of boots, and I rise from the bed and go to the opposite window, which looks back toward the driveway. With my face pressed near the glass, I see a man coming down the driveway.

In my dreams, as it was in life, my father is without fear, standing unarmed before a man who is armed. In a conflict there is a force of will one person can feel in another person. Lyman, his square hard jaw methodically grinding away at a plug of tobacco, understood this. Had he not turned around and left, had he insisted on confronting us, our father might have killed him. While he was a lovable miscreant to us, with his fantastic stories and claims of transmutation, his odd financial decisions, and his peculiar love notes written on boards, he was a hard man as well, a soldier, a man who had been indoctrinated into a life of violence in order to survive. And though he had left that life before it consumed him, that doesn't mean it wasn't still there. He had distracted days. Short-tempered days. Days when the slightest clap of sound collapsed him in panic or sent him flying into action. A threat to his family, real or perceived, would have lit all my father's worst fears.

Simon arrived upstairs in my bedroom as our father went out into the yard. While our father was eerily calm, my brother was winded and shaky. "Stay in your room," he blurted.

Down the hall a door slammed.

Simon turned from my doorway and stood in front of the stairs.

Link was coming toward him. "Move, Sy."

"Go back to your room."

"Knock that shit off. You're not Dad."

When Simon didn't move, Link rushed ahead and lowered his head into my older brother's chest. Link was low-built and compact, where Simon was tall and drawn out, but Simon was four years older. He pushed back against Link and swept his legs out from under him. Their bodies turned over each other in the tight upstairs hallway. I was scared they would both fall down the stairs.

Simon rolled over on top of Link and pinned him to the floorboards. I'd never seen Simon, who was gentle and often a little aloof, act aggressive. "You're staying here," he said.

Link got one arm free and pressed his hand up against Simon's chin. Then Simon hit Link twice, hard and fast, his right and then his left fist connecting with each side of his jaw. Link tried to get free again, lunging for the stairs, and Simon hit him a third time. This time, the snap of my brother's nose echoed through the house. The blood came in a wave, pooling for an instant atop his lip, then running around both sides of his mouth.

Simon was panting. "Just stop," he pleaded. "Each time I hit you, I'll hit you harder if I have to."

Link's white teeth flashed behind his swollen gums. The air went sour and metallic around us. "Why?" he asked, and held his grin as though he were deliciously proud of his mangled face.

"Oh Jesus Christ, Link." Simon pulled off his shirt and balled it up and bent down to put pressure on the wounds. "Because I love you."

Then Link made a great show of sitting right there in the middle of the hallway. He crossed his legs and sat on his hands and let the blood run down his chin and the shirt. "I know, Sy. I love you too."

Our father was shaking when he came inside and found Simon packing ice and gauze around Link's broken nose.

"I raised quite the thieves," he whispered. In his anger, I saw the fear of potential loss. He'd come through a war and built a tiny sanctuary down in the woods on the river partly to protect us, only to see us do this.

Then he simply walked past us without saying anything else, leaving us more ashamed than any scolding could. I was partly stung by the gesture and partly embarrassed at the performance of it. Of course we had been raised to be better, whatever precisely that meant. Lyman's treatment of our mother was simply no excuse.

There are sins for which not even children are excused. Those sins differ in different places. They are often tied to honor and loyalty and livelihood. Pulling pots and cutting traps was an unforgivable offense in a place like Seal Point. It didn't matter that Lyman had transgressed as well. We'd taken from another man's living and made his life more difficult, something our father knew wouldn't be easily forgotten.

SCHOOL HAD STARTED AGAIN. ON a rainy morning later that week, midway through my second-period humanities class, Cal Hayes walked into my classroom and pulled me out. Rain was lashing the windows, and the hallways were wet and cold. Cal took his coat off and wrung it out into the drain of a nearby water fountain.

"That's nasty," I said.

"I didn't ask you."

"So I guess this has to happen now," I said.

"I guess so." Cal sighed and slid back into his damp coat.

He had timed it perfectly so the bell rang just moments after we stepped into the hall. Other students flooded out from doors all around us. Walking through them, I made sure to make eye contact with everyone who stared at us, but I couldn't look up at Cal, who had been friends with my father and mother since before I was born.

In the east wing of the school Cal pulled me to the side by the lockers. "Stand here," he said. "Don't run off like they do in the movies. Don't be dramatic. Don't be dumb. Act like the kid your parents raised you to be, and just stand there and be quiet."

He went into another classroom. When he came back out, Link was with him. My brother and I walked a step ahead of Cal as he herded us through the hallways and put us in the back of his cruiser.

We spent half an hour at the sheriff's station in Cal's office, giving an unofficial statement about what had happened with Lyman's traps. No one was pressing charges, but Cal said he needed to know what had happened. Tensions were too high, and he was worried someone was going to get hurt. We detailed everything that had happened except for Wren's involvement. While Cal was writing up our statement for his records, a deputy ducked into the room and mentioned a call that morning about some footprints and a garden in the woods near Loomis Hill.

"Who cares?" Cal said, looking up from his desk.

The deputy shrugged apologetically. "I didn't know if it might have something to do with the fire."

Cal sighed and stared at both of us in turn. "What doesn't anymore," he said. "I'll look into it."

Leaving the sheriff's station, Cal drove out to the Douglas Road and up through the woods to Loomis Hill. He seemed to enjoy having us along as company. There was a large yellow abandoned colonial mansion up there, slowly being swallowed by the land. The garden was reportedly somewhere in the woods around the property. A hundred years ago a ship captain named Park Loomis had owned the house, which sat up on a hilltop clearing with a magnificent view of the same ocean that ultimately shipwrecked and drowned Loomis. Fifty years of unchecked growth had closed in the view now. In another fifty, the woods would fully consume the place. Up until the 1970s or so, people had gone out to the aging mansion to photograph it and smoke dope and mess around, but then it became too much of a chore to reach, and people forgot.

Rain was lashing down against the windshield and echoing off the cruiser's roof. I studied the driveway. It was a long, overgrown thicket, all brambles and broken earth and flowing mud. We could barely see the house through the mist and the rain. Cal stopped the car and waited. "You get the point, right. Of me making a big stupid show of picking you up at school."

A swarm of starlings moved between two maples in a swooping and perfectly spaced wave that curled through the rain. Link shrugged, and I said I understood.

"Enlighten me then," said Cal.

"Stop being knuckleheads."

"Well stated." Cal watched the birds move from one maple to another, back in the shadows. "They must roost in that one." Then he shrugged and put the car back in reverse.

"Aren't you going to look around?" I asked. "Find the garden or something."

"No," he said. "I'm going to get stuck or wreck the undercarriage out here, it's practically hailing, and your stupidity has exhausted me. No one has come out here for years. We missed lunch. You hungry?"

I'm not sure we were, but Cal drove down to the waterfront anyways. He parked the cruiser behind The Fish House, ducked into the side entrance, and came back fifteen minutes later with two large paper bags. "I was never very good at being the bad guy," he said. Sitting in the cruiser, we ate big greasy cheeseburgers from their wax-paper wrappings and hot salty fries, watching it rain on the misty water and listening to Stevie Ray Vaughan on the blues station out of Bangor. "Some of this will pass," Cal said. "But you fucked up pretty bad."

THAT AFTERNOON, AS THE RAIN trailed off to a light mist, we came home to a bonfire roaring in our yard. At the center of the rippling orange flames we saw what was left of our bateau. I was hurt and confused. Link clenched his fists until his fingernails cut bloody half-moons into his palms. At the edge of the yard Cricket stood in the glow, her head lowered to her chest.

Our father was standing in the fire glow too. For a moment he looked made of flames. "I build boats for a lot of things," he said. "But I don't build them to steal from fishermen. Stand there and watch it until there's nothing left. The mist will put the ashes out."

Then our father walked away from the fire and into the house, leaving us alone. Link and I stood there, watching the flames. We never spoke. An hour later, when our father came back outside and doused the fire with a five-gallon bucket of water, we were still standing there in the growing dark.

"I made dinner," he said. His voice was uncertain. I thought it held a note of regret. "Go scrub the smoke off your skin."

I walked over to the horse paddock and stroked Cricket's neck through the cedar rails. I stayed there for a long time, unable to look back at the ashes. Then I wiped the soot from my cheeks and followed my father inside to wash and eat and begin to atone.

Ten

A CHILDHOOD IS A BIT like a forest. You enter the world, and the trees and the stones and the creeks and the bright spots and dark corners are already there, waiting for you. I knew this business between my father and Lyman—the move toward the edge of constant violence, the fear of what would happen next, the volatility of two men who in their paranoia saw threat to their families, the desperation of it all—had something to do with the war. Though decades had passed, both men still carried it with them.

Beyond that, I was only starting to conceive of the harshness of my father's life before us. I had never known my grandparents on his side. I had never been to the scrub-grass farm downeast where the dawn light first brushed the land, and where he grew up staring out at the waters of the Quoddy Narrows, honing his urge to keep things alive on goats and draft horses and mixed-breed hounds, and wrestling to keep the tractors and crop dusters running. He'd grown up there with his uncle Harlan. When Harlan died, my father sold the farm and headed down the coast to Penobscot Bay and the little town of Seal Point. His life growing up must have been tremendously lonely. The only child, miles away from the nearest town, pressed against the easternmost point in the entire United States. Water and wind so heavy and present, you screamed to escape it.

Both his parents had more or less been children still when he was born. In his free time, his father was supposedly a canoe builder, and good at it, but he spent most of his life chasing road-crew gigs dumping fresh tar onto rural highways. It's an old and awful story: Two kids deeply in love. Two different worlds. A child with no place in either. The girl's family are not accepting or forgiving people, so the boy vanishes because he has to. One night the girl takes her father's car out on the roads, atop the cliffs holding back the sea, and skips a turn. In the child left behind, people see his mother's long eyelashes and brown eyes streaked with wires of gold. They ignore the dark, chiseled features that are his father's. The boy is not handsome but beautiful, like a doll, the type of child normally heaped with adoration, trailed by constant touch. They feel such guilt at what happened to his mother that were they to pick the boy up and comfort him or make a shadow puppet on the wall or slip a small toy into his hand, they would surely shatter. So they do none of these things. And the child is left behind, raised by an uncle who may be rough, but is at least composed of more love than hate.

My father chose to believe that his history began with us: with the river, the bay, our mother, our world. And I knew he would do anything to protect us. What I knew of my father's past, I had mostly learned over the years from Reggie, and it was again to Reggie I turned in the middle of our strife, for answers perhaps, but above all else for solace.

After Cal Hayes pulled us out of school and our father turned the bateau into ash, I headed to the hotel, knowing Reggie would be there. It was a Thursday afternoon before a four-day weekend, and I was relieved to have the space to do nothing and avoid everyone. The ceiling fans spun through heavy air. The doors and windows were open against the humidity. Having arrived at October, the true end of the tourist season, the whole place was empty, and I was grateful for this too.

The hotel was three stories tall and connected to a single-story bar built from the same weathered bricks. A faded wooden sign hung above each business, one announcing THE S. L. ROBBINS TAVERN and the other the E. H. COOMBS HOTEL. Around the turn of the century, when Seal Point was a shipbuilding center and thriving lumber port, a man named Sutton Robbins had run the bar, which also enjoyed a curious secondary life as a women's clothing store, while a man named Emmitt Coombs ran the neighboring hotel. Recognizing that drunks and boarders were of a common community, the two men knocked a hole through the adjoining wall and framed a door to connect the businesses. After flourishing for a few years, the partnership reached its point of division in 1907, when Robbins was caught attending a little too intimately to Coombs's wife in the fitting room and Coombs later walked into the bar and shot Robbins in the throat with a Colt single-action revolver. Reggie had never bothered taking the signs down. Convinced the whole place was haunted, my uncle and I had a routine that dated back years. I'd show up, pick a table, have him draw a salt-line circle around the table, and then sit down. When he stepped over the salt line and joined me, proving he was indeed my uncle, not some malevolent spirit, I'd settle in, order a grape soda, and stay until he drove me home or my parents picked me up. Maybe it was over-the-top, the whole production, maybe it was a bit foolish and childish, but it was ours.

When my uncle came over with a container of salt this day, I waved him off. "Not this time, Reggie."

He shrugged and sat down beside me. "Do you remember when I wanted to be a lawyer for a while? When I worked in Louisiana doing civil rights shit one summer and lived in that terrible hotel without air-conditioning, the one where everything smelled like ashtrays and cats."

"I wasn't born then, Reggie."

"That doesn't mean you can't remember it still." I didn't know back then what he meant. "Anyways, when I was in Louisiana, I started having these dreams. I was down in the south. It was the only time I'd really been away from home, from my history. The dreams were too vivid. And I guess I drank them right under, because they went away for a long time. Came back when I got sober and bought this money pit." He gestured out over the bar and hotel lobby. "These dreams, well, they weren't in English. They came from an entirely different life than the one I'd lived. That's what frightened me so much."

Sorting back through my own dreams, I was unable to identify any language in them at all. I could see people and animals and places. I could feel these things communicating, sometimes even see their mouths moving, but I could recall no sound, no spoken words. Reggie said he couldn't retain enough detail when he woke to identify the language, but he believed it was one of the languages under the Eastern Algonquin tree.

"You have to be real careful, though," he said. "I'm just some white guy. And it's real easy to open your mouth and become some white guy who's a real jerk."

Reggie told me one of his ancestors had fathered two children with a Maliseet woman in the Allagash up near the Telos Cut. He was pretty sure they'd survived the French and Indian Wars and been cared for by some later generation of cousins. "So I thought maybe those children accounted for the language dreams. I stopped fighting the dreams. Things got better."

"Accounted for them how?" I wanted to know.

"I think our ancestors give us gifts we're supposed to keep safe. Sometimes it's a trait or a tradition passed down by a parent. Sometimes it's really clear. Arnoux builds boats like no one can believe. You have Arnoux's hands. It doesn't matter what you do with them. Maybe you'll bake bread, lay bricks, be a doctor and save lives. The point of the gift is to hang on to it for future generations. I started thinking maybe those kids needed someone to leave something with."

I flexed my small, creased hands, which were indeed quick and capable for my age. They could tie an intricate bird snare, snap on three fingers, play my mother's piano, and throw a baseball with delicious speed and accuracy. But I had never thought about my hands saving a life. I liked the idea very much and was terrified by it as well.

I grabbed the container of salt from behind the bar and poured a thick line around the table. Then I stepped over it and sat back down to my soda. Reggie lifted an eyebrow. "Honestly," he said. "I liked the idea of not having to sweep for once."

"It's tradition," I said. "Didn't feel right without it."

"Funny how that works, isn't it? Go home, Almy, get some rest. Hug your brothers. Kiss your mom. Tell your dad he's an asshole for burning your boat. We need to get going early tomorrow."

"Going?"

"I need your help this weekend, and since you're here hiding inside a salt line and nursing the shit out of a grape soda, I'd say you might need mine too."

THAT NIGHT I FELL ASLEEP thinking of Reggie's words about family, about gifts, about what we're given and charged to hold for others. It was early when I woke. The rest of the house was silent. I found Reggie in the yard, sitting on the hood of his truck and watching the sun come up through the woods.

"You could have come inside," I said.

Reggie shook his head, slid off the hood. "Go pack a bag. Pack it light."

My head felt too full, and behind my eyes a sharp ache was developing. I could see the light getting full and green around the woods and hear the birds coming into the world and smell the mixing of gravel and sawdust in the wind.

A blue tarp was tied down over the truck bed. I was picturing the woods, camping for a few days, fishing, being free of the mess Link and I had made. When Reggie pulled the tarp back, I saw another truth: a pickup filled with sixty-pound concrete blocks and several squares of cedar shingles.

"That's a lot of weight." I did the quick math like my father had taught me. "Gonna ruin your truck."

Reggie shrugged, pushed the tarp back down, adjusted some shingles. "Probably. So go get ready before it gives out."

Reggie and my mother owned a rough cabin on East Grand Lake, out along the New Brunswick side of the Canadian border. The camp was surrounded by twenty acres of remote forest and sat high on a wooded ledge overlooking the lake. Seventy-seven stone steps led from the edge of the lake up the ridge to the cabin. On the other side, a mile-long gravel two-track connected the land back to a rural Canadian road. The cabin was sitting on posts that were starting to rot. Reggie's plan was to jack up the cabin and level the footprint, then lay a foundation of concrete blocks. When the new foundation was completed, we'd maneuver the structure onto the blocks using a come-along. Our final task would be re-siding the north face of the cabin with the cedar, a comparatively easy goal. I avoided the obvious observation: that a bit more help, from my brothers or even my mother and father, would have made this entire plan infinitely more plausible, if somehow less romantic.

We drove four hours north and east through the Maine woods. East Grand was twenty-two miles long and four miles thick at its widest point. While many were drawn there because of the abundance of landlocked salmon and various species of trout, I was fascinated by its natural beauty and strange mythical quality. The international boundary between Maine and New Brunswick sliced through the middle of the lake, and one could set out from the shore of America in a rowboat and within an hour be straddling the demarking line between two countries while listening to the ghostly call of a loon circle through the pines. My brothers and I would spend entire afternoons holding the rowboat on the exact line through the water where the two countries met. One hundred and forty feet beneath us, the teeming bottom of the lake peered up and watched. We had studied maps. Done our own surveying. Consulted area experts at length about the basin's geography. The great northern lake became for me a place that managed to slip through a crack in the known world. It was a little like being nowhere and everywhere all at once.

Finally we pulled down a fire road that ended in a clearing at the edge of the American side of the lake. Goldenrod and aster colored the land purple and yellow. A wide rowing boat was pulled up on shore. The boat had a tight lapped hull and was painted a striking white. I recognized the design as one of my father's immediately. The centerline was breathtaking, rising high at the bow and stern before swooping and flattening along the boat's middle. It reminded me of a smaller but no less regal version of the old Viking longships I'd seen in history books.

Across the water was a dense granite ledge. Atop the ledge, nestled among the trees, was the cabin. "We're on the wrong side," I said.

As I looked around, it became clear what was going on, and obvious that the point was grueling work, with no mind paid to the sensibleness of the method.

"Let me get this straight," I said. "You want to row hundreds of pounds of concrete and wood across a lake and then haul it up to a ledge."

"More or less."

"There's a road into the camp."

"Washed out two years ago. Never bothered fixing it. Plus I hate driving into another country. You make that type of crossing through water. It's tradition."

"This is insane," I said.

"I'm not asking you to become a French voyageur, paddle fifty-five strokes a minute, carry two hundred seventy pounds of fur pelts over your shoulders. Don't be dramatic about it."

"I'd rather not drown doing something preposterously stupid with my uncle before I even get a driver's license."

"Look," Reggie said. "You're a dreamer." It was no secret that I was an ill-formed and amorphous kid, lost in my own head, guilty of letting stories feel more real than reality, chronically watching others and imagining outlandish triumphs and defeats. "Lying around worrying about what's happening fixes nothing. You need to do something physical, exhaust the body to tame the mind. Plus think about how many people have undertaken something like this in a rowboat. You'll be a legend."

"If I live," I grumbled. I rarely questioned Reggie. But I wanted to be back home. I wanted to know what was happening with the mill fire. I wanted to know what was happening with my mother and Link and my father and Lyman. Mostly I wanted to see Wren, who I had hardly seen or spoken with since she'd rescued us that night on the water.

"I feel like we're running away," I said.

Reggie gripped my shoulder. "Being away for a bit isn't running away, Almy. Sometimes it's okay to get a little space to breathe."

From there, I could find no energy to argue. Instead I climbed out of the truck and got to work. The rowboat was fourteen feet long and could carry eight hundred pounds. We calculated we'd need to make three trips across the lake, and decided to begin with the concrete, saving the cedar for a respite at the end of this game of madness in which we were about to engage. By noon we had the first load ready and set out across the water. It was clear, calm, and hot, and after the initial fear subsided, the pleasant rhythm of rowing absorbed my body. I began to believe we would not only survive the trip but also perhaps enjoy it. Halfway across the lake something shifted in Reggie's body language. He stopped rowing, grabbed a pair of binoculars, eyed the trees around the camp for a long time without speaking.

"What?"

He tucked the binoculars back in their case, retrieved the oars, and plunged the blades beneath the surface. "Nothing. Keep rowing."

Farther on I saw it too, the glint of something in the trees, moving across the camp windows from inside. "Someone's up there."

"That happens," he said. "People come through hiking."

"Then how come you look so nervous?"

"I always look nervous. Less talking, more rowing. They've seen us too, so we might as well keep at it."

There was a man standing in the tiny camp kitchen when we got to the cabin. Reggie walked directly past him, opened the icebox, and pulled out a water jug nestled among several bottles of beer. No one spoke. The silence heightened the menace, and I felt every inch of my heart hammering in my chest. Though the man had kept his footprint tidy, it was apparent still—clothes hanging to dry around the woodstove, a sleeping bag rolled out in the corner, a few dishes washed and dried and stacked beside the sink basin—and I couldn't help but feel like we were the sudden, silent intruders barreling into his world.

Reggie moved his body two steps to the left, coming around so he stood between the stranger and me. "At least you packed in some ice," he said. A green canvas duffel bag was slumped in a pile by the door. Reggie pointed at it while drinking. "Special forces?"

"That was a long time ago," the man said. He was solidly built with deep blue eyes and dark skin. His eyes took their time moving around the room, taking us in, taking everything in. "I'm not armed," he said.

"Except for the beer," said Reggie. "I hear they make good bags, the army."

No smile from the man, no motion in him at all. In fact, he was eerily still. "You like a show, don't you?" he said after a while.

"It's a bad habit." Reggie blushed a little at being found out. "I'm afraid I was born to be the fool. Here's the deal. We've got at least five hundred pounds of concrete that needs to be unloaded from a rowboat. Good squatters make good workers. How about it, then?" My uncle extended his hand. "I'm Reggie," he said. The other man didn't move. "And this is my nephew, David. We call him Almy. He's the greatest human being you'll ever meet. He just doesn't know it yet. My brother-in-law left the war too."

"Who said anything about leaving any war?" The sudden edge to the man's soft voice was impossible to miss.

"I just did."

"Boy, you've got a nose for assumptions then."

The word fell across the air like a slap, bold and chiding. For a moment I thought Reggie might let his hand drop back to his side, but he didn't. Slowly the man reached out and gripped it.

"Let's start with names," said my uncle. "What can we call you?"

"When I'm being straight," the man said, "Roman Fitch. When I'm feeling grandiose, a patriot."

"Grandiose." Reggie smirked. "I might like you, Roman."

"This brother-in-law," Roman said to me. "Is that your father, great man?"

I blushed, nodded, and felt like I could have awkwardly stood there searching for something to say for days.

∨ ∨ ∨

WE SPENT ALL AFTERNOON AND most of the night rowing and hauling the concrete and cedar up to the cabin. In the morning we would start the construction work. The initial edginess of coming upon one another faded into the pleasant and distracted camaraderie of communal work. Sitting together at day's end with my muscles howling and my mind beat, I fully fixed my attention on Roman Fitch for the first time.

"Get a good eyeful now," he said.

"Sorry." It struck me that his complexion was as dark as the flat black spines of the Penguin Classics books that lined my mother's office shelves. I felt my face flame with embarrassment at the observation.

"Don't apologize for shit," said Roman. "You're just looking at me like everyone else does in the whitest place in the world."

"Can I be honest?"

"That remains to be seen."

"I was kind of imagining you as a book cover. Like those old Penguin Classics."

"A book cover? Yeah, you gotta look elsewhere now. That's messed up. I take it all back. Never look at me again."

It turned out Roman Fitch had been born outside of Cincinnati and had grown up in Jackson County, Kentucky. It was a pretty place, lush and green and thick with mountain heat and music, and it wasn't an overall bad place, but it was a vindictive place. He was drafted at nineteen and deserted at twenty-three. After that he lived in New York City, teaching healthy forms of dissent and conscientious objection, until his marriage fell apart and Gerald Ford's clemency program gave draft dodgers a path to redemption but made war deserters even bigger pariahs. He told us he'd left something awful and doubted that his punishment, as unjust as it was, would ever end. He said he'd ruined his marriage with booze and other women, blamed it on living too close to death during the war, when it was really driven by guilt, fear, and shame. He'd been on the move ever since. Guile, displacement, and fear had become his guiding principles. Sudden and intense bouts of camaraderie, much like what we were experiencing at the lake, and his nine-year-old daughter, Khali, who lived with his mother in Hell's Kitchen, were the only things that reaffirmed for him that the world was ultimately still good.

"Why here?" Reggie asked. The question had been gnawing away beneath our work the entire day. "What brought you to this place?"

"North is an old fantasy," said Roman. "North means safety, freedom. Maybe it is. Or maybe it's all bullshit. During the Civil War a bunch of draft dodgers fled up here. They started a community on a ridge. Locals called them skeddadlers and their spot Skeddadle Ridge. They called their home Musquash, and they stayed there for about a decade, living in a kind of communal utopia. Others came. Conscientious objectors. Deserters. Shit, they had fifteen families in Musquash at one point. Even had a little post office and a school. Then they all vanished. I thought I'd head up there and see what got left behind. This was as far as I got."

Reggie took the story in for a moment. "Desertion," he finally said. "It seems like the worst reason to kick a man off the ark."

"I'm sorry I broke in," said Roman.

Reggie shrugged. "I leave the door open and the solar battery hooked up. It's practically an invitation. Stay as long as you like."

"I don't stay well."

That night I struggled to shake the incongruity of my father and Roman Fitch's paths. I stayed up late thinking about how second chances were one of the great American lies. The war had ended twenty-five years ago, yet it hunted Roman still. My father had fled the same war but skated through to another life, what most would call a good life. I wondered why some people came through damage and arrived at wholeness, while others came through damage into more damage and heartache. It was impossible not to think of my father's exodus to Seal Point and his hermitage there, the result of which was our tiny family. The moment Roman Fitch deserted, an act that many saw as a declaration of war against one's own country, his blackness had made it impossible for him to ever have what my father had. With enough charm at his back, with enough value to the people around him, Arnoux might be tolerated. He might even be fully forgiven someday. But Roman Fitch had been born into a cruel America satisfied with its decision to give him the one and only act of forgiveness it thought he deserved: it had let his black body survive, let it scrape together an existence as a child and a son and then a young adult. It had *allowed* him to make it that far, and it had asked one thing in return: service. Roman Fitch had thanked it by becoming a betrayer. After his act of defiance, my father was given another chance, but Roman Fitch would never be anything other than a traitor in the eyes of his country.

The heat inside the cabin was stifling. Reggie had gone outside to sleep. Saddened by the world, I stood and breathed in the scent of the camp and its feeling of held time—the leather-bound books walling the loft on bowed shelves and the hand grinder for coffee and the black iron cookstove and the scuffed-up heart-pine floors. I had been here often over the years, and still it held all the rustic promise, comfort, and safety I'd loved when I first visited it as a small child. I knew nowhere else in the world like East Grand. Here everything had a place, and nothing seemed to move or diminish. The pairs of old slippers and mud boots lined up beside the woodstove. The massive brass jar sitting on a shelf and filled with pennies. Tattered purple and blue and plaid work shirts and barn coats arranged on nails, waiting to be removed for wear at specific times for specific tasks. Maps and stretched animal skins neatly tacked to the walls. There was a particular order to these objects that seemed to stop time.

The loft was designed in a horseshoe around the small upstairs. The north side was furnished with a Japanese platform bed my mother had built from harvested white pine one summer when she was a teenager. There was a dresser and a vanity that had belonged to my grandmother, and two expandable mahogany steamer trunks filled with winter gear and wool blankets. The south side opened into a windowed alcove that looked through the conifers down across the lake. It was furnished simply with a small roll-top writing desk. A few candles were set about in jars. Two twin mattresses were built into the walls on board platforms that could be pulled down and folded back up. A narrow catwalk connected the two ends of the loft.

I was in the loft looking at the books when Roman found me. "That's a good one," he said.

I hadn't been paying much attention. My finger was resting on *A Fable* by William Faulkner.

"Only time in history people decided to put down their guns and stop fighting a war. Too bad it's fiction."

"I don't get it. What's so bad about saying you won't do something awful?"

"You're as simple as a child, but the thing is you aren't a child anymore."

I was hurt but had no way of proving otherwise.

"Everyone *wanted* to leave. Only some of us had the guts to do it and shame our all-American mothers and fathers. I've been called scum, nigger, coward, cockroach, turncoat, traitor, and combinations of profanity I won't get into. But you gotta break a cycle somehow, even if doing it kills you."

Roman was studying the selection of books as well. "Try this one sometime." He pointed to *The Destruction of Black Civilization* by Chancellor Williams. "And this." And then to *The Varieties of Religious Experience* by William James.

"What are they about?"

"Being a fucked-up human being."

Silence filled the hot air between us. The old dusty walls seemed to draw nearer, as if we were standing inside some ancient wooden lung. I pulled both books off the shelf and cradled them in my hands, turning them over, studying their weight, their look, taking in their smell and feel.

"Your uncle's a weird dude," Roman finally said.

"Yeah, I guess he is."

"It was stupid calling him out earlier. I got it in my head that Canada was safer. But getting somewhere safer doesn't mean getting dumb once you're there."

"Are there safe places?"

Roman shrugged. "Some people always live underneath a bootheel. But sometimes the heel lifts up just enough that you can't see it for a bit."

I found my thoughts drifting back down the bay, to Lyman Creel, to the girl he had assaulted on the river, and to the assault Link and I had carried out on him, proving ourselves no better or worse.

"I'm tired," Roman said, "and it's foolish hot up here. Think I'll sleep in that rowboat down on the water."

"I'll read them," I said as Roman walked away. "The books."

He nodded slightly without turning. "That'd be a start."

WE LIVED ALONGSIDE ROMAN FITCH for four days, until the foundation had been dug and set, the camp moved, and the walls entirely reshingled. When we shook hands down at the shore before climbing back into the rowboat to leave, Roman said he didn't plan to stay too long. Probably just through the fall. He'd do what he could around the property to leave it better than he'd found it.

Our last night together, our muscles screaming from an entire day hammering shingles in place, we set out into town, a collection of rutted logging roads, bait shacks, a scandalous-looking roadhouse, and a small diner where the cooks and waitress switched between speaking French and English, depending on which choice would yield either the largest tip or the least trouble, as the area was as notorious for bumbling and entitled tourists as it was for loggers who liked to drink, fight, and grab.

Roman wanted to go to the roadhouse, a low-slung, concrete building. Old cigarette smoke bled from the walls. The floor was perpetually damp and sticky with beer and haphazard mopping jobs. We'd gotten inside and up to the bar itself, several long sheets of plywood butted together and propped on sawhorses, before the bartender spotted me, shook his head, and pointed at the door.

"Not happening, Reggie." The man's soft, reedy voice carried the slightest southern accent. He was wearing a leather apron and had a long silver ponytail, tied back with a piece of leather cord.

"Really, Tripp?" said Reggie. "You're picking now of all times to finally turn adolescent business away?"

"Gotta make a stand sometime." The proprietor, Tripp, disappeared into a room behind the bar. When he came back, he was holding a plate of fried haddock sandwiches. He tossed the plate down on a folding card table set up in the corner of the room. He poured two glasses of beer and then, of all things, a glass of milk. He looked from me to Reggie, and then to Roman. "This doesn't mean I like any of you. Anyone else comes in here and decides they want to stab or shoot you, which has been known to happen, it's not my problem."

A long and pleasant silence filled the bar. The fish was grilled to perfection and slathered with lemon-dill mayo. I realized that Tripp, like most people my uncle knew, was far less the outlaw than he tried to seem, and a certain heaviness sank on me at the sheer spectacle of having to watch all the men I'd ever known challenge, groom, uphold, and coddle each other's masculinity. We finished our sandwiches and, not knowing what else to do, rose to leave. As we were heading out the door, Tripp said, "Hey, you. Reggie's friend."

Roman's shift was slight but unmistakable. His body began to lengthen and bristle, while his head sank and his eyes swept sideways, as if trying to go small and slide from the scene. An instant later Roman's shoulders were back and his head up again.

"Fuck Vietnam," Tripp said. "It was a useless war." Then he went back to poorly mopping the roadhouse floor.

Eleven

SUMMER BURNED ON. ADAM AND Molly mostly lived off what they grew. They fished and hunted when they could, rotating both where they went and the routes they used to come back to the house. It was impossibly hot. Out harvesting beans and turnips and carrots, they stood dripping sweat. Adam noticed that his daughter never seemed to tire, never seemed to drink, never stopped to curse the sun or rest in the shade. He kept working, kept fretting over the dropping level of the pond as the heat rose into early July. Molly could see it too.

"The more water we take, the more fish are going to die," he said. "Eventually there won't be enough oxygen left in the water."

"We'll eat the ones that die," she said.

"*Who* die," her father corrected. "That's not the point. We're trying to do as little harm as possible."

But they were surviving. They were okay. Adam had become convinced this was a test. Not a test of one's spiritual faith laid out by a potentially sadistic creator, but of the self's ability to endure. Fall would come, and then winter. The world would become static, frozen. Then it would become passable again, and they would have to leave this place. Molly needed to be in school. He needed to be working. No one should have to live in the collapsing ruin of a dead English sea captain's house, taking game on the sly and battling a shade-flooded garden to survive. It seemed reasonable to head north, over the Canadian border and into Micmac territory, where the ways and land were not theirs but not so different, and where US laws couldn't follow them. They would start small. A rented room. A garage apartment. A bottom-rung carpentry job. He didn't want to leave Penobscot territory, and Molly of course would hate him for it, but he knew that the next white face that caught his daughter pulling fish from the river might kill her. What father could take such a risk?

SOME MORNINGS, WILD TURKEYS WANDERED out of the woods. Once, as the drought deepened, a starved and confused black bear came down from the hills. The bear was standing in the clearing on a rise in the meadow. Ragged patches of hair covered its body, and when the bear walked, it stumbled and sat down in a heap and then slowly rose again. Mosquitoes swarmed the bear, and it did not seem to have the energy to flee or to drive them away. As the bear lifted its massive arm to swat at the mosquitoes, patches of cloud burst into view behind the creature. Molly thought it strange to see a bear, powerless and painted against the sky, cupped by clouds.

"What's wrong with it?" she said.

"It's dying," Adam said.

"Why?"

"Mange. Stay with it. Don't go anywhere."

Adam went back inside the house. When he returned, he was carrying a rifle Moses had given them.

"Really, Dad?" she said.

Adam handed her the gun. "It's what has to happen. It's dying, suffering. We need meat."

Molly held the gun out away from her body. It was polished and oiled and immaculately cared for. It was the most valuable thing they owned. The bear was lolling its head about, trying to escape the mosquitoes. It turned toward the woods and then tumbled down on its haunches and sat.

When it tried to roar, nothing came out. *Get up*, Molly thought. *Please.* "It has its back to us," she said.

"Bear meat is bear meat."

"I'm not sure I can hit him." She had shot plenty before, but never at something living.

"You can hit him. Take a deep breath and hold it. Blink once and bring the trigger back slowly. Think of it as pressing the trigger back, not pulling it back. Steady motion. No exhaling, no jerking."

Following those directions, pressing back against the slender curl of steel, Molly fired, hit, and killed her first bear. The shot had taken the animal squarely through the heart. She felt both happy and sick at once. Her father did not try to touch her or speak to her afterward, and she was grateful.

They said a small prayer for the bear, thanking it. Then they spent several days with the animal, letting the innards and flaying the pelt back, running the knife between fur and fat and sinew. They would waste none of its gifts. The bear's fur would warm them. The bear's flesh would fill them. The bear's fat, rendered into grease, would protect their skin and ease their bodies and lubricate their tools. Molly still found herself trying to figure out if theirs was a good life or not.

ONE RAINY MORNING, AS THE leaves were beginning to change, a police cruiser appeared at the end of the driveway. It materialized from the trees as unexpectedly as the bear had weeks before. It nosed up the overgrown drive and then stopped after a few feet. Molly was in the woods, alone, foraging for mushrooms, and she watched in horror. Her father was inside the house. Squinting through the heavy rain, she was convinced she could see him up in the attic through the gable vent. She had the rifle with her in case she saw a partridge or pheasant or turkey, and now she lifted it to her shoulder. Sighted the driver's-side door of the car, waited in complete terror for the car to keep coming down the drive. The clouds had darkened. Overhead the trees filled with a violent gust of wind. Starlings broke in waves between the yard trees. In the distance she thought she heard the thunder. Molly urged the world to stay quiet, the wind to hide, the birds to shut up—anything to keep from drawing the attention of the car. She knew she couldn't shoot a person, but she knew she couldn't let a person come take her father away either. So she crouched on one knee among the hemlocks with her arms aching from the weight of the rifle and silently whispered *help* over and over and over again for what felt like hours. She was crying as the cruiser backed down the drive and disappeared. Terror knocked through her body, and she was unable to move. The car was about to circle back. She was convinced this was some sort of trap. Then she felt her father's hand on her shoulder from behind and heard him saying, "It's okay, Molly. It's going to be okay. Give me the gun." Her hands were white from holding the gun so tightly, and her finger was resting on the trigger. She let her father lift the rifle from her hands and set it against a tree. Then he gathered her into his chest, and she hugged him as hard as she ever had, sobbing and repeating, "I'm sorry, I'm sorry, I'm sorry."

THE LEAVES ON THE TREES began to curl and lift from their nodes. More fell each day, shaken loose by the wind or by small sudden waves of rain. A blanket of crimson and gold and orange replaced the lush green meadow grass. They went days without speaking. Then one afternoon in early November, just as the air was turning thin and brittle with the promise of snow, Molly woke to the sound of a hacksaw biting through wood.

Outside, rain still fizzled in the pines. Turning in bed, Molly watched the drops slip down the spines of the needles. They seemed to hang for a moment, frozen, filling with light, and then, with a gentle shake of wind, leap into the air. She had planned to explore the woods today, to see what this forest felt like as fall took over. But as she got up, swinging her feet down from the bed, she heard her father calling her name—his voice low and urgent, rising like a net from the steady sawing.

Molly went down the stairs and followed the noise into the backhouse. Adam looked up from his sawing, and she took in the room. Her father had pulled up the wide plank flooring. Golden boards were stacked all about him. The backhouse was built on concrete blocks. A foot below the exposed floor joists, Molly could see the packed dirt earth now. Adam had drawn an eight-by-eight-foot square by marking each joist with a pencil. Now he was sawing through the marked joists, effectively cutting a square out of the bottom of the house.

"It'll collapse," Molly said groggily.

"Not if I do it right, it won't."

"If you say so. What is it?"

"It's a cellar hole."

"For what?"

"Think about it, Molly. Use your head."

The ground was freezing against her bare feet. Her eyes were full of sleep still, and she had to pee.

"It's for us." Molly noted the shovel and the spade in the corner of the room. "We're going to dig."

"How deep?"

She thought about it. The big house provided shelter. But the big house was cavernous and drafty, and they couldn't risk a fire during the day. The backhouse was small, almost a shed, really, shielded from the elements by the big house, and it was sealed and insulated. The windows were intact. The roof was solid. "Deep enough to get below the frost line," she said.

Her father set the hacksaw down across two joists and stood. "Go on."

"If we can get below the frost line, we can get free heat. The earth produces heat, and the soil sucks it up during the year. The snows seal it in."

"Exactly." Adam was proud of his daughter for making the connection, for following the science. "Soil temperatures change daily at the surface," he explained. "But the deeper into the earth we dig, the more the temperature lags behind time."

"How much behind time?"

"Every five feet we dig saves us three months. Today is November fifth. The temperature at the surface is forty-seven degrees. The temperature five feet underground, however, is the same as the surface temperature was on August fifth."

"So if we dig deep enough, we can basically live in summer in the middle of winter."

"We'll have to combat heat loss somehow, but that's the idea. It's a place for sleeping, not living, not unless it gets real bad."

They spent the remainder of the week digging the pit, for that's really what it was, an eight-by-eight-foot hole extending ten feet into the earth. It was the hardest thing either of them had ever done with their bodies. They dumped the wheelbarrow loads of dirt in the woods. In spring, Molly said, they had to fill the earth back in, run new joists, and replank the floor. "Any harm we do to the house has to be righted," she said. Adam agreed. They used extra lumber in the barn to build a frame down in the cellar hole, and locked the structure by nailing horizontal boards across the studs. The frame prevented the hole from collapsing, but it was impossible not to look down at their creation from above and think of a cage.

"We're not animals," Molly said.

"We're no better than them either," said Adam.

They hung a ladder on one wall, and laid the bearskin out on the floor for insulation. They found several padded furniture covers and sewed them to the back of a blue tarp. Then they rigged up the insulated tarp so it could be pulled overhead to make a roof. *Home*, Molly thought, gazing down into the sleeping hole. It never looked like what you imagined. She remembered the pink ranch house she now missed more than ever. She'd watched it bend into sight each day she walked home up the hill. She wished she'd thanked it for being there.

AS THE DAYLIGHT HOURS SHORTENED and the warmth waned, Molly watched the finches flit around against the cold. She loved the little birds who made the whole world grow. They had developed beaks to fit certain seeds, carried life impossible distances, filled the most barren mountains with trees. Miracles in plain sight, her father had called them all her life.

She wondered which birds would stay, toughing it out with them, and which ones would go south in search of easier food.

Each day the plants seemed to droop a bit more. Molly methodically cut and collected as many stems and leaves and seeds as she could. Everywhere medicinal herb bundles hung about the old house. Finally a full heavy frost crystallized the earth. It was hard for Molly not to mourn the plants. Her father gathered up the dead stalks and stems. They would use them to further insulate the backhouse. They sawed the planks from the backhouse floor into three-foot sections. Then, to protect themselves from sight, they nailed the planks across the house's windows. On sunny days they removed the planks from the southern windows, and hot vanes of light fell through the house. They stood in the light for as long as they safely could. Molly thought of the bear and how when her shot felled it, the sun behind it came into view, and she felt the light that had filled the creature fill her.

That night there were meteors in the sky, little pins of yellow breaking through the dark and zipping about in lines. Sometimes they came in barrages, and other times only one or two an hour. The largest were a blazing white. Molly watched them through the dark, counting each flash until she could no longer stay awake. She swore she fell asleep to the sound of airplane engines.

Twelve

WHILE I WAS GONE, UNDERTAKING a ridiculous tour of labor with Reggie and contemplating why some deserters made it through the world almost charmed while others were chased like animals, news of my and Link's actions had spread. Sales of the paper had slowed in response. Simon brought back grim stories of how slow business was at the boat barn too. Some fishermen went all the way to Sedgwick to have their boats winterized. Others stripped barnacle and sanded hulls and recaulked seams themselves. That they would give up days of work to stay in harbor and struggle to mend their own boats with limited resources, tools, and facilities made the community's point. We were all being punished.

My mother was working the story of the fire harder than ever, and my father was spending more time alone down in his shop and staying later at the boatyard. He was distant when we spoke to him. Sometimes he would answer in a way that told us he hadn't heard a thing we said.

A noise stirred me late one night, and I opened my eyes with a suddenness that brought me fully out of sleep. The wolfhounds were sitting side by side at the window. I had not heard them push the door open or come in. I called groggily to Sam first, and then to Daphne, and when neither moved, I understood there was something out there.

We were not alone. And the dogs would not turn away until they knew what stalked us. I was terrified as I pushed the covers back and swung my legs off the bed. The floor was warm against my toes, and I closed my eyes. It would be so easy to stay in bed and drift back to sleep. Sam came over and licked my foot until I opened my eyes again. When I left the bed and reached the small window, I saw, across the moonlit yard, near the edge of the tree line, a figure. I had made no effort to disguise myself. The figure raised a single finger to its lips and then sank back into the forest. As I dropped to the floor with my back against the wall, a low growl sounded in Daphne's throat. Then the night silence returned. The dogs did not stop watching the window. They made no other sounds. And it was a long time before I rose and peered out at the empty yard and the wind blowing the shadows of the trees all about the night. I thought of Simon and Link, both asleep down the hall, and our parents asleep in their bed downstairs. I had always felt safe in this house my parents built. I had always felt that we had some power when together that would keep the darker things in the world away. For the first time I felt that sense of security vanish. With a single glance out a bedroom window, an era of innocence had ended. I got back into bed and pulled the covers tight about myself. I knew it must have been Lyman Creel out there watching us.

I TOLD NO ONE ABOUT what I saw.

We had frequented this river for four hundred years on my mother's side, and while our family stories of the strange, the mad, and the tragic were seemingly endless, I sometimes thought I was the only remaining one who actually believed the tales. Legend said a banshee had walked alongside my mother's family for generations, from the green hills of Donegal to the rugged shores of Penobscot Bay, ever since her lover, a young sheep rancher, had murdered her and loosed a curse on the family. While others in the family seemed unable to paint her as anything more than a child's fright—a banal white-sheeted ghost incapable of materializing any more solidly in the imagination than fog did in the air—from Reggie's lips she came in sheer terror.

"What makes her worth fearing is that she never leaves you alone," Reggie told us, gleefully oblivious to the terror he might be passing down to children. "Think cancer. Think having a bad heart. Think knowing all your time is actually borrowed. You live your whole life with death walking at your side. That's her particular form of torture. You flee across the Atlantic for a better life, and she stands right there beside you on the steamer deck, invisible and waiting."

According to Reggie, her dress was ornately stitched and an almost comic canary yellow. All levity stopped there. Blood matted her long hair. Her lover had murdered her with a rock in a winter field after seeing her talking with another boy in town, which is not a crime, which is not even wrong, which of course didn't matter. A faint layer of snow still dusted her face. Her eyes were not dead black things but a brilliant blue and achingly human. They were the eyes of the living, unjustly confined now to a departed body. Worst perhaps was the rusted wire. The young sheep rancher had wrapped her body in barbed wire, covered her with leaves, and left her in the woods. Though she no longer belonged to the forest floor, her barbed-wire bindings remained. Even in death the coils were twisted about her throat and torso, barbs tearing grotesque gashes into flesh, yet she never attempted to unwrap herself from her lover's iron corset, and she never bled from those hellish wounds.

In the tale it was autumn each time the banshee emerged across the forest or stepped grim and unapologetic from the sea to wail before another of our brood was taken into the next world. The women were always the most irreverent and brave among our family, and my mother and my great-aunts had named the banshee Screech. While the name was not particularly clever, I had always liked that. How these women who raised me and came before me were above fear. How as their husbands became increasingly anxious, they raised the volume of the taunts and jokes they hurled at Screech until the men walked out of the room, shaking their heads in timid protest. How they understood the necessity of knocking down what you most fear in this world with a little humor.

My sleep grew light and troubled: two hours filled with a frightening awareness of every sound. The wood heat moving through the vents in the house. The groaning of trees outside as the world grew colder. The rattle of wind blowing over the dormers. Dreams, some fantastic, others believable, flashed briefly. Then I would sense Sam and Daphne in the room and come fully awake. Slowing my breathing, I focused on the house, sought out the sound of Simon snoring, the refrigerator whirring downstairs. I tried to make sense of the vague dark shapes in my room, the dresser, the beanbag chair, the pile of shirts and shoes and socks and underwear that had been collecting in the corner. Finally, being unable to put off the visitation any longer, I slid to the window. Lyman was there every time, smiling as he stood beside the same tall beech tree in the moonlight. I knew what he was doing was insane, yet by giving audience and saying nothing, Lyman and I began to share a sinister intimacy. He would stand watching me until he stepped backward into the dark woods, as if being swallowed. Sometimes he was carrying a thermos or a mug of something. Most times he was empty-handed. He never gestured, except with his face, which contorted into all manner of expressions, sometimes lewdly grinning, sometimes straight-lipped with stoicism, sometimes turned down with disappointment.

On the sixth night, the moon was full, and I could see Lyman Creel cupped in silver light. He was munching on an apple. I was certain it was from the ghost apple tree. I felt the wind drop from my lungs. I wanted to run from the window but could not. Lyman lifted his pinkie finger and wiggled it in a coquettish wave as he brought the fruit to his mouth. I ran through all the symbolic ways I could read this. A violation of our Eden, Lyman as the serpent, Lyman as Eve, the apple-eater, and so on. Thinking of his teeth working a ring around the ghost apple, I remembered the careful way Lyman had built a fortress of sorts about his family, and I recalled watching him care so delicately for his ravens, chortling to them and tearing meat up for their frantic beaks. What I had seen then was not a serpent or a defiler or a tyrant but a nurturer. Perhaps his mad intimidation in our yard a few Saturdays back and his nightly visits—I didn't know what else to call them, for they didn't feel like threats or warnings or trespasses—were carried out to protect his family as well. What if all conflict was just a matter of perspective? He was smiling. He was easy. I wanted to believe he was just a man who was lonely and awake and a bit hungry. Yet there was something about Lyman eating an apple that seemed more sinister and symbolic.

The next day after school I went to the edge of the woods, where he had dropped the apple. The core was gone, picked up or eaten by animals, but a clear set of footprints led back through the woods.

I followed the tracks until they emerged from the forest. Lyman Creel was standing on the bluff by the ghost apple tree, as if he had known I was coming. I should have felt angry. I should have felt violated. But I could muster none of those feelings. The wind rode the bluff heavy. All about the clearing, whorls of color fell from the trees as they shook loose red, orange, and yellow leaves. After years of protecting this place from others, I was glad I wasn't alone. I shivered, wrapped my arms around my chest, and watched as Lyman reached out to touch the tree, thought better of it, turned, and sat cross-legged on the ground like a child.

"Do you know the story?" he said, pointing to the tree, and I nodded. "Would you mind hearing it again?" I shook my head, somewhat amazed he knew the story at all, but even more surprised he had asked permission to tell it.

Lyman told a slightly different version of the story of Nigawes and Sanoba. In Lyman's version, Sanoba did not die by his wife's hand, chopped to pieces and cast into the sea. He was killed by loneliness. He left his family because he felt disconnected from those he loved, not because he missed a life free of obligation. When he realized his error and returned, there wasn't a place for him anymore. His loneliness grew until he became his loneliness and nothing else. Finally, in his anguish, he cast himself off the bluff into the sea.

"You're trying to make him the good guy," I said.

"I'm just telling you the story the way it was told to me. There's no good or bad."

Then I found myself asking Lyman what I'd been too scared to ever ask my mother. "Whose story is it?" Sometimes you find the origin of a thing, and its wonder dies.

"You mean is it French, Irish, Penobscot, total bullshit, some mumbo from a book?"

"I guess."

He shrugged. "It's all of ours. It's been around these woods for a long time. It was here twenty-five years ago, when your mother and I were on this bluff with Billy. And it'll be here twenty-five years from now, when you or Wren or Galen or your brothers or your children or someone else's children are up here."

"Billy Jupiter?"

Lyman's face tightened. He looked surprised, then nervous. "You didn't know it happened here." Lyman pointed past the tree to the edge of the bluff. "Billy fell right over there. Maybe Moses was right all these years."

"You know Moses?"

"Everyone knows everyone here. Always have and always will. I was Moses's sternman for a year when I first started lobstering," Lyman explained. "He took me on even after my family's connection to the mills and Billy's death. I never fully understood it, and it made me uneasy, working with him. I spent my whole life thinking it would be better to be a warrior in the garden. But one time Moses told me the thing to really be was a gardener in the war."

I thought about the paradox for a long time, until the rushing waves slapping against the rocks had grown deafening.

"I'll probably die still wrestling with the right answer," Lyman said. He gestured out to the sound of the waves. "I was surprised Falon came back to the bay at all. Even more surprised when she and your father decided to build near here."

"Maybe it's better to keep the bad things in front of you," I said after some time.

Lyman grinned and rose. He reached out, and for a moment I thought he was going to tussle my hair. "Something like that, kid." Then he slid his hands into his pockets, curled his shoulders inward, and turned and walked away from the bluff.

That night, the seventh evening of our strange game, something shifted. I woke in the dark gripped by an eerie anticipation. I wanted Lyman to be there. When I reached the window, Lyman was standing outside, but for the first time his back was turned to the house. It was as if we no longer mattered. I watched him stand that way for an hour before I fell asleep on the floor with Daphne and Sam beside me. The dead came to me that night in my dreams. Faces I did not know, but understood were my ancestors. From the dark they drifted toward the window in my room. Gentle, weightless things, really. It was as if they had simply stood in the driveway and raised their arms and let the wind lift them up to the second story. More of these figures kept lifting from the ground and gathering in a line. Hundreds of faceless men and women, stretching back to the woods, beyond the woods, filling the air above the river, filling the air above the ocean, filling the world. Then the first hand touched the glass. I watched it move through the pane. Then I felt it move through my T-shirt, through my chest, through my ribs. Finally I felt the hand close around my spine and begin to pull. I woke curled in a pool of in-slanting sunlight, sore and shaken and scared, scratching at my chest to make sure I was still whole. Daphne and Sam were gone. Lyman was gone. I wondered whether the dead were gone or with me still.

AT THE BREAKFAST TABLE I fixed my eyes directly on the plate of burned toast my mother tossed down on her way out the door. But my brothers knew.

"What happened?" Simon asked as we stepped outside. After eating we would walk the three hundred yards out to Arnoux's shop, tell him it was time for school, and then drive into town. He liked that he could see us off in the mornings and head into the yard with the satisfaction

of having already put some work into the day. What he did most often at
the shop in those early mornings was sketch. He claimed he needed to be
down here on the river to draw a proper boat, never in town, never anywhere else. Drawing a perfect centerline or marking out a cabin were his
true joys. Building the things was the price he had to pay to draw them.

"Nothing *happened*," I said.

"Sam and Daphne," Link said. "They've been leaving my room in the
middle of the night. They never do that. I thought they were just going
downstairs or into the hall."

"But they're not," Simon said.

"They're going to your room," said Link. "Why?"

"I don't know." I felt trapped by my brothers.

"Your room looks at the woods," Link said. "Mine doesn't. Sy's doesn't."

Simon stopped in the middle of the path. "It's Creel, isn't it?" he said.
How could my brothers know such things? We were halfway to the shop. I
imagined our father looking up from his drafting table at us in puzzlement.

Simon took my face between his palms. His fingers smelled of chalk
and sawdust. He turned my head until our eyes met. "Being scared isn't
being weak," he said. "You tell us. And we'll tell Arnoux. Together."

WHEN WE CALLED AROUND THE shop for our father, there was no response.
The tools were powered down, the piles of sawdust swept up, and the radio
switched off, all sure signs he had not even been there yet that morning.
"Strange," Simon said. Outside we caught a faint, high metallic whining
sound, and we followed it deep into the trees. Its volume rose with each
step, until we came through the clearing in the deep woods beside the old
stone foundation. Our father was just outside the barn with the Citabria.
The engine was running, the propellers buzzing like saws. His face was
only feet from the whirring blades. At first I thought he had been injured,
that the blades had cut him open, or perhaps he had had a heart attack or
a stroke. But he was just sitting beside the running machine. He looked up
and noticed us then, but his face didn't change at all.

"Almost ready," he mouthed.

"For what?" I yelled, but my father didn't seem to hear the question, as he turned back into the machine, his eyes a bit wild, another wrench gripped in his fist.

Simon stepped up beside the plane and reached into the cockpit and killed the engine. The propellers ticked and slowed, bringing our father up from his trance.

"He's watching us," Link said. Though the propellers had stopped, the entire barn seemed to vibrate with stored energy. "Lyman Creel's been coming up to the house and standing at the edge of the woods and staring at our house for some stupid reason. And Almy's been up there, watching him right back."

Our father didn't react at first. It was as though he was trying to fully parse out a complex equation. Then he turned and walked out of the barn without saying anything. He didn't slow as he walked back through the woods, and it was all we could do to keep up with him. He veered from the path, taking the straightest route possible, not flinching or slowing when branches snapped or sawed at his arms and face. "Get the keys, Simon," he called without looking back at us. "Start the truck." And then he went past the shop and up into the garden shed while we scrambled to do what he'd asked. He came out a few minutes later carrying a logging cant hook and a massive pair of channel lock pliers. "This is how he has always liked it," he said as he tossed the tools into the back of the running truck, "how he's always wanted it."

Link said, "Make it hurt," and then went silent when my father glared at him.

"You don't have a clue what you're talking about," said Simon. His hands were shaking on the wheel, and my father made him slide over.

"None of you do," he said.

"I can drive," said Simon.

"Sit. That's all I want anyone to do."

His fury was so calm, so calculated, that I trusted everything would be all right. I wished one of us had had the courage or the knowledge to reach across the cab and touch our father's face to stop him, but fury is a contagion, and anger intoxicates young men. We drove without speaking or looking at each other. It was a raw gray morning. Gradually the woods thinned until power lines crossed overhead and the town streetlights swung color across the sky. We made the left on Wharf Street, and then another left, going down the marina road, graveled and pitted by too many years of too little money for road maintenance and too much hard weather. We were just beyond The Fish House, where the road went down a slight hill and turned around in a big loop dotted with pickups, traps, and buoys. The fish pier extended two hundred feet out into the water.

My father threw open the door and was gone. The truck had barely come to a stop. He reached back through the window and touched Simon's shoulder. "Stay here with your brothers," he said. "Keep the truck going."

I hadn't felt the fear until then. Suddenly my body felt weightless. I found I could no longer raise my hands or figure out how to push away what was happening. He was my father. I trusted him. Now he was halfway down the concrete pier. All around, men had stopped what they were doing. No one was stacking traps, coiling rope, checking gear. Everyone was staring.

Oddly enough, Lyman Creel was the last man to turn and look, and when he did, my father was already on him. The cant hook caught Creel across the face, tearing his cheek open. Lyman stumbled back into a stack of lobster cages but kept his balance. Then my father drove the wooden end of the tool into Lyman's stomach. With the ocean crashing against the pilings, my father lifted Lyman as if he were made of air and dropped him onto the pier. Lyman tried to sweep my father's legs out, but my father brought his boot down on Lyman's knee with gruesome force. His howl was almost as loud as the crunch. Then my father was on top of Lyman with his knee pressed against the other man's throat. He slipped the pliers from his back pocket and tried to peel Lyman's mouth open. Lyman swung his one good leg around to twist him off until my father reached back and punched Creel in his knee. Pain provided the opening. The pliers slipped into Lyman's mouth and gripped the man's thick pink tongue.

Lyman went completely still then, paralyzed with fear, eyes huge. "Your kneecap might be broken." My father's voice was eerily calm. "But it's likely just a dislocation. You have a deep laceration to your cheek. The blood in your eyes is from the laceration. Your vision is completely fine, don't worry. I'm putting approximately eighty pounds of force on your carotid artery with my left knee right now. The reason you don't feel tired from oxygen deprivation is adrenaline. Adrenaline is also the only reason you won't immediately pass out if I tear out your tongue. I told you to leave us alone. I think you understand why I'm here."

My father started to twist the channel locks, and Lyman tried to scream with his mouth full of fear and metal. Then my father let go. The pliers clattered to the pavement. He retrieved the cant hook and hurled it into the sea in disgust. No one had moved to stop the violence, and no one moved now to help Lyman, who had crawled up from the pavement and was yelling at my father.

"You've got kids and a wife." Lyman tried to stand and let out a piercing howl as his knee buckled and he fell back to the pavement. "You're crazy."

My father dusted a spot of sand off his shoulder, shrugged.

"I should kill you." Creel spat blood.

"You wouldn't know where to start," my father said. "Don't come to my house again."

MY FATHER HAD BEEN MANY things in my life, but for the first time I had seen him become a monster, and I needed to kill the image, to push it from my head and forget it had ever happened. At night I woke constantly to the sounds of imagined sirens—I thought surely someone would come for my father. The river gurgled and the distant ocean waves droned on, and some nights thunder bellowed about the woods, but no one ever came, and Lyman never pressed charges.

It was late October. The air was crisp and bright and thin. Red, orange, and gold leaves turned the skies otherworldly. Yet none of us seemed able to stand each other. Our mother said very little. Our father cranked his angriest Mahler records in the shop. Back at the house we could hear each furious note as clearly as if a hammer were being dropped on a nail beside our ears. Two nights passed without our father coming in for dinner—he stayed buried in his work, hunched over his drafting table, planning the winter builds, our mother doing her best to keep from looking out the window. We didn't know how to talk him back, to say, *Hey, Pop, look. Hey, we're here. It's okay. Just come back to us.*

On the third night, he came into the kitchen well after we'd finished eating. His face was tired, though his eyes seemed unnaturally wide and alert. Engine grease shone on his hands and smeared his coveralls. When he tried to help with the dishes, our mother lifted the plate she had been scrubbing and smashed it on the counter. "Don't come in here and be helpful now," she said. "I wouldn't want to take you away from planning your next barbarian lesson." He looked away, grimacing, and when he couldn't find the right words, he reached out for her arm. Our mother lifted and smashed a second plate. This time a shard caught his hand, and a small dot of blood bloomed through the grease. She lifted a small clear water glass and cocked her arm. My father turned and left the room. My mother brought the glass down anyway, smashing it against the counter and grinding the shards down with her palm. She seemed then to realize what she'd done. "Oh, I'm a fucking fool," she said. She held up her hand. Small chunks of glass sat in the skin. There was no blood yet, just light reflecting off the glass, so it seemed almost as though she were holding a tiny sun in her palm. Simon walked out of the kitchen and returned with tweezers and a bowl of warm, soapy water. He took our mother's hand and, standing there at the counter, removed each shard of glass. He hummed quietly the whole time, a movement from Stravinsky's "Firebird," of all things.

"Prideful, reckless, all grand ideas and sulking guilt after." Our mother jabbed her other hand around the room. "You'll be like that too," she said. "You'll break my heart, but you'll do it still."

I wasn't sure which one of us she meant. After he'd removed all the glass, carefully setting the bloody pieces on a dish towel on the counter,

Simon washed our mother's hand with soapy water and then poured the bowl of crimson water down the sink. Then he walked out the door with a plate of food and started for the shop, where Schubert was playing now—the impromptus, sad and contemplative. Link and I helped our mother finish the dishes. Link dried. I put the plates and cups away. No one said a word about anything.

When we came home the next day, our father had the truck running. "Get in," he said. "We're going into town."

"To the boatyard?" I asked. I thought perhaps he'd finished the winter build schedule out in the shop that morning—it was my father's habit to build one new custom wooden boat each winter, often a majestic sloop or a small ketch meant for day-sailing, in addition to the routine winter maintenance he did.

"To the hospital. To see Lyman."

"What?" I said.

"Gonna bust his other knee this time?" Link scoffed.

Simon cuffed Link on the side of the head, and our father roared, "Enough." Crows startled from the trees, darkening the sky around us. "He's owed an apology."

"He's owed," Link sneered.

"I owe him. You're all coming with me."

"Why?" Link asked.

"Because I want you to be able to remember what the right thing looks like someday, Link."

Simon put his arm around my brother. "Come on, Link. Just give it up."

I've thought of that drive often over the years. No one spoke. When my father rolled his window down, Link put his up. When my father turned the radio on, Link reached over and turned it off. Each countering action was another cut. I never again saw my father scold my brother. I think he knew there was nothing he could say to make Link forgive what he saw as weakness. In time he'd either see it differently, or he wouldn't. My father had called Grace Creel that morning, and she had told him not to go to the fish pier. She said my father had taken too much away from Lyman already in front of others. She told him he would be at physical therapy at the hospital that afternoon, and that was where we went.

When we came in, Lyman was lying on a padded bench as a man flexed and put pressure on his knee. He swore with every degree the knee flexed, and I thought he might begin to cry.

"You're hurting him," I said.

"Don't do that." Lyman grimaced. "I don't want your sympathy."

The physical therapist didn't seem to know what to make of the scene: a grown man standing with his head down, his three nearly grown sons around him, in the PT room in the middle of the day. "This is a hospital, come on, guys," he said. "Keep the circus shit out of here. I'm just trying to do my job and go home."

My father apologized for the intrusion. He seemed to realize now how inappropriate it was to be here. "Sorry, sorry for all this," he stammered. "We'll go."

He had started to turn to leave when Lyman struggled up off the bench and said, "You came this far. Do the rest of it."

My father turned to Lyman, and Lyman started to limp forward. The physical therapist moved to help him, but Lyman waved him off. He'd made it three shambling steps, his face all sweat and pain, when his knee buckled and he started to fall. I caught his arm and held him up.

"Jesus, Lyman," my father said. "I'm sorry. I'm so sorry."

"HOW'S YOUR MOTHER'S HAND?" MY father asked me a few days later. It was nearing dusk. Blue light gathered outside the boat-shop windows down at the marina. Since apologizing to Lyman, my father had been down here for days at a time, sleeping in the office with his work, grinding, calling his clients, trying to ensure that there would still be work as our family increasingly slid into the role of pariahs, trying, I suppose, to make his world normal again. I had stopped in after school to see him and spent an hour going around the woodworking and paint bays, cleaning up tools. Now we were up in the high office.

"She'll be okay," I said.

"I should have left her alone that day in the kitchen," he said. "Thinking you can fix everything is cruel. It ends up with people hurt."

"I'm sorry," I whispered. "For everything. So is Link."

I looked around at the boatyard in the soft late-fall light. The east end of the boat shop extended far out onto the pier, sitting only a few feet from the rock wall that held back the sea. During storms water would lash over the wall and smash against the shop windows and sometimes flood the building. The shop was laid out in a giant L, with boatbuilding bays set into the center, ringed by the woodworking shop and all its tools. The woodworking shop was two stories high, rigged with ladders and a balcony that hugged the L and whatever boat was at its center, allowing one man to work down below on the hull or keel, while another shimmied up the ladders into the lofted sky to work on the decks. Atop it all, as if set off in a garret, was a peaked third-story attic that my father made his office. It was walled and floored in rough-sawn, inch-thick hemlock, and he had cut the entire east-facing gable out and framed it in with windows so he could look out at the comings and goings of the sea while he made calls to clients or the lumberyards.

Walking by the boatyard in the afternoons, I'd creep toward the windows and peer inside. I thought it strange how this was the building, among all the buildings in town, that I was continually drawn to. It was simply a big barn down near the water filled with boats, and there was nothing particularly novel about boats: they surrounded us, supported us, were so common and expected in our lives that they faded into the ether, becoming as invisible and essential as oxygen.

"They speak to each other, you know," my father said to me one afternoon, years earlier. I'd been looking into the windows near dusk, and I'd missed him when he'd come around the corner. He must have stood there a long time watching me lift up on my toes and peer into the darkened windows, my breath fanning a hot gray mist across the glass. When I wiped the moisture away with my glove, the boats seemed to have shifted a little.

"What?" I said, scrambling down, feeling exposed and caught.

"Boats," my father said. "When they're in storage like that for the winter, they speak to each other. They talk back and forth to pass the winter nights. Everyone knows that around here."

"That's outlandish, Dad," I said. Simon and Link had long since grown bored and run up the street to the newspaper office, leaving me alone with the wild churning snow and the frosted glass and the gleaming, hulking ships inside.

"Nope," he said. "It's common knowledge, established fact, and why you all and every child who walks past that window has to stop to look inside."

Over the years I had come to understand that the possibility of a whole community of people being wrong, even about something as irrational as boats being able to speak, was less likely than their being right. I chose to believe. Soon after I found a key sitting on my bedside table, and I instinctively knew it went to the boat barn. I must have spent hours sitting between those stored boats on winter afternoons, reading, thinking, watching the snow drift across the windows, breathing in the scent of cedar and the sea, listening to those vessels whisper and speak.

"How about you, Dad?" I asked now. "How are you?"

My father looked at me for a long time over a table filled with unfurled blueprints. I was about to apologize again when he said, "I'm okay."

"Maybe it's okay to not be okay, Dad."

My father shivered, nodded. He grabbed his coat from the hook by the door, even though the woodstove was red-hot in the office. "Maybe you're right," he said.

I hugged my father, and we stood at the window watching the gathering dark for a long time. Thinking about his words, about time, and of course about regret, which was running beneath all he had said, I began thinking about the boats waiting to be built.

"I shouldn't have done what I did to Lyman Creel," he said. "That was too much. That wasn't human. Your mother deserves better. Loving someone is a fight to keep taking them for who they are. Your mother's as solid as the crust of the earth. She loves me stupid, but that doesn't mean I get to stop trying to be better."

"I know, Dad."

"And the bateau too." My father's face was ashen, and his eyes were sliding about. He touched his throat, right above his collarbone. "I think I need to lie down."

"Lie down?"

My father pushed papers and build plans off the couch onto the floor. I looked around again. Everything in the office was in disarray. My father did not lie down. My father did not do disarray. "Should I call someone?"

"No," he snapped, pulling away from me at the window. "Stay here. Stay where it's safe. The door is locked. Simon and Link are with your mother. I just need to lie down a few. Catch my breath. Think."

Thirteen

I WOKE TO THE SOUND of a plane roaring above our house.

Since the odd contrition of our visit to the hospital, my father had continued his feverish work on the Citabria. Now the distant, metallic whine of the engine grew into a wail. Then red steel flashed above our yard. I was shocked as I watched the little red-and-white plane bank down the river, turn at the sea, and pass overhead again. I could just make out Arnoux in the cockpit and Reggie beside him. Then the craft passed into oblivion, racing back into the forest. Surely the plane was too low, too fast, these woods too narrow—but Reggie and my father had done the math and determined that the clearing by the plane barn was large enough for taking off and landing. That was where my mother and I found my father, his flight finished, climbing down from the cockpit.

"It's ready," he said. His arms were crossed, and his face held a bewildered look, as if he couldn't believe he'd just been up in the sky.

"For what?" my mother snapped.

"Public consumption," quipped Reggie.

"I didn't ask you. And don't be clever right now."

"It's ready to *fly*, Falon," said my father.

My mother turned to Reggie. "Of course you thought this was a good idea."

"I wouldn't say I thought it was a good idea. But it was an idea." Reggie shifted his weight and glared over at my father. He said, "I'm sorry, Falon. I thought you knew."

"But you never bothered to ask. Every day I wake up and remind myself that I expect too much. What a foolish idea, to think I might actually know what the people I care about are doing."

"We need a different kind of attention," my father said. "I thought we could print something in the *Days* for publicity. Not an entire article. Just a notice. The event is publicity enough."

"You don't get it, do you?"

"I'll be safe. I'll do everything right, Falon. You know I'm not a careless person."

"No, but you're becoming a selfish person. Your safety isn't the problem. *The Lowering Days* is my newspaper. And this is my town too. Not everything is yours. Not everyone needs you."

My mother walked off then, leaving me with my uncle and my father and the plane. Looking around, I realized I was no better than either of them. I had assumed my mother knew about my father's strange early-morning tinkering with the plane, flesh and steel holed up together in that derelict barn in the deep, cold woods. Would I have told her, had I known of the deception?

I found my mother on the bluff, at the ghost apples. She was sitting with her back against the tree, picking blades of grass and whistling through them like a child. I came into the clearing and sat down in front of her. She looked like she was part of the tree. She looked like she had been there forever. We all went in pilgrimage to the ghost apples, but my mother was the only one who ever touched the tree. Our hands always stopped short of the bark, the branches, the fruit, as though we didn't have permission to enter that world.

"Do you want me to leave?" I asked.

My mother shook her head, pulled another blade of grass, whistled feebly. "God, I was always awful at this." She laughed. Overhead a raven circled the tree. I thought it must be one of Lyman's.

"It's not," my mother said.

"Not what?"

"His bird."

"How do you know that?"

"Because I pay attention to things."

My mother turned around and faced the trunk of the ghost apple tree. She reached out and touched a set of carved initials near the base of the trunk. They belonged to my parents. I had never noticed them.

"We carved them at the very bottom of the tree." My mother's voice was soft, tired. I realized I didn't pay enough attention to her voice, which was lovely, melodic and comforting. The tree had grown over the years, twisting skyward and spreading its otherworldly fruit in a huge canopy. It must have been twenty feet tall. "The letters were very small at first," my mother went on. "The leaves covered them, then the snow. You see, young love needs tenderness. It needs a lot of protecting. Over time we knew our initials would grow as the trunk grew. We thought we would grow too. Maybe we were being overly romantic. Maybe we were fools. But two people have to believe in something."

I watched the raven circling overhead and thought about the cost of love, which was the constant potential for loss.

"We discovered that plane," she said. "Your father and I made all these discoveries together. Sometimes I wonder what good they've really done." I put my hand on her shoulder, and realized it was not only her voice I hadn't paid enough attention to. We hardly touched anymore. Growing up had made the feel of my mother's body foreign, and I missed her even though she was right beside me.

"I only ever loved three men in my life," she said. "I lost one when I was just a little older than you. And now I fear I'm about to lose the other two."

"You're talking about Dad and Lyman."

"Yes. Lyman and I have tried to hate each other for twenty years. But that doesn't erase that we loved each other." I thought about that idea for a moment. If true, it meant that love perhaps remained under all things through time. "This has to be hard for you to hear," my mother said. "I should stop."

She was right. It should have been. But I'd been drawn to Lyman most of my life. The connection had felt powerful that day we went to see Grace about the letter, and Lyman was out in the yard with his birds. It had linked us on those nights he stood in the dark, watching our house. Then it had been solidified when I came upon Lyman standing in this very spot by the ghost apple tree. The truth was, I had always felt at ease in Lyman's presence, even when he seemed to cause unrest for everyone else in my family. I studied my mother's face. I had her round eyes and wide mouth, her dark hair and her freckles. If love did remain under all things, I wondered if it could be passed down in our genetic whirlwind as well. Unable to tell her any of this, I simply shrugged.

She looked up at the tree and then out over the sea. "She loved her husband." I knew she was talking about Nigawes. "Even when she was watching his color turn red and then black. Even when she was watching him fall apart. Even when she was hacking him to pieces. She loved him."

"I know, Mom."

"That was the problem. Loving him. And I guess that's what made it beautiful too. Until it wasn't."

Not knowing what else to say, I kept my hand on her shoulder, feeling the strong and solid curve of bone, the endurance of her body. She lifted her fingers from the initials. "Do you understand, Almy? About how something can be beautiful until it isn't?"

"I want to."

"I know, honey." She reached back and touched my face. "But that might not be enough. Lyman may never walk right again. Did you know that?"

My silence answered for me.

"Make sure you remember all of this. People think I don't care. That I'm just greedy for details and gossip, out to make everyone into a story. What they don't see is how much all these old rifts break my heart. I don't write about this place because I'm nosy. I write about it because I want things to change."

My mother walked out from under my hand toward the edge of the bluff then. I was worried about the winds. The wet earth. Loose rocks. I wanted her to turn around. The thing about the sea is how easily it takes what it wants.

"Your father's probably right," she said. "This nonsense with the plane will probably help. I just wish we hadn't gotten here. I'd like to be alone now, Almy."

When I looked back, my mother had moved away from the edge. She was standing at the tree, her forehead against the trunk. Her hair fell about the bark, and it was hard to tell where the tree ended and her body began. Her lips were moving, but I could not hear her words. Overhead, the raven kept circling. Each time it was about to land on the tree, it rose back into the sky and loosed a mournful croak.

AN AIR SHOW. IT WAS an absurd and childish idea, but oddly brilliant. My father knew that people from all over the county loved coming together for small gatherings: contra dances and barbecues and high school basketball games and maple syrup tapping parties. They also loved being mesmerized. Every year they amassed atop Hatchet Mountain to watch celestial events: the Perseids in August, the high bright point of Jupiter in April, glimpses of Venus and Saturn, lunar eclipses, blue moons and super moons. But the Geminids, the last sky-streaking bodies before winter descended, were their favorite. The Geminids were the debris of an asteroid called Phaeton that orbited between the sun and Mercury. The sun's great heat was slowly fracturing the asteroid, causing rock and dust to flame out in a comet-like tail. For two weeks every December, as Earth crossed Phaeton's path, this rocky, cosmic debris besieged our atmosphere, drawing meteoric streaks across the night sky. The beautiful thing about swooping through a field of interstellar debris every year was the unpredictability of the celestial show. You knew the show would come, but you didn't know what your eyes would receive. On the large grassy dome of this small mountain, people drank and danced and reveled and watched the sky, wondering what its meteor show would look like this year. Sometimes the Geminids passed in dull white streaks. Other years exploding yellow bursts painted the horizon with fire. Scientists said the meteor displays were intensifying every year as Phaeton passed closer to us with each orbit. I wondered as a child how many thousands of years it would take until the sun made ash of Phaeton. After that, how long would it be until space swallowed the remaining debris, and the December sky went dark? Would we even be here still to see such a thing? Not even Reggie, with his great and wandering mind, seemed able to answer this. My father wanted to fly for his community as his people gathered in the mountains to whoop and revel and wait. He wanted to perform. He wanted, I suppose, to make them love him again.

My mother hated the spectacle but agreed to it, and my father's notices showed up in the paper every week for the month of November. They were not large, and they were not flashy. There were no images, no color, no accompanying stories, just a simple printed notice in the bottom corner of the last page of the paper. But even the simplicity and the peculiarity of the placement seemed to add to the allure around town.

Local boatbuilder Arnoux Ames to take to the skies again.
Join him atop Hatchet Mountain to welcome back the Geminids.

Around the bay there was a general lifting. The communal ice around our family began to thaw. Arnoux had coordinated his stunt with the return of the meteors, and the brashness of it—a man flying around in the sky backdropped by flashing, aligning his metaphorical reemergence with the return of a group of heavenly bodies—was outlandish and oddly intoxicating. It was a transparent ploy. Some simply wanted to celebrate. Others came to stare in grotesque wonder at the spectacle of one man's bravado. Others came in hopes of seeing a stunning fall. I believe others were simply ready to love us again and quietly hoped this might provide that chance. Normalcy, after all, is a return to breathing.

In town the steady buzz of chainsaws let us know the Geminids were near. Giant piles of autumn deadfall were sawed up and skidded up the mountain. Fiddles and guitars and mandolins were restrung and polished and tuned and checked again. We wouldn't lament the shift toward winter. We would dance and celebrate in fevered appreciation of Gemini, a constellation that had for centuries guided eastern sailors and fishermen safely home across the hungry sea.

MY FATHER DID EVERYTHING LEGALLY. He had the plane meticulously inspected by an aviation outfit in Bangor. He filed flight plans with the municipal airport. He calculated his flight time, his fuel consumption, and coordinated his aerial maneuvers. He purchased and installed new radio equipment. He abandoned his rough landings in fields and meadows and clearings and made plans to both depart and land at the municipal airfield, which was to monitor his flight as well via its radio system. I didn't know my father knew how to do any of this anymore.

Early in the afternoon, on a cold bright clear December day, we headed up Hatchet Mountain. Grills were heated. Beans and casseroles put on to warm. At dusk the bonfire, which was twenty feet tall, was lit. The flames seemed endless. They turned the stars red. Swallowed the mountain pines at their back. Music started to slip out into the air, a tentative note here, a harmony note there.

At first I didn't watch my father's flight. I was too scared. I wanted to be proud of him, but I couldn't bring myself to risk looking up. What if by looking up, I caused some disaster? My brothers were staring into the sky. My mother made eye contact with me. Pride and anger filled her face. She nodded at me to let me know it was okay to look wherever I wanted. I listened to the gasps and murmurs around me. There must have been five hundred people up there, and I didn't want to be near any of them. I wandered away from the crowd, over to the edge of the woods, still refusing to look up. I hadn't been there long when Wren came across the meadow and sat down beside me in the dark.

Applause and hollering answered the whining engine as the plane zipped back and forth overhead. "Fools," Wren finally said. "If they skipped the fire, they could see the meteors better."

Wren sounded very tired and sad. I'd hardly seen her at all since she helped us escape that night on the water. She opened her mouth to speak again but seemed to collapse under the effort. She put her hand down on top of mine, and not knowing what else to do, I tipped my head onto her shoulder.

"I'll stay right here," she said. "You should look up. It'll be okay."

Overhead the Geminids had begun to streak, little pins of yellow tracing across the sky. My father made a few more passes through the night. I knew from the applause and the shouting that it was done, and that nothing awful had happened. I exhaled fully, and Wren squeezed my hand. I watched the plane disappear over the hills, imagined my father cautiously landing it at the airport on the far side of town, where Reggie would be waiting to pick him up.

"They're all mesmerized," I said, looking out at the gathered crowd. Flames shimmered through the trees. People were singing and whooping. They would do so for hours still, waiting for the meteors to reach their peak.

Galen and Grace, Simon and Link, my mother and even Lyman. They were all staring up at the sky. "Everyone is," I said.

"And you're not." Wren smiled. Her teeth were white against the dark. "The boy who thought himself above the cosmos."

"Nice title." I smirked. "Where have you been?"

"Around. Not that it's your business," Wren snapped. Then she let her head rest against my own, and I suppose I loved her for it all, and had honestly loved her for a long time.

"Sorry."

"Don't do that," she said. "I'm tired of people saying empty things like 'I'm sorry,' or 'Interesting,' or 'How's the weather?' when they don't have anything better to say."

"Okay," I said. "I missed you."

"That's much better. That's almost sweet." She lifted our hands and brought them into her lap as she rubbed the cold from my fingers. "He's going to be okay, your dad," she said. "So is mine. I think I believe that."

"Because it's true?"

"No, because I need it to be true. All this between our families." She gestured over the mountain and the sky and the river and the woods and the distant sea. "It really scares me."

I brushed her wrist with just the tip of my thumb. "Me too," I said. Wren turned my hand over and traced the veins and lines along my palm. I felt my dread leaving my body, and I became aware then of how close we were to each other. Her hair smelled faintly like garden dirt. She was chewing mint gum, and I could see the sweat along her neck from the fire.

"Were you really going to rob your dad?" I laughed.

"Oh Christ, I don't know. Probably. Maybe. You would bring that up now. I thought he was going to kill you both. But if he caught me with you, I knew he wouldn't hurt anyone."

"Then he could stay with you."

She wiped at her face. "Something like that. I know it's silly. He hardly talks to us anymore. He comes and goes to work, moves around the house, does laundry, takes the garbage out, cares for his birds, and he's somewhere else the whole time."

I understood. I had seen my father become an apparition as well. "They'll come back."

"I hope so." Wren pressed her lips to the top of my head. Then she kissed my eyes and then my mouth.

"We should probably be celebrating or something," I said when we moved apart. In the distance the notes of a mandolin danced around the fire.

"I think we're exactly where we should be," she whispered. "You could have come found me."

"I didn't want to presume."

"Someone always has to come to someone."

There was a great question in her eyes, and then it was gone. She took my face between her palms and kissed me more firmly. I closed my eyes and kissed her back. It felt easy. She rolled my bottom lip between her lips and bit it lightly, and I did the same, and we stayed there with our foreheads touching and our breath moving together. She pushed my hands down against her thighs and pushed her fingers up under my coat. When she traced my nipple with her thumb, I gasped into her mouth and could feel her smiling before she pulled away.

"Not here," she said. "Not with all this. Do you want to know the truth?"

"Yes."

"My father wanted your mother. Maybe he still does. And I think he hates her for it, like his desire is somehow her fault. And I guess part of me hates him for being that kind of man. You always think your dad will somehow be better."

I stopped short of telling her I knew exactly what she was talking about. I thought of my own father and his sudden violence on the dock, the way he'd delivered such menace and pain with such chilling composure, the way he had, in a few terrible moments, ceased being human to me. "I'm sorry" was all I could say.

Wren put her head on my shoulder this time. "So am I," she said.

I pulled a coat over us both and remembered my mother's words at the ghost apples—*Young love needs tenderness, it needs a lot of protecting*—as we watched the bonfire blaze beneath the Geminids.

Part IV

✴︎ ✴︎ ✴︎

Fourteen

S NOW FELL EARLY THAT YEAR, collecting overnight in great, suffocating banks that squeezed our houses. Windows rattled. Roofs shifted and groaned. Front doors met wet and sticky resistance when pushed outward in the mornings. The snow came unrelentingly, forty-eight inches in the third week of December alone, and for long stretches of time people were sealed in, entombed. Snow in the branches, snow in the creeks, snow in the marshes, snow in the distance, snow in the cracks of the world. For two months the temperature hardly rose above ten degrees. Some days the sun seemed dangerously bright in the thin, dry air. Heavy orange light, eerie in its absence of heat, layered the world until dusk, when purple shadows darkened the land. Other days an iron gauze seemed pulled across the sky. The roads became avenues of packed snow and ice. The snow got so high so fast we had to slide out an upstairs window and drop down into the yard to shovel. When the snows stopped and people dug free, the fog began rolling in from the sea. It blanketed the hills and coiled about houses, erased children tottering down the streets with their parents, choked brick storefronts and swallowed cars trying to pass through its belly.

In the fog Wren and I searched for and often found each other. We passed about town unknown and out of sight, finding empty houses with musty bedrooms, and for a few short weeks it was as if we were inhabiting a mysterious, unknown world.

Exhausted finally by the antics of my father and Lyman, talk turned again to the fire. Many assumed the arsonists had headed south or north, fleeing the state. Some thought they'd never be found. Others wondered if they'd ever existed. Talk started about tricks, about dark magic, devilcraft. Then a pair of hikers came across a set of moose tracks that disappeared mid-step at the base of Hatchet Mountain. Suddenly the ghostly fugitives were very much alive again.

My mother had reached her limits around foolish rumor. The air show had placated many. Papers were selling. Calls about boats trickled down through the woods. This treading-lightly nonsense would do no longer. As the rumors intensified, as the slander and the hate again teemed, she again turned to language. Over the course of a month, she published a four-part editorial series that traced the history of tribal rights, treaties, and land claim settlements in the state; explored the environmental exploitation of the river; considered the collapse of the timber industry and the economic devastation wrought by clandestine mill closures; dared to imagine the look of a postindustrial landscape; and combined the impact of those exploratory threads here in the bay. My mother expected angry readers and canceled subscriptions. None of that happened, and it came as a great shock when Galen Creel showed up at *The Lowering Days* out of the snow and the fog after the final article was printed.

The boy stood in the middle of the newspaper office with all his wide-faced earnestness. Snowmelt pooled around his boots. He waited as the steam banged about the radiators and settled. "I liked your stories," he offered, his voice cautious. My mother sat across the room at her desk, bent under a small green office lamp, scratching words on a yellow legal pad, wholly uninterested in humoring a child. Galen was standing in a deep puddle when she finally looked up.

"They're editorials. Not stories." She pushed a dictionary across the desk.

"I know I'm not supposed to like you," the boy said after a moment.

This caused her to pause. Like his father months before him, the boy had come to *The Lowering Days* during the middle of the week. At first she assumed he was there to right some perceived wrong to his family's honor. Now she wasn't so sure. She hadn't even mentioned Lyman's family by name in the articles. "That's an odd thing to say," she said. "It implies that you do like me."

"Maybe. I don't know. You haven't done us any favors, though. You could have stopped all this. My mom could have too."

"And what about you, Galen? What could you have done?"

"Me." The boy looked confused. "We're just children. People do things for us, not because of us. None of you would have listened."

This boy was not what she had expected. She swallowed her ego, which was colossal, and started to really listen.

"When I saw your husband up there in that plane," Galen said, "I didn't just see some smug bully. I saw something I wanted to be. It's not about being invincible or envied. Or being the center of attention. And it's not about being free either."

"Riddle me this, riddle me that."

"You aren't that nice for a grown-up."

"I have a busy life. And no, no I suppose I'm not. So what is it that you want, dear Galen?"

"It was about control. When I saw your husband up there, I saw someone in complete control of himself. His machine, his environment. All those people. Even me too, I guess. They were all under his control."

She saw now that, yes, she had misjudged this boy. There was more here to him. Some ambition, some hunger. "That can be a dangerous want."

"What if I said I just want to be good enough at something to get the hell away from here someday?"

The comment stopped my mother. The verbal barbs she had sharpened dissolved on her lips. She remembered her own life, her own attempts to flee and be someone great somewhere else, the struggle between belonging and ego, before she drifted back home to the bay and met my father. "You still haven't told me what you really want."

The boy swallowed hard. He lifted his chin a little higher, hoped his voice would not crack. "I want your husband to teach me how to fly."

THE BAY IS QUIET. IT is a Friday afternoon. The moon is full, and though it is not quite dark, bits of light seem already to be falling through the sky, sprinkling the pines. Overhead the stars will soon emerge, moving in unison in a great sweep of time. Some are near death. Some are just being born. Their cosmic dust lives here on earth, coursing down the rivers, growing through the trees, vibrating in the bones of the two-leggeds and the four-leggeds. Deep in this cold season, the river around the Ames's house has frozen solid. Bird, beast, and human all startle as the shift and whump of the river ice echoes everywhere. A giant is alive down there below the frozen surface. He pulls river water in through his great lungs and blows it out against the ice as though beating a drum. But no giant is as big as even the littlest river, and no matter how he beats and blows, he cannot get free. A boy walks cautiously up through the cold, covering his ears so the giant's whumping won't drive him back through the woods or to the realm of madness.

Flight itself was not an odd desire in a teenage boy, but Galen didn't just want flight. Since seeing the Citabria streak across the sky below the Geminids, he had longed to do only that: to soar. That meant he must go to Arnoux. He knew no one else in the bay who possessed such magic.

Full of an eerie calm, Galen sat in the Ames's kitchen with a cup of untouched hot chocolate and his hands patiently folded in his lap. He had been at the house waiting for Arnoux to come inside for nearly two hours. He had spoken barely five words.

Sound sometimes comes quicker than seeing. The river giant knows this. That is why he whumps against the ice instead of flashing his teeth. Now he stills and listens. A faint whistling comes first, brushing the frozen pines. Then boots crunch through the snowpack. Heels knock snow off against porch steps. A door sucks open.

In the kitchen Galen watched Arnoux strip down. First the older man set his gloves on the floor. Pulled his boots free. Set them near the heat. Unwrapped a ragged brown wool scarf. Unzipped and shimmied out of his insulated coveralls, stained by years of use. Carefully hung them from a nail by the door. Slapped his hands against his face five times in furious succession, reddening his flesh, reawakening warmth.

Wearing only a pair of long black thermal underwear and a tattered green sweater, Arnoux finally sat down across from the boy. The river giant strained to hear.

"I'm not like my father." Galen's voice was rusty with disuse.

"I don't know what that means. My hands hurt and my ears are screaming from running a table saw for three hours."

"I'm saying I'm different from him."

Arnoux seemed to take his time considering this. "Your father isn't a bad man. It's complicated."

"He's not me."

"Of course he isn't."

"Or remotely like me."

"That remains to be seen." Arnoux stood then, and the river giant stomached a whump, afraid of being found listening. "The plane is in the woods down a mile or so in an old barn. Get snowshoes. You'll need them. Don't freeze to death getting there."

"Is it magic," the boy asked, "flight?"

"No." The man squinted out the window at something the boy could not see. "It's imagination."

THE LESSONS BEGAN SATURDAY AND continued each Saturday after. They were carried out in secret, without Lyman's knowledge, and I have often wondered how much of the deception was necessity and how much was simple cruelty. The flying lessons should not have happened how they did: covertly, stealthily, not with blatant or reckless lies but with a string of calculated omissions. Looking back, I'm often amazed that Lyman never found out.

On Saturday mornings Lyman fished or hunted, while Grace took Galen and Wren, who had both chosen music over the woods or the sea, to the Unitarian Universalist Church in town, where they sang in a community chorus. For hours they sang, unhinged and celebratory, old songs and new songs, hymns and spirituals, gospel pleas and torch songs, folk laments and ballads and calls to arms. On their way to sing, Grace now stopped and let Galen out at the end of our road. The boy waved to his mother and sister. Lifted the gate. Eyed the green curve of pines against the snow. Then he walked down the frozen two-track to the river, while Grace and Wren continued into town. Grace and Wren said nothing about anything being different. Grace and Wren sang, and I believe everyone else simply pretended that Galen was there singing too.

The river woods swallowed the boy. If not for the snowshoe trails, he might have become impossibly lost. After a while he heard the high, desperate wailing of an airplane engine. It was never a natural sound, but in winter the metallic screech rose from unnatural to ominous. A plane is a thing of intense beauty, but it's impossible to consider a plane and not think of catastrophe. The troubling thing was how the sound of the plane didn't move on those initial Saturday mornings. It just stayed there in the trees, whining like some monster hovering nearby. An airplane engine is a dynamic sound. It approaches, growing more alive with each escalating decibel, before it breaks into sight overhead, freeing the nightmare of devastation to come, and eventually, if one is lucky, passes uneventfully, permitting the grounded listener to shed terror and again breathe.

Arnoux led Galen through all the flight systems and safety checks— battery voltage okay, fuel gauge and fuel valve on, flaps down, seat belts functional, oil level registered, flaps operational and up, carb heat, throttle position, fuel mixture, master switch on, magnetos on, brakes engaged. He was meticulous, speaking slowly and reverently of both the power and responsibility of flight. It would be months perhaps before he let the boy fly the plane, but he could test him still, try to overwhelm him. Just when the boy broke, when he could no longer keep up with the avalanche of technical information, potential catastrophes, and lifesaving troubleshooting techniques, Arnoux pulled back and turned almost maternal. He ceased talking *at* the boy and comforted him, told him no one can know it all.

But Galen harbored a perfect blend of tenacity and fascination and wouldn't let himself be overwhelmed. He kept up with everything Arnoux said. He took copious and detailed notes to later compare against flight-instruction manuals he sent away for. He entered into his obsession so fully that he closed out any space for doubt, let alone failure.

It was only a matter of time before the flying started. Teaching runs. Arnoux at the controls. Galen observing, chronicling every move from the copilot's seat.

At school, Galen was lost now in aviation dreams. Flight books and engineering manuals were his constant companions. Teachers didn't try to separate him from his obsession. Like Link, Galen had always been filled with rage, but unlike my brother, Galen despised the imprisonment of schools. While he was not following along in his biology textbook, he was at least engaged in something, not sailing off into fits of anger or disruption. He had become determined, and in his determination, manageable. He spoke to almost no one now, acknowledging only us. Nodded when I passed in the hall. Raised a hand in a strange fist of solidarity when he saw Link in the cafeteria. Lifted a chin at Simon in town. On these occasions his trance momentarily broke. His eyes cleared. His pupils narrowed, focusing, seeing. Then he was gone again.

THAT WINTER MY FATHER AND I ran into Lyman and Galen once. It was a Sunday afternoon, and we had gone into town for the matinee at The Grand. The theater was an old renovated opera house. Great Georgian pillars supported the lobby ceiling. Gilded mirrors covered the walls. A thick and dusty red curtain hung in front of the screen. The radiators knocked so loudly and so viciously that they often eclipsed the sound of the film being shown. There was a balcony, and four elevated seat boxes. The owner, a German hunter who'd moved to the bay from Tunisia and mounted his kill from all over the world—silverback gorillas, wildebeests, Kodiak bears, Nile crocodiles, Sumatran tigers, diamond-back rattlesnakes—about the theater, colossal and terrifying in death. It was impossible not to feel the eyes of the world's most fearsome predators bearing down on you from above while the screen before you flashed combinations of moving light. What disturbed me about the theater's grotesque collection was the randomness of its narratives. I'd seen complex dioramas in museums, with predator and prey and flora all arranged in a perfect encapsulation of stopped time, but the theater's collection was entirely one-sided and without any context or supporting environment whatsoever—a Burmese python coiled about a railing, a shortfin mako shark splayed across five seats—so I could never tell who was the watcher and who was the watched. All that winter they were showing a rotation of the old *Star Wars* movies at The Grand. We were there to see *A New Hope*. When my father and I rounded the corner, we saw Lyman and Galen coming out of the auto parts store and heading for the theater as well.

The two men narrowed their eyes. Then Lyman noticed me beside my father, and the air between them softened. My father ran a hand through his hair, hooked a thumb in his back pocket. "Lyman," he managed to say. "How are you?" When the civility of the greeting faded, he cast about for a conversational topic. "Your ravens," my father said. "How are the birds taking all this snow?"

"Fine, fine," Lyman said, stumbling a bit at first. "They enjoy it. They're like children, really." He looked at me and then at Galen. "Constantly playing, always up to some mischief. They've all decided to stay through the winter," he said. "The young ones are roosting in the same woods as their parents."

I saw my father catch Galen's eye and look away.

"Is that unusual?" I asked.

"No," Lyman said. The ease between us all was shocking. "Not unusual, but not common either. Sometimes the adolescent birds go off on their own. Sometimes they stay close to their birth sites for a couple years. It's their variance, their complexity, really, that makes them so much fun."

Lyman stopped then, hit by a wave of self-consciousness, and looked down at the sidewalk. I wanted desperately for him to go on, unburdened and at length, extolling all the fascinating behaviors of his birds, but he said no more.

"We're going to The Grand," my father said.

"I suppose we are as well," said Lyman.

"Then it's settled," Galen added.

For two hours we sat together inside the theater, that chorus of death above us in the dark balcony, watching the powers of good and evil battle in a world of dreams. Then we walked out into a blinding orange sunset. The western edges of town smoldered. A deeper red frosted the rolling crests of the coastal mountains. Hardly anyone was in town. Lyman and my father looked at each other one more time. To the east, blue twilight bathed the brick buildings sloping down Main Street to the harbor. Soon the world would go black. For a moment I thought they might shake hands, but they did not, and we went our separate ways, my father and I walking westward into that fading red glare as if chasing more days, Lyman and Galen heading east down the hill, deeper into the cold, where their car waited among all that blue.

Fifteen

T HE HAUNTED FEELING THAT HAD begun to hound Lyman that
night under the Geminids seemed to grow with the cold. A group
of Penobscot kids had been staring at him as they all waited for
the meteors. He wondered if any of them were related to the kid in the
river. How could he go over to them and say "I don't hate you"? He had
been too near the bonfire. He couldn't breathe. The sound of the plane
engine came first, before the actual aircraft broke into view, and he hated
how everyone had experienced that flight, that glory. The little red-and-
white Citabria rose above a wall of white pines. When it reached a perilous
height, it seemed to stall and float for a moment, this small metal speck no
more than a black feather now, could have been a whisper, could have been
a dream. Then it was plummeting, diving, but with control, nose down,
its wings pivoting around like a top. When it fell behind the trees into the
ravine, a gasp shook the mountain. Then the roaring plane shot up again
and burned a low pass over their heads. Lyman had staggered, covered his
face, almost falling on his wrecked knee.

Steadying himself, he had searched for his family. Grace and Galen
were staring at the sky. Wren was slowly moving away from him. Lyman
wanted to yell out to them. But it was as if the plane had erased his ability to call his family back. Searching for relief, his eyes fell on his son,

who momentarily met his gaze. Then the boy's eyes traveled right through Lyman, swinging back into the sky, where they widened in a desperate search for the plane.

When the plane had roared overheard again, emergent, Lyman heard music, a piano. It was as if the notes were being drawn through the sky. He was losing his mind. Then the ground was coming up to meet him, and he didn't understand how an entire mountain could tip over. This time he had gone down. His knee struck the earth, pain like a howl he had never dared dream. No one turned away from the sky. No one saw him at all.

And Lyman's fall had gone on and on.

Since then, he had kept half his traps in the water, fished deep into winter. He was trying to outwork this dread, this thing—that was how he had taken to thinking about it, as a living and potentially parasitic object that was festering somewhere in the tissues of his body—that was drawing down his energy and his mood, his courage really. Some days he was short of breath and dizzy. Other days his body was so rigid and sore, he felt as though his spine had been packed with cement. He tried to outsmart it by reading books on trauma and rage and how pain can linger in the body. Instead of answers, he found only frustration, divining knowledge of what was perhaps happening to him but no clear solution. He would be miles offshore, trawling through rolling black waters that kicked freezing seafoam up over the gunwales, when without warning his mouth filled with the pungent tang of metal. The memory was everywhere: the pliers being forced between his teeth, steel cracking and scraping off enamel. He would double over, short of breath. The ocean would disappear, his sternman too, leaving him alone again with the awful, helpless panic of being violated. He spat, scrubbed his tongue with seawater he'd palmed up from the deck, clenched his fists as tightly as he could and counted backward from one hundred. The memory always broke, but it always came back too, triggered by forces he had not been able to exactly identify.

Back home, he turned to his ravens instead of his family for comfort. At the kitchen window now he studied the woods, watched dark shapes flit and dart about the branches. The three juvenile ravens foraged about the river woods. At night they roosted in a stand of tall, shaggy white pines behind the house. They all seemed quite content here. Not domesticated, but not exactly wild either. Acclimated—he and the birds had acclimated to one another and entered a mutually beneficial partnership. He built pecking stands around the woods. He left more food out than he had in the birds' infancy, supplementing their foraging. At night he fell asleep thinking of ways to keep the birds close for longer. Grace asked him where he was, and he answered, "Right here, silly, like always." Obsession was only interesting to the obsessed. Obsession cut the strings to the rest of the world: where I am going, you cannot follow. In the wild the ravens would have fled the area by now, flocking up in their own teenage gang and soaring about the woods and cliffs to get a taste of the world before pairing off. When he thought of them leaving him, he came close to crying.

Outside now, the three young birds were playing in the snow. They hopped up to the crest of a hill, rolled down the slope, and then burst into flight, exploding in a whirl of black feathers and white powder. He had had another episode at sea today, and his sternman had somehow found the guts to suggest that maybe Lyman should take a few days off, "even see someone, you know." Watching the birds play now, he hated them for their confidence, their unburdened ease.

He retreated to the bathroom and closed the door. Sitting on the floor in the dark, he waited for his mouth to fill with the taste of metal. Then he almost began crying, this time in relief, when it did not. If his brain was indeed perched on a narrow ledge above a racing canyon of madness, he knew that ledge was eroding, the wind tunneling in at him intensifying. He got nervous when he was out in the world now. He ducked away from people in town, hid in the cabin of his boat at the waterfront. He had hated many things in his life, but this was the first time he had resented his birds. And he knew that this too was somehow Arnoux's fault. It was Arnoux who had come with his apology that day at the hospital when Lyman had faltered, unable to stand without the help of a child. And it was Arnoux who had shown up in town and acted like a movie meant an end to everything. Something had broken in Lyman when Arnoux pinned him to the cement fishing pier, and it occurred to him now that the key to recalibrating his own sanity might be to do the same to Ames. Not to harm the man, not to confront him, not to ruin him, just to lower the bastard a bit.

Buzzing with the idea of it, Lyman limped out into the yard. Knee-deep in a snowdrift, he watched the ravens hop up the hill, somersault down, and burst straight up into the air. They seemed with each run to be trying to outdo each other. They spun and they chortled. They somersaulted faster and flew higher. Their ascents grew dizzying. Lyman almost fell over, craning his neck to follow. The largest of the birds did a spiteful and somewhat brilliant thing then. It picked up a chunk of ice in its talons and took off into the sky. When the next bird finished its roll and burst into the sky, the bully released the chunk of ice. The rising birds banked to keep from being struck, tumbling back to the earth, and nearly crashed. Enraged, the lowered bird croaked loudly, as high above it the antagonist slowly rolled over in the air, showing off its back and then its belly, belting black laughter. For the first time in weeks, laughter split Lyman's jaws too. Perhaps shock was the key. If he could tame Ames through fear, perhaps he could reset the racing clock he felt enveloping his life.

So IT WAS THAT LYMAN turned further inward that winter. Like his son, he began reading about planes in secret. He never risked speaking a single word about flight out loud. He drove two counties away to do research at a library where he wouldn't be recognized. Had books he ordered mailed to a post office box in the same town. Like anything in the world, a plane operated within a system and was operated upon by the laws of other systems—the natural laws of inertia and gravity, and the mechanical laws of aerodynamics and internal combustion. You could toy with those systems and change the end results. A sudden burst of fear, a plane that for a moment lost an engine, a landing arm that deployed midflight and sent a drag ripple through the fuselage, an altimeter needle that dropped to zero and then flicked back to life—those, he thought, might change something. So Lyman studied and waited. As he trawled back from the fishing grounds at the end of the day, schematics and emergency flight scenarios cluttered his mind. He had no more fits, and his sternman kept his mouth shut.

At night, Lyman dreamed of a plane that rose into the sky. At its peak the aircraft turned black. It folded its wings down against its body like a raven. Then in a silent dive it dropped through the sky and fell. At the last moment it unfolded its wings and croaked back to life, returning to steel and soaring back into the sky.

But a pressure builds with any idea kept to the self. The fits crept back, all claws and talons at having been ignored, and finally, like everyone else he had ever known here along the sea who lived with distress, defeat, or weariness, Lyman started drinking to escape his hauntings.

On a brutally cold early March afternoon he came off the sea shaking from his first episode in weeks and went into The Fish House, hoping to silence his dark idea with a bottle. He drank two beers at a table in the back. Everything was too loud. A radio was hollering in a hockey game from up across the border. Voices coiled about the room. Each time the door opened, the massive cast-iron farm bell some fool had wired up above the hinges hammered with such concussive force he thought his skull might cave in. He couldn't stand to be here with these people anymore. He walked behind the bar and grabbed a bottle of gin. No one stopped him. No one said a thing. He shouldered outside without paying, nearly knocking Ruston Garvey over in the parking lot. When Ruston muttered, "The fuck, Lyman," and flipped him off, Lyman didn't even register the slight. Dazed and shaken by the complete lack of a reaction from the other man, Ruston went back into his restaurant. "What's the score?" he asked instead of sharing his unease. Someone answered, "Five-four midway through the second, real shootout." Then the winter night slid on like any other.

In his truck, Lyman cranked the heater and spun the windows down. He drove, shivering against the delightful combination of frigid air and hot wind. Five miles became ten, and ten miles became twenty. He watched the near hills go gray and the distant slopes fall purple and noted the blackening of the world by the way his headlights lit the passing road signs more brightly. Finally all was black and yellow, and a metallic glare came off both the snowpack and the road signs that ticked by with each small town. He didn't stop until he had driven all the way around the other side of the bay and reached Bar Harbor.

Parked at the waterfront, he stared at the same sea from which he had just fled. The pilings that held up the wharf were crisp with ice, and when the wind slashed down from the east it came over him in a scream. All about the water huge black waves rose and crashed. In the distance the Porcupine Islands churned in icy tidal froth that bubbled like acid. He shuddered to think that this same ocean was the beast on which he made his living, that it had not somehow broken and devoured him after all these years.

Up the street, lights and music spun from some jazz bar built for rich tourists. It was the off-season, but the bar was a tight buzzing lair among the shuttered hotels, icy streets, and deadened storefronts. He felt different here, at ease. Christmas lights were still strung around stoplights and streetlamps shone blue and silver. His chest softened. His breath no longer felt like a razor blade. The world, he thought, heeling out a cigarette and hurrying into the bar, truly was a magnificent place when you were the only person in it.

The place was all black walnut and mirrors. Instead of chairs, old oak barrels were pushed up to high tables. A tapestry of vintage license plates framed a backbar mirror that extended over nearly the entire rear wall. Not liking what he saw in the glass—this bustle of bar-goers against the dead white skin of his own reflection—Lyman looked up. He'd been hoping somewhat preposterously for a skylight in the ceiling, a glimpse of the moon, but instead saw a burnished sheet of hammered tin. The music was hard and fast, and he avoided looking at the stage for a moment longer, standing in the doorway somewhere between awe and terror, until a couple politely tapped him on the shoulder and asked him if he'd like to close the door and sit down and have a drink. They were young, and Lyman realized they were being genuine, not trying to start something or whip fun over him, so he apologized for his paralysis and cut to an empty table in the corner.

Onstage a six-piece jazz band wailed against the night and the air swung with color. A young black kid was bent back at the hips and howling into an alto sax, sending a flock of high green notes about the room. At the back of the stage a woman attacked the neck of a double bass. Sweat beaded her skin, and with each double stop and run, the room's edges vibrated a deep yellow. Beside her a scrawny white kid was battling a giant baritone saxophone. The massive horn seemed to float in his hands. The only sign of his strain: the way his squinted eyes jiggled as he belted out his wall of breathtaking cobalt blue. Each time the drummer bent to his kit and struck the snare, a rich orange snapped across the air. A pianist sat with her eyes closed and her head cocked in concentration, tendrils of purple and alabaster heat lifting from her hands. At the front of the stage was their leader: a young, bold trumpeter who seemed to be both battling and making love to his horn as he wrestled and wept and the world went scarlet with his story.

Lyman watched the set with all the joy of a man who loves music but does not see it performed live nearly enough. He drank, and he hollered. Outside sleet tapped against the black windows. There wasn't a single fisherman around. There wasn't a single person he knew for miles. It was every bit as terrifying as it was intoxicating.

The band broke between sets, and Lyman went to the bar. Everyone was sunk in conversation already, and he stood alone with his reflection in the backbar mirror. For the first time he felt on the outside here, and he was scared. The music dead. The colors fading. Why was he here at all? Drunk and deep into a late winter's night. His family home alone. Not a soul aware of where he was. In the mirror he saw the couple that'd tapped him on the shoulder when he first came in. He sent a drink to them both, seeking something. Camaraderie, connection, assurance—he wasn't exactly sure what. And when they sent back a note on a cocktail napkin that read "You can come closer," he stared openly at them both. Under their table the woman was rubbing the inside of the man's thigh. Her fingers pushed up dangerously high, and he imagined the man aching to be touched. The woman opened her legs a bit more, her body loose with the

booze and the music, and Lyman saw shade. He watched the man's crotch
bulge powerfully, watched the woman work her knees open and closed
to the soft house jazz now playing. The woman smiled at Lyman, and the
man did the same.

The staring, the drink sending, this desperate, lecherous watching—it
all exhausted him. He wanted to be at home. He should have been in bed
with his family around him, all of them inside the stone wall he had lovingly built so many years ago. He missed his life—the woodstove, the
smells of garlic and cinnamon and lavender. He wanted to undress in the
moonlight, watching Grace curled in their bed, and slip under the covers, bend his body about hers, kiss her face and breasts, whisper "I am so
sorry."

Lyman tasted steel at the back of his mouth, bubbling up behind his
molars. The musicians were about to start playing again. The woman
closed her legs. The man shrugged. Lyman rose and stumbled outside. The
Christmas lights were off. Even the bar seemed a black, silent pit. Fear
came in a crippling wave. He reached into his mouth and squeezed his
teeth, prayed, *Not now, not again.* But no answer came, and Lyman started
his truck and drove back around the bay, repeating everything he had
learned about planes in the last weeks. It was hard to tell how much time
had passed. He didn't know where he was going or what he was doing until
suddenly, he was at the cattle gate cutting a thin metal barrier between two
worlds: the state highway that rolled on through the night and the gravel
two-track down which the Ames family lived. He deadened the engine.
Excavated a cardboard coffee cup from the mess of gloves and tools on the
floor. Out in the night he scooped a bit of snow into the cup and opened
the bottle of gin he'd taken from The Fish House.

It was two forty-eight in the morning. The moon was nearly full. He
was too angry to be cold. He thought he saw a bird across the moon, just
a ripple of shadow. From his childhood bedroom window he'd watched
swans migrate at night. He would sit in complete stillness with a spotting
scope to his eye and wait for the birds to breach the moon with their fantastic, winged silhouettes. There was something magical in all things that

lived in the sky, but unlike planets or moons or the stars, the migrating birds told a story: we were there, and now we are here, and soon we will be there. But those were long-ago times, and long-ago times don't come back again so easily. He poured the cheap gin over the snow in the cup to soften its edges. Kicked the cardboard back and hissed as the liquor seared his throat. He drank, thinking of the moon, until the gin was gone. Then he got his tools out and grabbed a metal can of diesel fuel. He had two hours until dawn, and it was dark and cold enough that no passing gossip would stop to explore a parked truck. By the blades of light silvering the woods, he began his frozen trek out to the plane barn. Months of hurt and aviation research stumbled with him through the snow. Do this, and that happens. Fail to do this, and this happens. To the west, the hills waited. To the east, the sea turned. Between them, a single, reverberating thought seemed to sweep all reason into dust: *I'll mess with it a bit, just enough to put a scare into him, just enough to bring him back down to earth.*

Sixteen

I N THE MORNING ADAM AND Molly watched the sky from inside the belly of the sea captain's dilapidated house. A storm was coming up from the east, and Molly was sad because she thought it might be the last snow of the year. Spring would bring something else. They'd been living in the house up on Loomis Hill for months, but the shrubs and flowers and weeds had long died back, and now it felt like living inside a dead thing. The cold never stopped. Her skin split and bled from the dryness. Her father tried to hide his coughing by turning into the piles of wool blankets at night, but in the cold, the unrelenting everywhere cold that had become their life, the sound cracked against every surface. Still they danced and told old stories, and still they were together. With the plants that had once so magically grown up around the rooms now gone, they could see outside so easily now. The worry was that the world could see back in.

Today was not a bright day, but Molly had asked to take the planks down from the windows anyway. "I want to watch it snow," she said.

"It's cold out."

"Not that cold."

"Not that warm either," her father cautioned.

"If we had a TV, I'd watch that instead."

"Fair point." He moved over to the small camp stove they'd set up and stirred the contents of the small, dented pot of soup. "Just for a while."

Molly didn't know the exact date anymore—sometime early in March—and her father thought she was crazy for mourning the last snow. "A last snowstorm," he said, "is not a bad thing when you're living off rice and dehydrated rations and using blankets for heat." Watching his daughter's face sadden as he looked about the house, the meadow, the woods, he understood. It wasn't the storm, but the leaving: that's where all the terror lurked. The real world would come with only teeth, and his heart filled with a great sadness as well. Molly had seen the maps north he'd been studying. She'd turned away in disgust, angry, sulking, swearing at him for being weak, but in the mornings she always apologized, and he caught small moments when she would stop and study them as well. "Eventually the shadow draws back," he told her, pushing his head down to her scalp and kissing her soft, black hair. It was not just the peace she would miss in living in a world that seemed to have little to no need for human influence. It was everything. It was her father. It was their life, a life that while hard had been clear of purpose and filled with love, a life that had, perhaps for the first time since Molly's mother left, felt whole.

All of this was running through their minds when Molly softly said, "Dad, look." She was pointing out the open window.

Her father heard it before he saw it. The sound of a plane was suddenly everywhere overhead. The aircraft passed over them and spiraled out over the hills. It was dropping fast, struggling to rise, falling again as it veered through the fog toward the ocean. "It's going down," the man said, shaking as he stood. Molly was already heading for the door.

"Molly, wait," he tried to call after her, but she was gone already. "If we go," he said to himself, "we might not get to come back." Then he turned off the stove and crashed after his daughter.

Dead in the air, the plane was in a glide now, slowly falling toward the sea. The man thought the pilot might be able to land at sea if he weren't moving so fast. The storm was barely a whisper still. The seas might be calm enough. Miles away a distress call was coming through the radio to the municipal airport. Molly watched with horror as a small speck peeled off the plane, and she knew it was a body. She ran harder, her legs twisting in the snow crusts, wet air flooding her dry lungs. She waited for a chute to open, and it did. Then the plane disappeared below the ridgeline and was gone. The ocean absorbed most of the sound, which would have ripped through the hills, ripped up the river, ripped over the entire world with its fire.

THEY FOUND THE BOY BESIDE the sea, his body splayed among the rocks, the wreckage of the parachute coiled about him. The boy's arm was severely burned. A ragged diagonal gash ran from his left shoulder down across his chest. His leg was bent beneath him at an awful angle, surely broken, and possibly dislocated at the hip. He was unconscious. A soft white dusting of snow skinned his body. He was very cold. They were two miles from any road. It was not far, though, through the state forest to the boy's home.

"I don't know what to do," she stammered, moving around the boy, bending to him, queasy with fear. The man knelt down in the snow and took out a knife, severed the parachute's suspension lines as close to the pack as he could.

"Kneel down and put your knees on either side of his head," the man told his daughter. "Put your hand on his forehead. Comfort him."

"He's not awake."

"That's not going to matter. I have to reset his hip."

Molly dropped to the snow on her knees beside the fallen boy, who was not much older than herself. The boy stank heavily of the sea, and he was soaking wet. He'd come down in the water, she realized, and the waves had brought him back instead of taking him out. She wasn't sure where to touch him and where not to, so she bent low to his heart and began to sing, voicing the haunting melody of the piano piece she'd started composing in the woods so long ago.

"That's good, Molly, that's good," she heard her father say somewhere above her. "Let him know he's okay. This is going to hurt some awful." The boy seemed to be lifting into the music slightly, and she gently placed her hands on his chest and thought, *Don't die, no matter who you are.*

As delicately as Adam could, he lifted, turned, and pressed the broken leg back into the boy's body until he felt the grind and then the pop of the bone returning to the socket. A long scream punched the woods. Adam watched Molly bend her forehead down to the boy's. "You lived through the bad thing," she said. "You're going to be okay."

Then the boy who had fallen from the sky and survived slipped back into unconsciousness. Adam splinted the leg with saplings and ties cut from the parachute while Molly dressed the wound according to her father's instructions. Working quickly, he cut more strips from the parachute and folded them repeatedly until he'd created a thick pad like a rolled-up towel. He had Molly gently lift the boy's head, and then he wrapped the pad around the boy's neck, using sticks to reinforce the makeshift brace. He was worried about a possible spinal injury, but not knowing what else to do, unable to reach the outside world and unwilling to leave the boy to go for help, he and Molly lifted the boy into their arms.

This was never how they were supposed to leave the peace of their life here. As the sky darkened and the wind cut voices through the trees all about them, Molly saw how little she knew about anything. Her act of destruction had brought them here, and now another tragedy would take them away from this place. Bearing the weight of the boy alongside her father, she thought of flaming meteors and dying bears and what it meant to be a thief and what it meant to be a survivor as they carried Galen Creel home.

THE SHAPES MATERIALIZED ON THE edge of the woods. At first Grace Creel thought it was a trick of the frozen mist, or twists of blowing snow lifting from the trees. Then the mist turned human and began to walk. It had not been snowing long, only an hour, but the world had taken on enough of a dusting to alter its composition. The familiar suddenly seemed strange, wondrous. Two figures emerged in the mist. One was a man, much larger than the other, a child. And before them both, cradled across their arms, was a third shape. At first Grace thought it was a bundle of firewood, or perhaps a small deer. Then she realized.

She moved her arm to set her mug on the counter but missed the surface by a clean foot. Clay shattered against the floor. Hot coffee splashed back against her shins. Paralyzed, she watched with horror and fascination as the cradled deer slowly rematerialized into the shape of her son.

By noon, what had happened became clear. Sirens and radio talk buzzed about the bay. Responders went into the sea to search unsuccessfully for my father. An ambulance raced Galen Creel through the snow to Eastern Maine Medical Center. Cal Hayes went looking for Lyman Creel, who hadn't been seen since his gruff exit from The Fish House the day before. Later that evening, Lyman turned himself in. So did Molly and Adam Greenwind. Before being renovated, the sheriff's station had once been a Congregational church. The carpenters had left several pews along the edges of the station. The man and his daughter sat on those pews, being interviewed and fed pizza and coffee and hot chocolate long into the night, while Lyman Creel sat at the back of the building, down a narrow staircase leading to the concrete basement, behind a wall of one-and-a-half-inch bars spaced three inches apart. A small ground-level window was at his back. By morning, the snow had eclipsed it completely. There was no justice in any of this. It was simply how things were.

I was shocked that my mother did not immediately know about the crash. We were home having a quiet Saturday together. She had been edgy since she woke up, but no more so than usual lately. Sam and Daphne were circling and whining at the door. After breakfast my mother spent an hour at the kitchen table with a seed catalog. When that failed to hold her attention, she pulled a yellow legal pad close and began outlining a story about the vanishing days of sea-run fish in the river, and what it would take to get rid of the remaining hydroelectric dams spanning the river and blocking fish passage.

As she fell deeper into her notes, she became more and more agitated. She rose repeatedly to fill a mug with coffee. She tore sheets from the pad, mashed them up in fits of rage, burned the discarded ideas in the sink with matches. She kept looking out the windows down the river. We watched her with slight amusement. Simon offered to go to the store for more matches. Link offered to go for more paper. I said nothing. My mother laughed, told our smart asses to be quiet, and went back to pacing about the house and glancing out the windows. Arnoux and the boy were flying together. They had gone up early for a practice run to beat the weather. She trusted her husband would not challenge the storm gathering over the sea. She knew he would come back. He always had.

But sometimes love cannot call love back. Miles away, the steel machine she and Arnoux had brought back to life slipped into the sea.

GRACE CAME TO US LATER that morning, accompanied by Moses Jupiter. Wren was at the hospital with her grandmother. Her brother was stable, thanks to the heroics of Molly and Adam Greenwind.

Grace was standing at our door, looking like she was holding all the sorrow in the world on her back. My mother slapped Grace across the face hard and then screamed at her. Then she was somehow in Grace's arms.

I don't remember who tumbled out of the house first, but I was running with the cold snow cutting at my feet and Link was running and Simon was running too. We ran past Moses's truck. We ran by Cricket in her snowy paddock with her head lifted. We tore into the forest, Sam and Daphne on our heels. Link ripped at snowy branches by the fistful. Simon was moving so fast we could hardly keep up with him. I tugged at my hair and kept swallowing the words *Don't cry, don't cry, don't cry.* We tried to channel the ferocity of monsters, a savagery we were sure could forever hold back loss. But no matter how loudly we yelled, we were just boys.

Our chests heaved as we crashed through the last stretch of woods and rode out into the clearing, understanding where we'd been running. The sky was leaden beyond the rocky edge of the bluff. Black waves rose, crested, and crashed down against the cliff. Cuts from slashing branches lined our faces red. Snow and ice clung to our clothing.

The ghost apple tree stood before us, alone. About its base the bright red fruit, finally fallen, littered the white ground.

With our wrecked hearts and burning lungs, we stood upon the bluff in bafflement.

He was supposed to be here. Running through the woods, my brothers and I had asked for one more miracle. We had asked the sea to return our father to us.

Seventeen

NTSB Crash Report
Event Details

DATE:	21-MAR-1994
TIME:	10:04
TYPE:	American Champion 7ECA Citabria
OWNER/OPERATOR:	Arnoux Ames
FATALITIES:	Fatalities: 1 / Occupants: 2
OTHER FATALITIES:	0
AIRPLANE DAMAGE:	Damaged beyond repair
CATEGORY:	Accident, sabotage
LOCATION:	Penobscot Bay, ME, USA
PHASE:	Approach
NATURE:	Private
DEPARTURE AIRPORT:	Penobscot Regional Airport
INVESTIGATING AGENCY:	National Transport Safety Bureau (NTSB)

Event Narrative

THE WEATHER WAS REPORTED AS 10 statute miles of visibility, scattered clouds at 300 feet, and a temperature and dew point of 25 degrees Fahrenheit at flight time from the departure airport. The pilot and passenger reported they were on a training flight. The plane climbed steadily to a reported cruising altitude of roughly 4,000 feet about 25 miles from the runway. Early in the flight, the pilot reported faulty altimeter and airspeed readings but clear visibility still. Heavy fog settled into the area, confusing visibility and terrain considerably. Taking into account malfunction combined with the lack of visual clarity, the pilot reported that he was preparing to return to the departure airport, following standard safety protocols. Moments later the plane's engine failed unexpectedly. The pilot was able to maintain control, stabilizing the craft. The plane began to lose altitude in a sustained glide before descending into a fog bank. With low visibility to confirm actual altitude or topography for an emergency landing, the pilot banked the plane out over the ocean after having the passenger eject using the craft's sole parachute, as a glide landing in foggy conditions over the ocean without functioning instruments presented extremely low prospects. With malfunctioning instruments, no idea of his actual altitude or airspeed to adjust the glide path, and heavy fog, the pilot was unable to successfully perform an emergency landing. Shortly after, the aircraft struck the ocean and broke apart against the sea.

Event Probable Cause

COMBINATION OF MECHANICAL FAILURE (SABOTAGE) and pilot error. From the beginning of the flight, unbeknownst to the pilot, the plane was operating in a compromised state due to mechanical sabotage. The static port had been plugged, negating accurate airspeed readings, altitude readings, and instrument control. Additionally, diesel fuel had been poured into the off-wing fuel tank. When the pilot switched tanks midflight, diesel fuel was forced into the engine, resulting in a stall that forced the plane into a glide. The pilot maintained control but turned out over the ocean and into a fog bank. In a departure from controlled flight at low altitude with limited instrument functionality or visibility, the pilot failed to manage the energy state of the aircraft and apply proper recovery techniques.

ᴠ   ᴠ   ᴠ

What we knew of the accident was painstakingly pieced together by experts in aviation accidents, connoisseurs of disaster, who investigated the crash and spent hours interviewing Lyman and Galen Creel and Adam and Molly Greenwind. "It was just a bit of putty in the static port and a bit of diesel," Lyman said in bewilderment, freely confessing to his sabotage. "How didn't he notice? It was just supposed to be a little shock, an inconvenience . . ." He trailed off, his head sinking into his hands.

Tourists and fisherman found bits of debris as far south as Matinicus Rock and as far east as Blue Hill. For months after the crash we lived with these sporadic reminders of catastrophe coming in on the sea. Among the found items: a modified cockpit voice recorder my father, ever the documentarian, had installed on the small plane for his own research interests and that survived the crash, giving us and investigators a final recording of his voice as it fell through the sky, calmly relaying every bit of terrible information. Once a boy I knew mentioned a bit of wreckage that had come in, calling it flotsam. I wasn't familiar with the word, and after I looked it up, I wanted to hurt him, but Link dashed across the school gymnasium and wrapped me in his arms. "We've done that too much already, Almy," he said. "Look where it gets us." The boy had not meant any harm, but in my grief I saw insults and affronts everywhere. The word meant discarded things. My father was not a discarded thing.

They never found my father's body, but for years I dreamed of its return. In the dreams I was there when they pulled him from the sea, though I was only a child and shouldn't have been allowed to see such a thing. But in the dreams the sea crept up the river to our house and told me where my father was. *Hurry,* the sea whispered through my bedroom window, *hurry before they stop you.* My father lay atop a large, flat rock in an inlet so narrow and tightly forested along its banks that it seemed the sun must never touch it. He was stiff, inert. I thought of driftwood brought back by the sea. I thought of Nigawes and Sanoba and their children. My father was one of those people who are always in motion, spinning from one thing to another, and I could hardly remember him at rest. Oddly enough, it made me think of him as a child, before there was always so much to do. His skin was so blue, it shone almost black. His body was not twisted or flame-scorched at all. In fact, he looked peaceful: a blue slab of flesh resting atop a blue rock in a wash of blue ocean light. But his hair was gone. And his eye sockets were empty. You see, fish had eaten the eyeballs. They had also chewed each of his fingers down to wet, boneless nubs. I bent down over my father's body with the strongest desire to touch his hands, to somehow put them back together. Every time I reached for his palm, I woke screaming.

IF THERE HAD BEEN A body, my father's ashes would have been spread about the ghost apple tree he had loved so much. Instead we gathered on the bluff to say goodbye on a Sunday morning in April. The sun was just coming out from behind the clouds. Soon the dogwoods would bloom, dappling the woods with white flowers. Soon the hyacinths, my father's favorite flower, would emerge. I remembered him telling me the story of the flower's sad history. Hyakinthos was a Greek boy adored by both Apollo and Zephyr, the god of the west wind. Apollo set out one day to teach the boy how to throw the discus. In a jealous rage, Zephyr blew the discus back. The discus struck the boy in the head and killed him. His blood soaked the earth, and the hyacinth grew from the boy's blood. I turned to ask my father if I had remembered all the details correctly, and then I remembered the hole in the world.

People who loved my father and wanted him returned filled the bluff. Together we sang and we wept. When I let myself acknowledge my grief, I felt my breath turning in on itself, swallowing my lungs, threatening to take me from the world as well, and for a very long time after, I chose to feel nothing at all. Near the end of the service, Link came across the clearing with an axe, heading straight for the ghost apple tree. It was Grace Creel who stepped out of the crowd and stood in his path.

"I know you're scared and angry," she whispered in that gravelly voice of hers that somehow always brought the comfort of an embrace. "But that isn't going to happen."

We could do nothing but watch.

"You'll have to cut me down first," Grace said, and crossed her arms.

Link looked about to run at her with the axe. Then he let it fall to the ground and began to scream at us that it was all of our faults. Grace stepped over the axe, now lying on the ground between them, and gathered my brother in her arms. "I know, child," she whispered. "I know."

Neither Adam or Molly Greenwind were at the funeral. We had not seen them at all since they rescued Galen Creel. They were in state custody as the battle began over what would next happen with their lives. I knew Moses would be there with them at each turn, and Reggie too, who had already started raising a legal defense fund. The ruins of Loomis Hill were again simply ruins. "People come and people go," Reggie said. "And sometimes the debt to the departed ones long outlasts their presence." The sun sank behind the western hills, and another day fell into blackness as our grief continued.

OVER THE YEARS MY MOTHER had planted peach trees all over our property. They struggled, hardly flowering or producing fruit, and she struggled right along with them, fighting to keep them alive. She added sugar to the soil, then coffee grounds. She spent long afternoons simply sitting out with them, often speaking to them or reading aloud to them, sometimes singing. We asked her why she bothered, why she tried so hard. "There's a Taoist story of a peach tree that produces a single fruit every three thousand years," she told us. "Whoever eats that fruit receives the gift of immortality." We let that sit for a moment. And then she said, "And that's why I try so hard," as if she had actually answered our question.

The next time we saw Lyman, he was on television wearing prison orange. Throughout the early days of his incarceration and arraignment, a stunned expression had crept over his face, and it seemed he might never escape it. The same question that assaulted all of us—How had this happened?—seemed to haunt him as well. He'd said very little to anyone, but what he had said to authorities and investigators and lawyers and his family was that the plane was not supposed to crash, that Arnoux was not supposed to die, that it had been a prank, choking on the foolishness of the idea now in the aftermath of what he had done.

"They kept it all from me," Lyman said to the state prosecutor, his voice rising to a plea. "My boy wanted to learn to fly. I didn't even know it. That's a beautiful thing to want. I would have let him. I would have driven him a hundred miles to the finest flight instructor we could find. I didn't even know he wanted it," he repeated, baffled.

I hated Lyman in his threadbare Sears suit as he stood in that courtroom, but I couldn't bring myself to disagree with him. Keeping it all from him had been cruel.

"I see," said the state prosecutor, who was tall and covered in a heavy sheen of sweat, constantly pushing his glasses back up his nose. "But the matter here is not what they did, Mr. Creel, it's what *you* did."

"I know it," Lyman said. "I know it, but it wasn't supposed to happen this way."

"But it did, Mr. Creel," said the prosecutor, as Lyman lowered his head to his hands. "It did."

Grace Creel was not at the courtroom with her husband. Instead she was standing with us by the woodstove in our living room. "Don't say a thing," she said. "I'm right where I'm needed."

Link moved to turn off the television, but Simon grabbed his wrist. "Don't."

Our mother had started smoking again. She went days without speaking. When she left the house to do errands, she insisted on going alone. And when she was at the house, she mostly stayed in her bedroom with the door closed, or up in the small attic full of Christmas decorations and boxed-up toys and clothes, where she didn't think we would find her. Along the river, everything smelled of ash all the time. She motioned to leave the television on.

"What will happen to his birds?" I asked. Wren had started to cry. She looked away to hide it. My mother ground the cigarette out on the counter-top and walked out into her gardens. By four that afternoon she had up-rooted all her peach trees and tossed them into the edge of the woods. In the distance, the ravens croaked and called. Perhaps they understood that their world too had been turned to ash.

That night Grace went out and replanted the trees and pressed sugar and water into the roots. She sat outside with the trees all night long, speaking to them. In the morning, I asked her what she was doing. "I'm keeping things alive," she said. Thick black garden dirt streaked the sink.

Under the weight of grief, life takes on strange shapes. My mother and Grace had always been close, but now, with Lyman in jail and Arnoux gone, they seemed to need each other in a new, powerful way. During the months after the crash, Grace and her family gradually slid into nearly living entirely at our house. Though my mother and Grace rarely spoke, they seemed able to read each other's thoughts, and I often wondered how much of our togetherness resulted from guilt and how much from love. Lyman had been refused bail. Soon he would be headed to prison. Most nights the TV was quiet. The air grew hot. The world was green and filled with possibility—chortling tree frogs and snapping fireflies and great spinning shows of stars. Our world along the river, though, was still a hole through which you could fall forever.

Galen and Wren readied for school with us in the mornings and rode to school with us in Grace's car. But I can remember very little of how they looked or what they said, only that Galen was crippled by night terrors and awful dreams. I would wake from my own heavy dreams to the sound of his yelling. I mostly wished he would shut the fuck up. He was alive, at least. I barely spoke to Wren, even though she never stopped speaking to me, seeking to draw me back into the world. I no longer dreamed about her body. I no longer woke up tasting her lips or neck. Instead we fell into a ghostly orbit of circling each other, returning, passing, never sure where the center was, who was a planet and who was a moon, which direction was the sun and which direction was the cold, dark side of the void.

Eighteen

IMMORTALITY IS A FUNNY THING. My father did not live, but in each of his sons he lived on, albeit in slightly mangled ways. The fall after our father's death, Simon dropped out of college and moved home. His plan was to complete every one of our father's unfinished builds. He moved a bed into the office at the marina and started living there. The task took two years. My gentle older brother was gone. What emerged was sharklike—composed, confident, calculating. The new boatyard he would later open, a modern ship-building conglomerate that far surpassed anything our father had dreamed of, was well under way in his imagination. Two years later, Link and I would graduate. I knew then that I would move toward a life in medicine, while Link was spending more and more time hanging around the US Navy recruiter's office in town.

"Do you remember my peach tree story?" my mother asked one afternoon.

We were boxing up shirts and blankets in the house. The photo albums had been packed already. Cardboard boxes and bubble wrap littered the kitchen, waiting for the dishes. Link was going into the military, and I was heading to college. My mother was leaving the river as well. She had decided to close up the house and move into an apartment above *The Lowering Days*.

I had long since stopped listening to her tales. I had stopped reading. I had stopped dreaming of the dark shapes of old ancestors and visiting ghost apples and believing in banshees. Like a fool, I thought then that I'd become too old for stories, too smart for fairy tales. In truth grief had slayed my capacity for wonder.

"Of course," I conceded.

Had things gotten any better? My mother was still smoking. When people asked her how she was doing, she screamed at them in the streets, in the grocery store, anywhere and everywhere, until people simply stopped asking. Through it all, *The Lowering Days* came out each week, never missing an issue. Was that better?

"Some people give up." My mother held up a charcoal-gray sweater to the window light. It was my father's. "They get to a place where they're ready to go and they go. Other people, they keep wanting to be here, and here they are. So you can stay, but you have to want it."

She neatly folded the sweater and placed it in a cardboard box and came across the room. She cupped my face and held me there until my anger had nowhere else to go. I wanted to strike her for leaving. The only reason I didn't hate her was because of how much I loved her.

"Don't be mad," she said. "I'm not betraying him. I'm not abandoning him." She waved her hand across the sky, fanned her fingers down the river as it slipped among the woods, around the ghost apple tree, and out into the ocean. "He's right here still, and he's coming with me."

MY MOTHER, REGGIE, AND MOSES drove me from Penobscot Bay with my meager possessions loaded into the back of Moses's truck. I didn't understand why it took all of them, and my mother simply brushed away my concerns by saying, "Maybe it's not about you."

I hadn't thought about that. Instead of asking further, I settled for a general air of sullenness and self-pity. Reggie was driving. We were headed into Canada, where I had decided to study. We should have headed north and then east over the Canadian border. Instead Reggie put his right blinker on, and we veered to the south, heading for Machias Bay and the mouth of the St. Croix River. No detour was surprising with Reggie, so I said nothing.

"I was hoping you'd get a little mad at least," my uncle said. "There has to be some type of orientation schedule up there."

"Probably," I mumbled.

"I need to show you something before you go," Reggie said.

"You always did love an agenda," I scoffed.

"He means we need to show you something," Moses added. My mother said nothing. She just stared out the window at the green trees bending past us.

It took another hour to reach Machias Bay. Moses told me about how it was Passamaquoddy country as we got out and stood shivering on a rocky beach while staring out at the tossing sea. The French had come and established New France just up the coast in 1604. Their first settlement was on an island in the icy jaws of the Bay of Fundy, where the St. Croix River met the ocean. By December of that year the river had frozen solid. The tides rose and fell and smashed the ice until the waters around the island were an impassable field of jagged terrain. Cut off from the mainland, they began to starve.

"For them it was the lost place," Moses said. "The Passamaquoddy helped them survive. Then in the spring the French went farther up into what's now Nova Scotia to start over."

I studied the terrain, baffled at the stupidity of trying to colonize a cut-off island in the grip of the Atlantic. They had brought things like gilded dressers and ornate furniture but not bothered with heavy coats, winter boots, or extra provisions. Looking more closely at the shore, I noticed giant slabs of rock with faint carvings etched into the stone.

"What are they?" I asked.

"Petroglyphs," my mother said. It was the first word she had spoken since we left home. "Some of them are three thousand years old."

"Shamans used to carve an arc into the rocks," Moses added, "before the French and other Europeans came. It showed them going up to the spirit world to seek guidance and then coming back down to their people with the knowledge they'd discovered. You saw these arcs, completed journeys, all over the place. Then Christianity took hold, and they started carving vertical lines instead. Arrows that showed them going up but never coming back."

"I can't do this right now," I said. My father, the one not with us, hung heavy over the landscape.

"Death is a circle," Moses went on. "But they made it a line. Over time the link between the world of the living and the world of the dead got broken in the people's minds."

"Arnoux isn't some pre-Christian shaman," I said. "Arnoux is gone."

"I know," Moses said. I felt the world level some with his admission.

"Maybe some people are more open to possibility than others," said Reggie.

I didn't want to hear what he was talking about. My chest felt hot and tight. I wrapped my arms about my body and shivered at a blast of sea spray. I thought I might cry. It had been years since I'd let anyone see me cry. I realized there was something terribly sad in that truth. "I'm tired of a life where every moment is a lesson."

Moses nodded, and Reggie looked away. I thought it was over, until my mother spoke. "You've been hard ever since he died," she said. "If you go away hard, I'm afraid you'll never come back."

Of course she meant more than geographically back. I raised my head and met Moses's eyes, which were dark and patient. "Your father loved these rocks," my mother said.

They would not look away from me, my people. The rocks waited. The roiling ocean waited. The breaking waves never seemed to end, and the wind was a constant battering ram. I shivered, imagining the barrage of a life lived at the edge of the world. I felt suddenly that the coast must have turned itself into rock and cliffs just to survive. Anything else would have been bent in two and broken in half over time. Yet people had persisted here for millennia.

Moses traced his hand along one of the larger stones. An image took shape under his fingers. Moments before, the rock had seemed smooth and gray and in no way unusual. It was like confronting anything that exists closer to another world, say the life of a bird or the consciousness of a tree: once I saw the truth of the stone, I could not stop seeing it.

"They call this spirit the Meda," Moses said of the image. It was the rough shape of a face with large eyes and long ears hanging down to the sides. It had no mouth.

"The pictures don't show themselves to everyone," he said. "It was not a lost world for the Europeans, but a hidden world. This picture?" Moses questioned. "You know it."

I suddenly remembered an old story my father told about a man with extraordinary powers. He had long ears that heard everything and large eyes that saw anything. In the story he didn't need to speak to know everything that was happening. Now he was here before me in the stone.

"I had forgotten," I managed.

My mother quietly took my hand. "That will happen from time to time."

"That's why we're here," added Reggie. "To remind you."

I was embarrassed, ashamed, and enraged at the spectacle. I was also grateful to be here with all of them, though my father was gone, and the truth of that absence seemed to cover the entire sea, stretching from whitecap to whitecap, until I could no longer ignore it. I hugged Moses and then my uncle and finally my mother.

WE DECIDED TO CAMP THAT night on a small island not far off the shore, surrounded by more petroglyphs, which seemed to emerge everywhere we looked. As we crossed the darkening water by canoe, my mother pointed out a great blue heron doing aerial maneuvers under the full moon.

I had the acute sense that a period of time in all our lives was ending. I pointed to one of the drawings beside our campsite. "When did Dad find these?"

"A long time ago," my mother said. "Before you were born. We came here looking for your father's father. A man who had known him put us up for a few days. He told us stories. Said it had been a hard life for your grandfather. He said he talked about his kid a lot but never knew him. The man said he drank too much. That he never got over your grandmother's car going off that cliff. The man said he'd lost touch with your grandfather and that he could be anywhere now—working road crews still, in jail, building boats, dead. Then the man brought us here before we went home." My mother went quiet then. I could tell she didn't want to leave the memory. "He said it had been one of the only places your grandfather ever seemed at peace."

"Arnoux was fascinated by this stuff after that," Reggie added. "He'd come into the hotel for lunch and start telling me about shamans who had access to both good and evil spirits. He told me about different books on petroglyphs. Asked me to go to the folklore archives in Orono with him to do research. He said they could leave their bodies behind and travel from this world into others. Sometimes the other world detained them, evil spirits tricked them. Sometimes they couldn't get back to their people."

It hurt to learn something new about my father after he was gone. There were so many things I wanted to ask him. Moses seemed to sense my sadness and put an arm around my shoulders. "He would have brought you here himself," Moses said. "He just ran out of time."

Reggie rose, walked through the moonlight, and pressed a key into my hand. I knew it was to the cabin at East Grand. "You don't lock it," I said.

"You can start if you want." Reggie gripped my shoulder. "You'll have a place to go now to decide if you believe in arrows or arcs."

"The ones who could go between worlds," I said. "What happened if they stayed away too long?"

"They sat in a trance until they starved," my mother whispered. "They died."

"But what happened to their souls?"

"That's the great mystery, sweetie."

Part V

✔   ✔   ✔

Nineteen

I WOKE UP THIS MORNING full of the belief that three fried eggs and a good ten-mile hike up some remote and deep-wooded mountain would cure all the ills I'd ever known. It was a very good plan, simple like the best ones. The woodstove was crackling in the semidark. The frosty cabin windows looking out on East Grand Lake had begun brightening with the day when the phone I try to ignore started buzzing. When I answered, I was knocked from the present and flung into the past. What type of world is it where a tiny electronic device can overturn our realities with such devastating ease?

I had not heard Wren's voice in six months, when we'd gone out to Nova Scotia for a weekend trip, eaten far too much cheese, drank far too much beer, and hiked all over the barren cliffs of the Annapolis Valley. We'd traveled down to coastal Queens to visit the rural community of Mill Village and the surrounding forests, which held the ruins of an abandoned Teleglobe satellite ground station Wren had read about years ago. In those old woods we stood among decommissioned radio satellites being swallowed by moss, amazed the giant discs had held a thirty-year-long conversation with space. Then we traveled back north, listening to Acadian fiddlers at bars and roadhouses all along the way. Again we joked about making love, both of us having slipped into a state of what seemed like perpetual bachelordom, but chose not to mess things up, feeling perhaps after all these years that the boundary was firmly here to stay, and that perhaps it was the boundary that would keep us together for the rest of our lives.

The voice on the line was not the voice I had heard just six months ago, though. It was Wren's voice from our youth, high in timbre and low in control, the exact opposite of the instrument into which her voice had matured. It made me want to be young with her again, and the shock and power of that realization caused my throat to close and my hand to release the cast-iron skillet I was transferring from stovetop to countertop. I was no longer standing in a camp kitchen I'd known all my life, frying eggs and dreaming of the mountains in early spring. I was in Wren's house, looking at six perfectly round and smooth blue stones. I was atop a mountain with the Geminids streaking overhead. I was on the Little River, hollowed out with grief and dreaming of an airplane that never stopped falling through the sky.

"Are you crying?" I asked.

"Actually," she said, "the ten seconds we've been on the phone is the only time I've stopped crying in the last two days."

The news was that Lyman Creel had died in prison. With my plunge through time, I realized I was not just sad for Wren, but sad for myself. What a hammer to the throat, to stand with a black iron pan rattling around at your feet and your favorite teenage voice sounding in your ears as you realize that you too will mourn a man you should have hated but never could.

"He'd been sick for a long time," Wren said.

"People always say that, 'He'd been sick for a long time.'" I struggled to hide my anger, shocked at how suddenly it rose.

"It happens that way sometimes. It's no one's fault."

"I didn't know."

"I didn't tell you."

"Sorry," I said, reading the edge in Wren's voice. "I'm being an ass," I said. "I'm just shocked."

"That he's dead, or that you didn't know?"

"I'm not sure."

"I didn't want to tell you."

"You should have. I could have—"

"Helped?"

"Maybe. What's so wrong with that?"

"Nothing. I'm not mocking you, David. I didn't want to burden you. You have your own life. You can't be managing the lives of others and trying to forestall the inevitable."

"I'm a doctor."

"And you couldn't have done a damn thing, though you'd have gone crazy thinking you could."

She was right. Wren is a cosmologist at McGill University. She does research on time and the relationship between different types of matter and teaches a few classes up in Montreal. Wren does not see the world through a simple lens, and she decries the simplicity of my doctrine— we're here to keep people here—as an unrealistic and impossibly sentimental value cribbed from an incomplete understanding of my father, who I was never able to get to know as an adult. Wren says this philosophy confirms I've yet to have an original thought in my life, which may be true, but of course is a hyperbolic viewpoint. Having loved her in various iterations since we were fourteen years old, I'm of course compelled to listen with great attentiveness to every word she says. "You may be right," I always tell her. "But I still believe doing the right thing, whether it's legally, philosophically, or scientifically defensible, is better than doing the original thing." To this she just rolls her eyes or hangs up the phone. Wren thinks my morality around all this is somehow about male ego and, though largely disgusting, also slightly noble as well. I'm too close to it all to confirm or disavow her suspicions.

"Are you down in the bay, then?" I asked.

"Why? Do you miss me?"

"This isn't the time for that."

There was a pause. I watched a phantom of mist coil up through a colossal black pine out in the yard. It was the hour before full light, a lost time between night and morning, and my favorite time of day. At the base of the ridge the lake would for the smallest of moments lie solidly black before the rising day painted it with color. The ice had only been out for a few days. All the ghosts who slumbered through winter on the bottom were surely still waking up.

"I suppose I'm trying everything I can to avoid this conversation being real," Wren said. "I'm home in Montreal. I know I *need* to leave. It's just that I can't *seem* to leave. Picking up the phone almost killed me dead." I choked on a laugh at the timing of the phrase, and Wren said, "This is no time to start being polite. Let it out."

"Should I come up?" I asked. "I could travel down to the bay with you."

"That's not what I want. I was thinking I'd rather come to you."

"Come to me."

"Yes."

"I'm over in East Grand."

"I know. Despite the fame and fortune of being a good country doctor, you don't have many places you go."

This was true. I spent most of my time between downeast Maine, where I lived and worked, and the cabin in East Grand. I had some money in bank accounts from a horrendous five years spent as a resident physician in a large Boston hospital. The only things I really much cared about were my patients and of course Cricket, who traveled everywhere with me via a cozy horse trailer. "You want to come to East Grand?"

"This is the part of the conversation you find difficult? Yes, I want to come to East Grand."

"You sound like my mother," I said, aiming for an insult and a compliment all in one.

"One could do a lot worse," Wren said. "Remember how you always used to tell me you loved East Grand because it was between two places, how it was like being everywhere and nowhere at once?"

"Of course."

"I need to be between places for a bit. Even just for a day or two. Even if it's a bullshit illusion."

I understood then and was ashamed. She was not ready to move forward and face what waited for her back home in Penobscot Bay, which was the reality of a death.

"I'll be there tomorrow," she said. "We'll have a bit of time. The funeral's Monday."

I remembered that today was Good Friday. "That's the day after Easter."

"I guess it is."

"Are you bringing Harold?"

"I'd not deprive you. He's already planned a route. He wants to drive."

"Isn't he fourteen?"

"Almost fifteen. Not that it much matters. There isn't much between here and there, and any dummy who can reach the pedals and see over the dash ought to be able to make it alive. I'm in no rush, really. Lyman's already gone."

I was amazed at her composure. I thought for sure she was posturing. "You don't have to perform for me."

"That would be the male ego speaking. I don't perform for anyone. Sometimes life forces you to get used to the idea of someone being gone long before they actually go." Wren's voice had become a whisper over the line. "So I'd been preparing."

"But the reality of it," I said.

"Hurts like hell. I'll be there tomorrow," Wren said. "Don't go anywhere. Don't get arrested. Don't marry anyone. Don't get anyone pregnant. Don't die."

"Don't change," I said.

"Exactly," she said and hung up the phone.

I felt a great yawning emptiness spread through me. It was a feeling I had not known in years. Death, I thought, looking out at the still lake, beginning now to gain its fire as the light broke overhead: there was nothing

more confusing than a death. The wind was down and the water as undisturbed as glass, and I was reminded of what I had first realized years ago as
a young child—a lake is simply a window into the earth. Some see through
it, some don't. I believe my father had seen. I believe Lyman had as well.
Prison had been hard on Lyman. He had tried to commit suicide once,
after my mother bitterly launched a merciless stream of opinion pieces
about him and the leniency of our justice system. Of course there were
other factors. He lived in a place that was a hell. Each day a procession
of dehumanizing defeats tore him further down. My mother didn't help
things. Lyman's defense of temporary insanity wasn't enough, and he was
convicted of second-degree murder. My mother wanted more. People cut
the articles out and mailed them by the dozens to Lyman. He tried to die
by hanging himself with a bedsheet. But he lived. Of course he smoked too
much and didn't work out enough, and when he was finally nearing the
end of his sentence, it appears he developed lung cancer.

I have a patient who spent thirty years of his life in prison. I treat
him for a variety of physical ailments—diabetes, angina, gout, macular
degeneration—and he swears that none of those things are what's actually wrong with him. "I'm afraid they're symptoms," he once told me, "of
a deeper ruin." The man's name is Anders Hines, and he was a Norwegian carpenter. When Anders first came to see me, he was struggling to
continue his work. His comment gave me pause. For weeks I lived with
it turning around in my head. Anders had been a concert pianist in his
youth and somehow got it in his head to rob a Halifax bank with a group
of other young men. A guard had died of a heart attack during the rob-
bery. After that moment, his life was never his own again. First he became
a prisoner of the correctional system, and then a prisoner of his own body
and lingering despair. One day I watched him slowly remove his clothing
in my examination room, marveling at just how gray he was. His skin and
his hair and his lips, even his fingernails, were all the color of ash. When
he saw me looking, he said, "They don't let you take much back out with
you." A few nights later he swung by my house with a flank of venison
for me—he never had much money to pay for his care and always felt bad

about that, though I swore it didn't much matter—and stayed for dinner. He talked about his growing belief that the death penalty was the only humane solution to the problem of incarceration. The moment one is imprisoned, he argued, he or she ceases to be human. It had gotten quite late, and the cabin had become a balloon of darkness. When Anders rose to turn on a light and take our plates to the sink, he slid so fully into a mode of stealth that it was almost as if he ceased to exist in the room. I knew he was there, but I could barely see the shape and weight of his body. When he returned to the table, he asked me if I lived with a variety of emotional registers attached to my memories. Some being sad. Others joyful. That sort of thing. I thought about it for a time and then said I did. Anders told me I was one of the lucky ones. He said fear had become his only emotional association to memory. Even the memories from his boyhood days, long before he went to prison, were accompanied now by a shaky terror. "Guards move up and down all of my memories, jumping locations, jumping decades, morphing from my jailer one moment to my mother the next and back again, and they are always black-eyed and unhappy and provocatively swinging clubs or rifles down around their hips," he said. After, I was consumed by a despair I had not felt since I was a child. I fell asleep shaken, and I have thought every day since then of how little was left of Lyman Creel after all his years in prison.

Twenty

I PUT THE PHONE DOWN and was struck by the overwhelming and somewhat abnormal urge to be surrounded by people. East Grand was a place where people came to pursue the opposite impulse, and there simply weren't many spots to toss one's self among the living. So, full of old and new heartbreak, I grabbed a wool jacket and an empty green thermos and left the cabin without cleaning up a thing.

Cricket was waiting for me in the corral above the cabin. I'd cleared an acre up there, abutting the long granite ledge that overlooked the lake. Though I'd fenced in the area, fearful Cricket might spook and plunge over the cliff, I mostly left the gate open, and for years she'd followed me around at the hip, showing no hint of accidentally plunging to her death. I cracked a scrim of ice from the water trough and spread fresh oats for her breakfast. Then we walked out to the ledge, Cricket nuzzling into my side with each step, sensing, I suspect, as only animals can, the strangeness of the morning. I'd left a row of tall pines as a windbreak between the pasture and the ledge, and we passed through the trees like this, two beasts nearly enjoined. The ledge extended north-south for one hundred feet. Pines at its back, straight bedrock drop at its front. I'd set a bench out there and a rough table made from an old shed door and some scrap lumber legs. Far below was the wide expanse of East Grand. Cricket leaned in to me. I pressed my face to her warm body and felt my fear leave. "Thank you," I whispered.

The wind was blowing the mist about the lake. Long blue tendrils rolled over the water. They struck the shore and then scaled the cliff. They swallowed the paddock and the stable. They broke around my truck below us in the yard and swept about the cabin, so all the world became for a moment soft and blue and vague. I imaged Lyman Creel in the bardo, wondered where he was in his passage between this world and his next. The news of his death had taken me deep into the past, and I shuddered at the realization that my world had become a field of ghosts.

The thought of an hour-long drive out through the woods to a population center like Fredericton gave me the urge to walk into the lake with an armful of rocks, so I left the ledge, took Cricket back to her paddock, and turned the truck down the two-track toward Duster, nothing more than a handful of rough buildings thrown up for hunters and fishermen, but a town nonetheless.

Green needles shagged the pines and hemlocks, but the hardwoods were still leafless. Driving through their bare, skeletal spires, I thought of my father and our road through the woods to the Little River. I could remember his voice more clearly now than when he was alive. Yet I struggled to recall his face. The news that Wren was bringing Harold was a balm. The young can be an anodyne to the greatest sorrows. Harold has a dad, but no one really knows where he is these days, so the boy, to his benefit or regret, gets all of us. It had been eight months since I'd seen him, but I always thought fondly of Harold, this tall and stocky kid who carried a peculiar openness to people, a bit like his uncle Galen before the crash. First seeing Harold, one might perceive disdain and contempt, a boy with long hair falling into his eyes, a boy who kept his head down and turned his body away and seemed to melt back into the walls. Until you spoke to him. In an instant the boy's posture would right, and his attention would swivel to you like a beacon. Harold's problem was that he enjoyed being somewhere else, in his imagination, in his dreams, until there was a person directly in front of him. Nothing fascinated him more than that. "He likes people who are passionate about things," Wren once told me, shrugging. "He wants to hear them talk about all the things they love and why they love them. That's what makes him happiest." Very few people are as curious about other human beings as they claim. Even fewer are more curious than they claim. Harold, who claimed nothing, was at fourteen years old more curious about other people than anyone I'd ever met.

In town the lights were on in Tripp's windows. Four cars were in the parking lot: a rust-bucket pickup truck with just a cab on the frame, no bed, an El Camino that seemed lost in time, a Toyota sedan, and a flashy new one-ton pickup. I pulled in beside the new truck and did a double take when I caught sight of a dog in the cab. It was a hulking, shaggy black-and-white thing, surely a Bernese mountain dog, with ears that flopped down around its massive square head and a brown patch around one eye. It was lying on the passenger seat, shaking. Its ribs showed through the heavy fur. When I spoke to the dog, it buried its head beneath its paws, breaking my heart even further.

Over the years Tripp had managed to nudge the roadhouse toward respectability. An actual bar now extended across the front, though I had to admit I missed the old plywood one that had for so long sat up on sawhorses. The lighting had been brightened. Beer no longer lingered all over the floor but was promptly mopped up. The pool table was gone, and the Keno machine as well, but an old dartboard and a jukebox remained. Tables, chairs, real menus, ceramic plates, and metal utensils had been added in the pursuit of becoming a proper restaurant. Tripp was older now, but he still ran breakfast, lunch, and dinner wearing his leather blacksmith's apron, his silver ponytail tied back with gutstring.

"Who's the jerk with the new truck and a thing for animal cruelty?" I blurted out when I walked in.

All the faces came swinging around. Only Tripp's was grinning. I supposed he was proud of me, having watched me come, or fall, depending upon who you asked, a long way from being the bookish kid he'd first met all those years ago.

"That's a rude way to say good morning, Doc."

"Call me Doc again, and I'll shit on your floor. Then we can talk about rude mornings."

Tripp did a little mock bow, took the thermos from my hand, and started filling it with fresh black coffee. "Belongs to some guy up from Connecticut," he said. "He's here to fish and drink and fuck pine trees for the weekend because there aren't any women around and the ones who are around are smart enough not to fuck a man from Connecticut with a new big-dick truck. He stumbled in earlier wearing about five grand in freshly bought Orvis gear and reeking like piss and Wild Turkey. Can't say we encouraged him to stay long, and can't say we've seen him since."

A newspaper sat on the counter, loosely folded and stained with coffee. I noticed a story about the Cassini space mission to explore Saturn and its moons. The satellite images of the ice and rock rings of that strange leviathan of a planet pulled me through the pages. The shuttle had launched in the late 1990s. Now NASA was asking the world to "wave at Saturn" as Cassini peered back at our tiny planet from hundreds of millions of miles away and took a picture of Earth. We would all be nothing but a bright dot in a dark sky, not unlike a star. On each page the images of Saturn's moons were more stunning. Polar storms and the scarred and cratered surface of Hyperion, a moon that had refused to be made ovular by gravity. The underground sea of Enceladus. The mesmerizing surface of Iapetus, which was half black and half white. I imagined both Lyman and my father, whose feud so long ago had escalated against a backdrop of celestial objects, sitting in a diner much like this one but nestled on Penobscot Bay instead of the remote boundary between the United States and Canada, bent over a coffee-stained newspaper and putting their differences aside long enough to receive with awe the news of this far-off space mission's progress through the cosmos. I very much wanted things to have been that way, if only for an instant. I was suddenly weary beyond belief, and I folded the newspaper under my arm, took the filled thermos back from Tripp, and turned for the door without offering a word.

I sat in the parking lot for ten minutes, rereading the space story and debating the plight of the Bernese mountain dog jailed beside me.

I thought about Wren and Harold again. I tried to envision where they were, what the road looked like around them. I remembered how Link used to sit at our kitchen table, full focus, drawing pictures of where he thought our parents were whenever they were away. I thought too of the principle of indeterminacy, which Wren had first explained to me years ago when she was doing her doctoral work. It posits that you cannot know both a particle's velocity and its position. The more accurately we identify location, the less accurate becomes our measurement of momentum, and vice versa. And so the world around us stays slippery.

Seeing no other option, I got out and grabbed a pry bar from the toolbox in back. I wedged the bar into the top of the truck's window. I put all my weight into the lever and worked it up and down, listening to the glass give and crunch, until the motor released and the window dropped six inches. The dog eyed me curiously, then put its head back down under its paws. I went back inside and filled an empty milk jug with water and dumped it through the cracked window until the driver's seat, which was of course leather, was pooled up nicely. The dog came over and cautiously lapped at the water before curling back in his spot. Patches of fur were missing all over his haunches and stomach. One of his teeth was badly chipped.

"I'm sorry you lost the human lottery," I said, and dumped more water onto the seat.

THOUGH I SPEND MUCH OF my time here at East Grand, I live farther down the border, not far from Passamaquoddy Bay, the rugged place where my father's life began and my grandmother's life ended, and it seems my path of living between things continues. If you follow East Grand south through the rest of the Chiputneticook Lakes—Mud Lake, Spednic Lake, and Palfrey Lake—you'll eventually spill out into the St. Croix River, which drains into the Bay of Fundy. There in the wooded highlands a bit west of the river, you'll find the family practice center I run with two other enterprising doctors. We still do things like house calls. Sometimes we go to people by boat. Sometimes by snowmobile. Sometimes there's a treatment. Sometimes we just sit and listen. The goal is always to follow the grand rule of medicine: first, do no harm. And to remember its equally important partner: all people deserve equal care. About half my patients are white, and about half are Passamaquoddy. In some of them I imagine my French grandmother, in others my grandfather. Every so often a patient reminds me I'm living along the wrong river, cocking a thumb west in the direction of the Penobscot. I'm never very easy with the joke, which cuts a bit too close, I suppose. My house is a simple log structure built by Anders Hines, the Norwegian carpenter patient who left his spirit behind in prison, and it sits on the western side of Porcupine Mountain in the Moosehorn National Wildlife Refuge, near the town of Meddybemps. The country there is eighty-three percent forest. With a population density of about ten people per square mile, more bear and moose exist than people. While it's perhaps a mad way to live, I've been doing it nearly a decade now, since Lee and I went north together after our residencies, seeking to escape Boston, which we thought, rather unjustly as it turns out, was ruining our marriage. Lee left, and I stayed behind. I wanted to help care for a rural community with a desperate need for medical services, but I couldn't muster the courage to do so back home along the Penobscot. I wanted a big family. Dogs and goats and horses and all manner of trucks and tractors and gardens and things. And the clinic. I realize now my desire to carve out something of a homesteader's life in the middle of nowhere was my parents' dream, which I had blindly tried to repeat. Such is how disasters are born.

After my stop at Tripp's, I drove out into the snowy back roads of New Brunswick, gaining elevation, until I was among the wooded ridges overlooking the lakes. I pulled off in a fresh logging cut and left the truck on a high spot in the clearing. Then I set out for Skeddadle Ridge. It was a six-mile hike into the remote mountain valley of the old ghost town and back. A few families supposedly still lived out here, though I'd never found them. The schoolhouse and the post office once anchoring the makeshift community had long since returned to the earth. Only stone walls and fieldstone foundations remained.

Climbing the tight switchbacks, I pulled my coat close against the wind, which carved over the exposed bluffs in ferocious bursts. I had not brought ice spikes or snowshoes, and my boots slid and skidded in the half-frozen slush, but I traveled on, pushing up through the woods. Civilization fell away. Clouds rolled in over the sun. The gray solemnity of March filled the trees, the cold, dull casing of a winter-blasted boneyard with none of the hints of the transitional season to come. Frogs lay frozen at the bottom of ponds and streams. Bears slumbered. Sap ached to run but waited. I missed the birds most of all, and wished I had heard the news of Lyman's death a few weeks later, when the world was free and green. I had no idea where I was walking to, precisely, not that I ever much did, the walk up and around Skeddadle Ridge having long been a favorite meditation of mine. The logging road, which had not been used in a decade, rose and turned through the forest until it reached a fork. To the right the road continued up the ridge into the old settlement. To the left a half-mile-long spur led deeper into the woods before opening onto former pastureland and an abandoned farmstead on the western ridge. A steel Quonset hut hunkered at the apex of the two paths, filled with the bones of harvesters and tractors.

Walking, I thought of Virginia Woolf, whose work I had returned to recently after many years, staying up deep into the night reading those circular passages by the light and crackle of the cabin's woodstove: ". . . and Mrs. Ramsay could not help exclaiming, 'Oh, how beautiful!' For the great plateful of blue water was before her; the hoary lighthouse, distant, austere, in the midst; and on the right, as far as the eye could see, fading and falling, in soft low pleats, the green sand dunes with the wild flowing grasses on them, which always seemed to be running away into some moon country, uninhabited of men." Yes, I thought, there are worlds like that, serene and unoccupied, moon countries upon which snow and darkness fall undisturbed by footsteps, places like this ridge, places like Iapetus, slowly circling Saturn with a clear view of those interstellar rings of singing ice.

Walking, I listened as my body changed the world's sound. The gusts howled around boulders and barely moaned as they broke about my bones. My boots scuffed dully on rock. Crackled on ice. Crunched through drifts of wet, heavy snow.

Alone with the wind, I grew scared I might never find my way back. So I began to sing, and found in my mind the face of Lyman Creel. I sang old songs of mourning, mercy, and release from bondage that my mother had taught me—"Swing Low," "Down in the River to Pray," "Long Road to Freedom." And even though death was still hanging about me, I began to feel like things might be okay after all.

At the Quonset hut I broke from my usual routine, veering left toward the old farmstead. A few hundred yards down the road there was a chain gate, and I ducked under it and continued on. The air had darkened and grown colder. I'd heard about the homestead, but never visited it. I realized now it was simply an old house, long forgotten. I thought of Molly and Adam Greenwind, who had created a utopia under the harshest conditions in a place not so different. There aren't really many happy endings in most American lives. There are honest endings, though. Despite the best legal efforts of my uncle Reggie and others, Molly was ultimately convicted of arson. Though the judge reduced her sentence, based on the nature of the act, her rationale, and other extenuating circumstances, she was sentenced to five years in a juvenile facility. Once a month I visited her. We rarely said more than a few words to each other. Sometimes Molly never spoke at all. That was okay too. One day she said, "Thank your mother for me. She listened."

Then she said, "Do you know what it feels like to stand in a room full of people who hate you?"

I searched all the moments of my life I could retrieve. Of course I did not.

"I couldn't become another woman who balled her anger up and quietly imploded," Molly said. "So I did something."

I nodded.

"You've come enough now, I think," she told me, and I nodded. "Maybe sometime I'll see you again."

Then I rose and left the facility for the last time.

After she was released, Molly crossed the bridge over the Penobscot River back to the Penobscot Indian Island Reservation, returning to her people, who helped her walk toward forgiveness. She lives there still and teaches Penobscot language classes to kids. I imagine she has a big garden, can beat any fool up Bald Hill in a footrace, and sees her father as often as she can.

Saplings had begun growing up in the fallow pastures around the house. A barn had caved in on the property, and an outhouse as well. Passing the house's black windows, I felt watched, not by the structure or the woods or the trees but by time. Behind the house, the road thinned to a trail that wound through a field and then passed into a dense wood of gnarled hemlock trees. I hesitated before entering. No light penetrated the canopy. Patches of orange needles and lush green moss carpeted every rock, trunk, and root. I realized it was a stand of ancient old-growth forest, never touched by human saws. The trees seemed impossibly tall. Lichens spotted their trunks a hairy, fluorescent green. Great webs of moss wove between the canopies like spooky cloaks. There was only a foot or two of space between some of the trees. With each step, the black wood drew down more tightly about me. Overhead I heard the distant song of a raven. Just when I feared I would have to crawl to find my way forward any farther, the woods relented, and I broke through the trees.

Dry wind bit at my throat as my eyes adjusted to the light. Before me was a small frozen pond. I took another step and stopped cold. There was a man standing at the edge of the pond, facing the ice. To one side of him were the embers of a fire; to the other, an overturned rowboat painted white. He was at least six and a half feet tall, standing perfectly straight, with his arms at his sides. He wore black canvas pants and a black T-shirt. A pair of black suspenders slipped off his shoulders and hung down around his hips like folded wings. I was certain the temperature had dropped into the twenties, but he didn't seem cold at all. His head was bald, and his clothes were far too large for his body, which was corded and stringy with muscle.

"Your singing was off," he said. The man's voice was a dry croak. He

turned then and said, "I mean no harm. I'm just a tired traveler resting."
I realized he had once been a much larger man. Though something about
his body seemed wasted away by time, his features were youthful.

He cleared his throat and continued. "I don't mean to say I didn't enjoy your singing. I haven't heard some of those songs in a very long time.
There was just a hesitancy to them, which seems odd to me, considering
there isn't anyone anywhere out here."

It was true. In a decade of walking these ridges and hilltop woods I
had never seen another person. "Except for you."

The man smiled. His teeth were straight, and so white they looked
nearly silver. His skin was immaculately clean. His fingernails, pulling up
the suspenders now, were very long and yellowed. "I suppose that's true."

I thought about my singing and realized the man was right. "The hesitancy," I said. "I wasn't feeling self-conscious. It was more a question of
whether I should be singing at all. I'm not sure the man I'm singing for
deserves it."

"I see, then." He curled his lips into his mouth and then pushed them
back out. "That I can understand. Are you hungry, cold? It wouldn't take
much to get the fire going again."

I thought to ask his name, to ask why he was here, but didn't. "No," I
said. "Thank you, though."

"I really don't mean any harm. This just seemed a nice place to rest
for a bit."

Back among some boulders near the shore stood a stick tent wrapped
in a canvas tarp. A clothesline was strung between two oaks. "Looks like
a long rest," I said.

The man scratched his bald head. "I suppose it has been some time,"
he said. "Last night I dreamed a boy came down to the pond here. In my
dream, he was trying to sing, but there weren't any words in the air. In the
dream everything felt quite cold, and I woke around four in the morning,
feeling very sad. I've been standing here waiting to see what was going to
happen next ever since. I let the fire burn out while I was waiting. And
you can imagine my surprise when my dream of a boy who couldn't sing

turned into a man who could." His voice seemed to be coming from different directions with each sentence. I couldn't make sense of it. I was staring at his mouth as it made the shapes, but the words rose from the ice at his back and the boulders to his right, from all around. I thought about how ventriloquism was thought to be a spiritual art form, originally practiced by shamans. I was not scared but instead felt a strange, soft comfort. "You aren't the person from my dream, though," the man said. "He had different mannerisms." Suddenly the man's voice was directly in front of me, hard like a punch to the chest. "He was a child, a pilgrim. So what are you?"

I shivered. I didn't want to tell him I was a doctor, so I said, "I don't know. I've had loss on the mind. I guess I'm just a man who felt compelled to walk."

The man looked me over for a long time. Then he gestured to the rowboat. "This boat is for going back and forth. I'd take you across so you could continue your walk, but the way isn't clear yet. The ice. I was a boatman in the navy once. It was my job to take people from dangerous places to safe ones."

"Is this a dangerous place, then?" I squinted but could no longer see across the pond. A heavy mist had come out of the ancient woods.

The man shook his head. "I don't believe so."

"Have you ever heard of Iapetus?" I asked.

He shook his head. "I haven't."

"It's a moon of Saturn, half white and half black. They say it's a trick of science, mineral dust settling on one half of the planet while only snow covers the other. It gets stranger. An equatorial mountain ridge circles the entire moon along its center, eight miles tall and twelve miles wide. I keep asking myself what it actually divides and whether we'll ever know."

"A natural wall. Eight miles tall rising out into space."

"Yes," I said.

"I have seen miraculous things. Awful and beautiful. I've ferried and befriended grand people. But when I leave my body for good, I'd like to go to a place like that."

A great sorrow for all the things I had never experienced in my life filled me then. At the edge of this pond, I felt as small and lonely as a young child. People never talk about the loneliness of childhood. "Today is Good Friday." My voice didn't sound like my own. It sounded eerily like the man's, but perhaps an octave lower.

"So it is," he said.

"I feel I need to be honest. I'm a doctor."

"Why."

"Why what?"

"Why are you a doctor?"

The question gave me pause. "Because I want to understand how things work. Because I want to help people."

"Empty answers."

"Most are," I said. The truth makes itself unutterable: because my father's body never rose from those waters; because I knew that if it ever did, I had to know how to put it back together or put it to rest; because my world fell over during my youth and set before me two paths, devouring rage or infinite compassion, and I needed to find a way to walk the latter, however hard.

As if responding to my thoughts, the man said, "You wanted to hurt this man once. The one who died. Maybe you even wanted to kill him."

I remembered Lyman Creel in prison orange on the television, all those years ago. "Maybe," I said.

"But you didn't. How come?"

"Because I became a doctor instead," I said. "Because I learned to see that being alive alone is a fatal condition, so we have to treat it with the utmost attention. Because," I admitted, unsure whether I should go on, "a part of me loved him too."

Something about my answer seemed to please the man. "That's a hard circle to break," he said. "Anger. They say it's like the family dog. It holds on and on and on. You should be proud."

Somehow, I still felt like a fraud and a traitor. The thing is, these generational circles of violence don't live outside our bodies where we can see them, like a ring of fire, for instance, and simply step around them. They live down inside our cells. We are the circle. To step free is to break away from your people and leave a gap, and I'm convinced it's this fear of loneliness and displacement and trespass against one's own that keeps so many forever turning around the same violent track.

"When were you in the navy?" I asked, hoping to shift the subject.

"A long time ago."

"My father served," I said.

The man nodded. "It's a special place here. Though all the earth is a special place, I suppose. An impossible concept that's somehow possible."

"You sound like him, my father. He used to say, 'The earth moves us to dream, but no dream is worthy of the earth.'"

"For all you know I could be him," the man said, and grinned with those strangely blinding teeth.

Nothing about this notion made sense. But who was I to say that I knew what I was seeing? We stand at a faucet and turn on the water and watch it drain down the sink clockwise. Who's to say a man or woman, some shaman without a lick of the narrowing trap of public education or societal groupthink, wouldn't come down out of the mountains, turn on a faucet, and see the water draining down the sink in the other direction?

The man said, "The hardest thing to sustain is a pure heart."

Then he slipped a card from his pocket and handed it to me. It was slightly smaller than a playing card, and its corners were rounded. It felt quite heavy and warm. One side was solid red, as bright as arterial blood. A pencil-line drawing of the Greek Minotaur against a white background filled the other side. The drawing was a portrait, really. It began at the beast's chest and moved up to detail its throat, head, facial features, and horns in menacing specificity.

I held the card up and turned it around in the soft blue light coming off the pond. The card contained no words. The image was static, but like the best art it seemed to vibrate with emotion and movement. "What is it?" I asked.

"A card, obviously," he said. I felt seen through, and it was hard to hold his gaze. "Don't despair, son," he said. "The thing about people is that each one deserves to be celebrated, and each one deserves to be mourned."

I slipped the card into my pocket. "I have a cabin and a small paddock up on a ledge over East Grand," I said, not knowing what else to say or do. I wanted to hug him, but didn't know how to ask. "I'll be there," I said. "At the cabin."

The man smiled at me again. "I know," he said. "I'll come to you some day. You have to wait for it. And you have to keep singing."

Aimless and blind, seeing but hardly thinking, I wandered the wooded ridges for hours. Morning curved into early afternoon and then into late afternoon. The sky darkened. A storm was gathering far out to the west in the hills. The temperature dropped below freezing. The wind ignited. In the gray light it began to snow, and I was shaken from my reverie by a momentary glimpse of mortality. I was ill-prepared to be caught out in a New Brunswick snowstorm at night. Of course I hadn't brought a light, and in the growing dark I treacherously navigated back through the rip-rap and the ice and the howling pines. Twice I got turned around in the wind coming down. Twice I heard the wingbeats of large birds passing overhead. Ravens. In their race to get clear of the storm, they didn't pause to croak down at me. I avoided the route past the pond and the farmstead and the Quonset hut, terrified the man might not be there, terrified really that the whole experience was a delusion, though I believed in its absolute truth, and by the time I made it back to the turnout, a few faint stars were doing their best to mock me from above.

I found my truck already under five inches of fine snow, the keys tucked behind the front tire just like I'd left them. Both my father and my uncle had the habit of simply leaving the keys in the ignition when they ditched their vehicles on the side of some logging road. When Reggie went up to the woods, my father would often drive up after and move my uncle's car a few miles away, and vice versa. It became an ongoing game, and as a child I often emerged from the woods with either my father or my uncle, only to find our vehicle nowhere in sight. It never caused much issue for Reggie, who never had to be anywhere at any specific time. But my mother would be spinning with fury when Arnoux came home four hours late because he'd lost the car and spent half a day backtracking through the forest. "I don't care about the time so much," I remember her once saying. "It's the fear I can't do. People die in the woods, Arnoux. And I can't stand sitting around, wondering if a tree fell on you and smashed that body I love so much into a bloody stump, or if my brother was just flirting with you again and moved the fucking car."

My stubborn father never did start taking his keys with him into the woods, but he did begin unhooking the battery, and though that was an easy enough deterrent to get around, my uncle understood and left things alone after that. "She thinks I won't be here that long," my father said to Reggie one night. It was fall, and we were making stone soup as a family around an outdoor fire. I'm sure it was a conversation I was not intended to hear, but I was a child who never wanted to miss a thing, who was always quietly lurking at the edges of adult conversations. "Who knows, maybe she's right and maybe she's not. But why make life harder for one person so two people can get a laugh?" Reggie nodded and lit a cigarette. Wrapped my father in a great, endless hug.

Coming through town, I saw that the new truck was still parked beside Tripp's, covered now with snow. The driver's window was still cracked. There was a little steam-melted patch on the window where the dog had pressed out his nose and breathed while straining to look through the growing skin of snow. The clock on my dash was busted, but it must have been after nine. I did the math and almost put my vehicle into a skid swinging back around.

Inside two women were sitting in the back, eating pie. A man sat at the counter with a beer and a coffee. All locals. The dog's owner was nowhere in sight. Tripp was perched behind the counter on his elbows, reading a *National Geographic*. "David," he said. "You look cold."

"Grill still on?"

"It is."

"I'll take ten cheeseburgers."

"Ten cheeseburgers." Tripp closed his magazine.

"Yes."

"You realize if the doctor dies of a heart attack, it creates quite a calamity for the community."

"Good thing I'm not your doctor. Just a paying tourist."

"All factual statements."

"So I'll take ten cheeseburgers."

For a moment I thought Tripp was going to argue with me. Charlie Parker and Count Basie were playing from the juke. I could picture sweaty couples spinning and swinging through the air. I watched Tripp's eyes drift over my shoulder to the frosted window. The truck sat quietly under a white robe of snow now.

"God knows where that asshole is," he said. "Yvette took water out a couple hours ago. We added it to the front seat. I'm reading an article here about coyote populations in Wyoming and the caldera in Yellowstone National Park. They say it poses one of the greatest threats to the human species. Someday its fire will supposedly reawaken and devour most of North America. It's cheery stuff. You'd absolutely love it." Tripp passed me the magazine, tied on his apron, and walked back into the kitchen.

"Happy Cataclysm Day to us," I muttered.

"I'll take a Happy Easter."

"Happy Easter, Tripp."

"Thank you, David."

IN THE PARKING LOT I waved a cheeseburger in front of the cracked window. The Bernese didn't stir. Seeking some mode of universal communication, I took a bite, chewed loudly, breathed the cheeseburger air into the cab, rubbed my belly, and watched the dog slowly rise. I angled the rest of the burger through the gap. He was tentative, licking at the bun first. Finding no trick, he ate the burger in two bites as I pulled another one from the sack. Suddenly the poor, misbegotten ghost of a thing became a dog again.

He started to pant, giant slab of a tongue lolling out, body shimmying all over. "You seem highly evolved," I said, "but I don't think you can unlock this door. That means I'm going to have to shatter the window." The dog tipped his massive head thirty degrees. "I know. I don't condone destruction of property either." I shrugged. "But desperate times. This is going to be loud and messy. It could be scary. I'm going to need you to sit on the other side of the cab so you don't get hurt." I thought my explanation was direct and full, but the Bernese didn't move. "Okay, I get it. You're no dummy. Never do anything for free for a man holding a cheeseburger." I tossed the burger as best as I could across the cab and the Bernese followed it to the passenger's seat. "Good boy," I said. "Now stay."

I wrapped my jacket three times around my elbow and forearm and smashed the window. The dog started at the sprinkle of glass and then went to leap free. I held a hand up and raised another cheeseburger, and the dog sat up and watched me. "I've treated plenty of people for glass cuts. It's nasty business," I said. "I'm going to reach in here now. If you bite me, I'm eating the rest of your dinner."

It was like wrapping your arms around a sack of doorknobs. The dog should have weighed as much as a small man, but he was all loose fur and skin over bone. He had a prong collar on. A name tag hanging from it: DOG. "Jesus Christ," I whispered.

I lifted the animal over the broken glass and was about to set him down on the pavement but stopped and carried him across the parking lot and set him down beside my truck on the passenger side. I got down on one knee, and the animal licked my face and wagged his tail. Cautiously I undid the prong collar and pushed it into my pocket. I opened the passenger door, climbed inside, and slid all the way across the bench seat. I kept my hands out of the cheeseburger sack and waited. The Bernese jumped in beside me and settled down on the seat, snout atop paws. Then the real test. I leaned over the resting dog, watching the contour of its fur for bristling, and gently closed the door. Together we sat in the truck, watching it snow. The flakes had thickened into a heavy curtain. I was very tired and confused. For perhaps the first time ever, I wished this place was big enough for streetlights. I wanted to watch the end of winter spin through the soft yellow cones of light.

"You're right," I said to the dog after a few minutes. "We should leave one." I took a pad of paper from the glovebox and scribbled out a note.

My name is David Almerin Ames. I'm a doctor. The Bernese, who I'm thinking of calling Otto for reasons you need not know, is with me now. East Grand, Green Mountain Side. To be clear: This is a notice, not an invitation.

Otto followed me as I crossed the lot and left the note on the dash. I reached into my pocket and left the prong collar too. In the driver's seat the shards of glass would be frozen in the puddle of water by morning. Together Otto and I drove home.

It was well after ten when we got there, the night cold and dark with a howling wind slipping between the stars. Still I took the dog all around. We walked down the seventy-seven steps to the water, where I pointed and said, "East Grand Lake, Rowboat, America (be leery)." Otto bounded through the woods, scaled glacial erratics, and leapt over stumps. In the yard, I pointed at everything I could, saying, "Window, gable, shed, spring box, woodpile, shitter." At the ledge I introduced him to Cricket and stood in the starlight and swept my arm in a giant circle over it all. "Home," I said, and he wagged his tail. The snow had thinned to a fine icy mist, and winter felt very alive. I pointed up to the sky and said, "Venus, Saturn, Gemini, Orion."

Inside I set up a big bowl of water to wash down the cheeseburgers and showed Otto how to start a fire. Then we climbed the stairs into the loft. I wanted to read more Virginia Woolf but was exhausted. The glow of the fire was rising up from below, while from above the full moon cut down through the skylight, filling the cabin with white light. Climbing into the loft, I had the distinct feeling the stairs were multiplying. As I rose toward the moon, foot lifting over foot, hands pulling against the stair railing in desperate battle, I became convinced I would never reach my destination.

I feared for a moment that I was having a heart attack or a stroke, until my rational brain again dissolved and I continued to rise. I climbed on into the night, weary and gasping, with Otto and his great heart at my side. I climbed until I was sure I had left the world of East Grand far behind and had risen through the stars.

Otto bulldozed into the bed and wrapped his body around mine. After five minutes, I forced him onto a pile of blankets on the floor, fearing the long-term effects of a life together completely without boundaries. The howling wind kissed every corner of the house. Through the skylight I watched the shoulders of the swaying pines do their joyous and macabre winter dance. I was very tired, and the day had been strange and taxing and full of madness, but sleep would not come, so I went downstairs to write a note at the table.

The firelight cast eerie shadows all about the kitchen. Ash logs snapped, and warmth settled through the house in waves. Snow pelted the windows and softened the roof. The wind came around the walls in a loop, sharp and then flat. Surrounded by the peculiar music that exists only among the woods during a snowstorm, I listened for a river I knew was many miles away. For a moment I was sure I heard its trickle.

Not knowing who else to write my note to, I wrote to my mother.

Mom,

Wren called today to tell me about Lyman. I didn't know what to do with the news, so I started to walk. I walked until I hardly knew where I was. Then I encountered a strange man. With him, I felt oddly and powerfully in the presence of a great love. Have you ever met a person who you felt was more than one person? Do I sound insane? After we parted, I walked for hours in the cold. A thick fog engulfed me. A storm had come in. I realized if I continued to walk, I would freeze to death. So I came down from the mountain. I stole a dog. I cried for Lyman. I sang old songs you taught me as loudly as I could to the woods. None of my behavior today has been very rational or even feels very real, yet the day feels more real than so many others I have lived. I wonder if you know the feeling. The spring equinox just came. You'd tell me we're in a liminal time still, when the borders between worlds are thin and fuzzy. Maybe it's okay to be with the ghosts for a while. I'm trying not to be scared. I miss you. And I miss Dad. I'm coming home soon. You'll not see this note before I arrive. In fact you'll likely never see this note, but I know you are listening. There's no reason to fear. We're not so very far away from each other now.

Love David

Twenty-One

I WOKE JUST AFTER DAWN, thinking I heard my father's car coming up the road through the cedar trees. I could recall very little of the dream to which I had been lost, but coming up from sleep, the sensation was one of great joy. My father had never visited me in my adult life, and here he was in the yard. I had forgotten I was at East Grand. I had forgotten also that my father was dead. This happens more often than I like to admit. In most of North America there's real risk in looking like a complete loon if you admit these things, so you keep the voices and visitations to yourself. Instead we go to dreams, where we are all eternally together. All I could remember from the dream was my father saying, "We must go to the shore."

Being a fine opportunist, Otto had abandoned the floor in the night and snuggled his bulk under my arms. The snow had ended, and the cabin was very cold. There was nothing in the yard but golden cordwood drying in the soft blue light, a murder of crows mobbing in a tall pine. My father tried to talk to every living thing in its own language. If he had come up the road through the settling dawn, he'd be standing in the yard, cawing at the birds.

Five years ago I was stopped at a country store way out on Cape Breton when I became convinced I saw my father's truck. The vehicle was backed around in the parking lot at a terribly disjointed angle to all the other cars but sat as fully as possible under the largest shade tree. This was a key reveal when it came to my father, who refused to "properly" park between parking lines in parking lots, opting for whatever patch, side, or corner presented the most shade. He claimed he couldn't see the lines on the pavement, and when we pushed him for the truth, he would just shrug and say, "Can't see 'em. Too bright, I guess. Best go find a shady spot."

The truck was a beat-up GMC. Just like my father's truck, it was missing the passenger-side mirror and sported the same oxidized green-and-blue patina. My heart was hitting like a sledge, but the possibility of some strange and mystical reunion broke when I peeked inside. This truck had a floor. No truck my father ever owned had a true floor for very long. When the floor rusted out of his GMC, he drove it for a summer with no floor at all. When Cal Hayes finally threatened to arrest him for child endangerment, he went and hammered out the cedar strapping from a dozen lobster traps. He pinned the boards together and fitted them into the bottom of the truck. For the rest of his life we rode to school with our feet resting on boards that had once lived beneath the sea.

I have no idea what my father and I would talk about now. I'd like to hear about what boat he was building and for whom, and I imagine he'd be captivated by even the most banal of my patients. I suppose we'd probably share a meal together, something I miss awfully. I'm sure he'd be intrigued and pleased that each of his sons grew into a different professional iteration of himself. I've often wondered if we would have taken the courses we did, had he been with us longer. I think we would have. Simon was destined to keep building boats. Link was destined to lead people. And as the youngest, I was destined to watch and try to help those I could.

There are things I'd like to tell him: how Simon built a house up the river a ways, on a high hill, a simple place, and lives there happily with his wife; how Link is stationed in Afghanistan in a special forces outfit; how Galen lives in the area still and became an artist and works for Simon as a painter, and though he has burn scars from the crash along his neck and arm and doesn't speak much, most days he seems okay; how two years after my mother left the river, Grace sold her own house and convinced my mother to move back home. Together the two of them unboarded the windows and hooked up the water in the house my parents had built, and vowed to never again leave. And there the two of them remain, wild, strong, alive, and more or less happy in the woods, alone and not alone.

Obviously hungry, and possibly a critic of long reflections, Otto reared up on his hind legs and started slapping at every glass, plate, and appliance in the kitchen. His paws were the size of a bear's. The cheeseburgers, of which only three remained, had suffered an awful night out on the counter. I told Otto it was too early to bother Tripp for more, so we settled for coffee, bananas, oatmeal, and dates. I was delighted to find that the mess of eggs I'd left on the floor the day before had been cleaned up nicely during the night. Exuberant with my decision to get a dog, I told my father I loved him and watched the light coming up and listened to the coffee percolating.

I went outside to survey the storm and tend to Cricket. In the yard the sound of a car brought me back to reality. I had forgotten all about Wren and Harold.

"You're early," I said as my visitors exited an old burgundy Saab coupe caked in slush.

"He drives fast," Wren said, and hugged me. Harold was standing behind his mother with his head down, shuffling his feet. He'd grown a good three inches since I'd last seen him.

"Good practice," I said.

The boy looked up and beamed.

Otto came bounding out of the house, made two frantic and playful circles around Wren, leapt over a snowy puddle, and came to a skidding stop within inches of barreling through poor Harold.

"You got a dog," said Harold, laughing.

"Kind of."

"Kind of," said Wren. "What does that mean?"

I shrugged. "It means I suppose I did."

There wasn't much for luggage, but Wren launched into unloading the few bags on her own. She seemed like the Wren I knew, though there was

a tightness to her gestures and mannerisms, as if letting too much movement into her body might break her open. It took me a moment to realize
that what I was seeing was a great effort at concentration. Even the act of
reaching for the front door was executed with extreme attention, and I
tried to understand the great sadness that had engulfed her since she'd
received news of Lyman's death.

Harold's hair was long, spilling over his forehead and his ears, giving
him an unearned height. But he still had the wide, solid facial features of
his uncle and his grandfather.

"I'm sorry about your grandfather," I said.

"Thank you." Harold went on scratching Otto around the neck and
chin. "I guess. I mean, I'm sad because somebody died. But I'm not sad
the way I think I'm supposed to be, considering I lost a grandparent. Does
that make sense?"

Wren moved from the porch back to the car, where she grabbed one
last bag, an olive backpack I suspected was stuffed with about seven books.
She paused for a moment, the first break in her focus, and watched a string
of snow geese curve through the leaden clouds above the lake. Then she
turned away and was gone again, drifting like sand back into motion from
car to cabin.

"It does," I said to Harold.

"I barely knew him at all." Harold was looking off to the empty porch
where his mother had just stood.

"You must be hungry," I said. "Come inside. Come get warm. Come
feel safe and loved. That's why I got the dog."

"Kind of got the dog," said Harold.

"You don't miss much."

"We've established that, Uncle David."

AFTER HAROLD AND WREN SETTLED in, we went into the remaining snow
to go sledding. The idea had been Harold's, and his argument, which was
entirely built around time and opportunity—*What else do we have to do*

right now? and *Come on, even Canada gets stingy with snow after Easter—*
was sound.

"I want to follow the river home," Harold said to me after a final pass
down the hill. We were walking back up into the hot sunlight. Above us, at
the precipice, Wren was standing with her hands on her stomach, staring
out at the pines.

"What do you mean?" I asked.

"It's pretty simple, really. You cross this lake back over the border.
Then you take the Mattawamkeag River west to the main stem of the Penobscot. Then you take the main stem all the way south to the bay." The
boy opened his jacket like some huckster about to deal me a fake Rolex.
He had an old state map neatly folded and tucked in his pocket. "I know
the way," he said. "I've already showed my mom."

Over the lake, a pair of eagles darted into the open, flying circles around
their nest pine. They were the first eagles I had seen since fall. I pointed to
the birds, and Harold looked up at them twisting under the clouds. What
Harold had said was completely true, and I was stunned I hadn't thought
of it myself. I had been following the Penobscot River out into the world
my entire life. Somehow, I'd never thought to follow it home.

"I really want to paddle it," Harold said. "The ice is probably out. But it
would be a really hard trip, and I'm worried about my mom. We can still
drive the route though, all the way there."

"Okay, Harold," I said. "I think that's a wonderful idea."

We were inside, hanging our wet clothes around the woodstove, when
I heard the suck of heavy tires on a slushy hill road. Harold had heard it
too. He paused with a pair of borrowed thermal underwear in his hand and
looked at me. I looked at Otto. Wren looked at me and smirked, sensing
a certain victory, I suppose. Thirty seconds later the sound materialized
in the form of Frances Hurdle's brown-and-white sheriff truck weaving
between the trees.

Frances's knock was not unkind, but I could tell she wasn't happy
about a fool's errand like this, having to drive out to the high side of the
lake on a cold afternoon near the end of winter.

"There are at least two advanced degrees in this room that I know of," she said after I let her in and she took stock of our little gathering. "It's good to see you, Wren," she added. "Been a while."

"Likewise, Frances," said Wren.

"So you're probably sharp enough to know why I'm here."

"Otto," I said and hung my head.

"Who?"

"The dog."

"Ding, ding, ding," said Frances. "I don't like to approach strange animals. I see this one doesn't have any collar on or identification of any kind, but the markings and his size match—"

"Sorry about that." Harold spoke up from the corner. I supposed I looked as shocked as Wren. Harold was an almost nauseatingly polite human being, and I couldn't remember him ever interrupting someone.

"What?" said Frances.

Harold cleared his throat. "I'm sorry he's not wearing a collar. We left in a rush, and I forgot it at home. I'm not usually so reckless."

"Who are you?"

"Harold."

"He's my son," said Wren.

"I see. Well it's good to meet you, Harold. Now what is it you're saying? Are you trying to tell me this is your dog?"

"I am telling you this is my dog, miss. So yes."

Harold made a clicking sound with his tongue, and Otto uncoiled from the floor and shambled over to the boy. He collapsed at Harold's feet and rolled belly-up for a scratch. For a moment Frances seemed more amused than angered, but as the implication of what the boy was saying sunk in, her face drew down into a hard, dark mask.

"Actually," Wren chimed in from the corner. "That's not exactly true. Otto is technically my dog."

"Harold, Wren," I said. "You don't have to do that."

"Nope." The voice came from behind Frances, and at first we all turned to her in confusion. Then it registered it was drifting in from outside. "It's not that they don't have to, it's that they better not try." The voice was my uncle Reggie's. We had not heard the second vehicle arrive during the showdown. My uncle walked into the house now with his arms raised. "Frances," he cried. Reggie had known the sheriff for close to thirty years. "You found him!"

"What is all this, Reggie?"

"You found my fucking dog." Reggie threw his arms around Otto's massive brown-and-white neck. Otto's panting grew thunderous. "That's what this is about. I've been looking for this guy everywhere."

"Your dog?" Frances lifted an eyebrow and looked at Wren.

"Wait." A second voice came from the porch. "I thought he was mine."

Roman Fitch was standing outside, a wool suit coat draped over his arm and a cigarette in his hand. He was doing all he could not to crack into laughter. It had been years since we'd seen each other, though we'd talked often over the years. He lived in Toronto now with his daughter, who was grown, and together they ran a large bank. I was not surprised Roman had eventually made it in the north and ascended into some position of power in the business world, but I was surprised anyone had ever convinced him to wear a suit.

Frances put her hands to her face and held them there for a good thirty seconds. I could practically calculate her weighing the ethics of returning the dog versus not while also doing the math on the work involved. Frances was a small-town sheriff and a Buddhist, a combination embodied by very few in this part of the world, and much to her credit she brought to her job an idea of justice that was more karmic than legal or punitive.

"The dog looks loved," she said.

"Smothered, even," I quipped, watching Harold and Reggie coo and chortle and stroke the beast with levels of attention and joy that essentially erased their fifty-year age gap. They had both become children.

"I'm going to go home now," Frances said. "I'm cold and I'm tired, and it's obvious you all have more important things to do than entertain or frustrate me. This is not me agreeing with what I've been told today, because unlike many here I value truth, but it is me willing to let things be, for now. The guy from Connecticut, he wanted to come out here with me. I told him to stay put."

"Thank you."

Frances moved to the door. "Oddly enough, he didn't really seem to care that much. My sense was that he wanted blood more than his dog back."

"The confounding beast that is man!" Reggie hollered from the pile of dog and raised and shook his hands.

"Don't push my patience," said Frances.

When Frances had left, I turned in shock to Reggie and Roman and hugged them both. "How?" I managed.

"I called them," answered Harold. "We should be together."

Wren turned to her son. "And who else did you call?" I could not tell if she was angry.

"Falon, Grace—I mean grandma—Uncle Galen, Link, Simon." Harold listed off the names as if they were just names, completely detached from history or context, old bitterness or old joys.

"Are they coming here too?" she asked.

"No," he said.

"But they've been called," Reggie said.

Harold said, "They've been called."

"Good boy," said Reggie.

"Should we go tonight then?" I asked. "Back to the bay."

"No," said Wren. "I need more time. In the morning."

"An Easter drive," Harold said.

"An Easter drive," Wren agreed. "We can see the grove in spring," she added. The grove was what we called the improbable patch of life that Molly Greenwind had started in the ashes of her fire. As her court case made headlines across the nation, several conservation groups banded together and purchased the mill site, then wildly growing into a returned forest. That alone seemed a great coup: How often in the history of our country had a mill site been sold off to become forest again? Then, a few years later, the site was returned to the Penobscot Nation, where it persists today as a medicine forest nurtured by the tribe.

"I don't know how to say this." Reggie cleared his throat and paused. He was looking at Wren. "It's been with me the whole drive up here, and I can't be with it the whole drive down to the funeral."

"Just say it then," said Wren.

"I hated him," Reggie said. "But I love you more. So I'm here."

Wren looked hurt, but she nodded.

"*Nətɑpi-nisóhsepənɑ*," Harold said, surprising us all with the phrase, which I could tell was Penobscot.

"Did Moses teach you that?" I asked.

Harold shook his head. "Molly, actually. By way of Uncle Galen."

"What do you mean?" said Wren.

"Uncle Galen said she whispered it in his ear when she and her dad carried him out of the woods that day—"

"When one father died," I interrupted, and then saw Wren trying to hide that she was crying. "And another may have too," I added, coming back from the edge of anger.

Harold nodded.

Wren wiped at her eyes. "What does it mean?" she asked.

"We return together."

WE COOKED AND ATE AN afternoon meal of skillet cornbread and chipotle-seasoned rice and beans with a winter squash and cheddar frittata. Then Reggie and Roman went outside and began stacking wood and cardboard for a fire. Other things would wait. The dishes could be done when we returned from our journey, which would begin in the morning. I wondered if I should take Otto. I wondered if Frances would look in on Cricket. I wondered if she would look in on both Cricket and Otto. I wondered how much was pushing it.

Outside Reggie had the fire started. The blaze was six feet high and cutting a strong orange cone into the darkening sky.

"I brought marshmallows," Roman said. "Graham crackers. Shit like that."

We all pushed back from the table and made our way out to the fire. It was still light, though not much day remained. In the corner of the yard, Harold sat on an Adirondack chair with Otto lying on top of his feet, undeterred by the cold, snowy ground. The boy spread his maps out on the Bernese's back and leaned in to study the routes in the twilight.

"Do you think you'll ever go?" Wren asked at my side. We were in separate chairs, but under the same wool blanket. She was looking at Harold looking at his maps. "To the bay."

I shrugged. For the first time in a long time, I wasn't sure. I'd been here a long time. This place, East Grand, felt permanent, eternal. But my work, the clinic downeast, it could have been nearing an end. There was never enough help, never enough money, and lately rarely enough patients. The caregiver's dilemma persisted, of course—How do I leave my patients, few as they may be?—and its near enemy as well—How do I learn to live without being desperately needed? But starting over in the bay, there was that chance.

I told Wren the truth. "I honestly don't know."

I thought of my yearly trips down to clear the brush around the ghost apple tree on the bluff. How I would pull into the yard, and my mother would come out of the house in an old field coat with a green thermos of sun tea and a bright orange cap on, no matter the time of year. Grace, who was usually off visiting her clients, was never at the house when I arrived, but she was there when we returned from our work. Food was often cooking. My mother hugged me. Never asked too many questions. Then we made the trek through the woods to the bluff with the clippers and shears and scythe and started the delicate work of clearing brush and cutting and trimming and knocking back the long grass. My mother would help for a while and then wander off to the tree, where she would sit with her back against its base, still the only one after all these years to ever touch it, and stare out at the ocean. Sometimes she cried. Sometimes she swore. Sometimes she was silent. When we were done with the work, she'd press her hands against the bark and whisper goodbye before we walked home. I understood the truth now. Like Sanoba, my father was the man of flight and flames, a victim of the violence and the aggression and the insecurity of a certain male world stalked by shadows and old hurts, all brilliant color and terrible darkness, pride and hubris and wonder and love and heartache, forever doomed to be taken by the sea. My mother was the ghost apple tree, strong and ever-present, no matter how much quiet pain she carried. And I was one of the children, the boy still searching.

"The ghost apples," I said then to Wren. "Have I ever told you the story of the tree?"

"No," she said, "I don't believe you have."

"All these years." I shook my head. "That seems almost impossible."

Wren reached across the space between us, took my hand in hers. "It's surely criminal, David." I turned to her with the same wonder that had always been there, knowing that through the years, Wren had lived the stories right alongside me in her own way.

"Soon," I said. "We have a long drive still."

Roman was in the yard, staring out at the hills. Reggie was on the porch. Harold was lost in his maps. Otto was snoring. It was just Wren and me, and while I realized how much I had missed her company in my life, I had really missed the company of them all.

"He was a good father," Wren said.

"I know."

Harold rose and put another branch on the fire and went back to his chair. I could not hate Lyman when I was a boy, and I could not hate him now. They were both gone now, my father and the man who had taken my father's body from the world, and in every glimpse of every old green truck, and in every sauntering fisherman, and in every black bird passing overhead, I look up and remember them both. No, that's not true. I look up and snap around, expecting to find them beside me.

"There's so much I still want to know," I said.

"About my dad or yours?" Wren asked.

"About both of them."

"Me too." After a long pause, Wren said, "In a different life, I think they would have been friends."

According to Wren, we can only account for about seven percent of all the matter in the known universe. What this means is that you'd be a fool to believe that what you can see, feel, and comprehend is more important than what you cannot. Probability would dictate that what exists in the other ninety-three percent of matter may hold great importance. So the perplexing truth is that there are quite possibly other worlds playing out that we can't see or even begin to comprehend. It's not just that our fathers might be living different lives in some different dimension, but that different concepts of father and of friend and of enemy may exist, or not exist at all.

"There were"—I paused, looking for the right word. "Similarities."

I could barely see Wren beside me. It was nearly dark.

"I think it's time," I said.

"Time for what?"

"To go to the lake shore."

Harold looked up from his maps. "Why?"

"I don't really know. It was in a dream."

Roman looked back from the horizon and nodded. Reggie stepped down into the yard and shrugged. I could see Wren doing the math in her head, looking for the logic, tapping into cosmic equations to calculate the likelihood that walking down seventy-seven steps together in the freezing near dark on Easter Eve would matter or make any difference to anything. "Fuck it," she finally said. "Maybe the adventurer isn't supposed to understand the adventure."

On the wind, the pines were fresh. A soft rot was there too. The new snow was melting. Easter would bring a return to fertile ground. I could see the buds beginning on the trees, and I closed my eyes and followed those buds down into their stems, forcing my consciousness through each branch, funneling into the warm trunk, falling down through the roots into dirt that was frigid at its surface yet warmed with each descending inch. From there it was just a matter of imagination, of flight, to travel from root to root through the earth, marking the world, hearing the bodies of insects shift and awaken, diverting my trek around bedrock, pushing up through damp earth into the vernal pools where life would again emerge. If I paid enough attention, I was convinced, the earth could carry us all home where the ghost apples waited.

In the morning we would leave, while the world here went on opening without us. Across the lake the sun was sinking beneath the western hills. A vane of red spread across the sky, and I gasped.

"What is it?" Harold asked.

"That sunset," I said. The red line of the horizon was the same shade as the odd card the stranger had given me the day before.

"It's gorgeous," said Wren.

I reached into my pocket and traced the cardboard edges of the Minotaur card. It truly was. I looked at Wren and Roman and Reggie. I looked at Harold and Otto. Squeezed on the shore, our bodies seemed to form a strange mosaic. I heard the call of a newly returned loon. The wind spoke up and down the trees. The stars were waiting to emerge. To the west, out over the long indigo lake, we could see into America. To the east, where twilight mottled the vast conifer-swept valleys, we could see into the heart of Canada. We could see north and south as well. I had the great sensation that together we could see anywhere.

No one spoke. At my feet the still water reflected the dimming sky, and I was taken back to a day with my father when I was a child. I am eleven years old, and we are standing on the banks of our Little River. The water holds a perfect reflection of the sky. I can see white clouds, blue light, rust-colored branches, golden leaves, my father, myself. It is October, just weeks before my father's birthday, and on the ride home from school I have been watching the whorls of color blend in the trees while trying to think up a suitable gift. My father has been eerily silent on the drive. Now at the river he holds up a long and narrow bedroom mirror he removed from the back of a closet door and carried down to the water earlier in the day. I can tell he has been waiting all afternoon to show me this. His movements are incredibly precise, yet I see the nerves harrowing his face. He wants this to work. He wants me to be impressed. He turns the mirror so it is facing down, lifts it as high in the air as he can, and then extends it out over the river like a plank. He tells me to scoot under it and look up at the glass. Suddenly the water is a mirror of the sky, and the mirror is a mirror of the water-sky. But the magic is only beginning. Between glass and water, between mirror and mirror, the reflections multiply. Cloud and sky and tree and my father and myself nest inside one another endlessly. My father tells me this is an infinity mirror, and I can hardly breathe with wonder. My father tells me the reflection will go on forever.

Acknowledgments

Little we do is done alone. Writing a novel is no different.

First, I'd like to thank my wife, Heather, for her love, her support, and her intelligence. Through the years, no one read this book with greater heart or insight, and this book, much like my life, is so much stronger because of your presence.

To my daughter, Aloma, thank you for your miraculous ability to deepen my world each day. There's nothing as special to me as being your dad. And there's perhaps no greater gift to a writer than becoming a parent.

The author Linda Hogan wrote, "Walking. I am listening to a deeper way. Suddenly all my ancestors are behind me. Be still, they say. Watch and listen. You are the result of the love of thousands." To my ancestors, thank you for that love, for the ways you made a path before me, and for the ways you have stayed with me, bringing strength, belief, and stories.

Thank you to my agent, Jonah Straus, for your unwavering faith in this novel. Your attention, insight, and feedback strengthened this work with every revision. And thank you to Alec McDonald, as well, for the many hours spent working on this novel.

Thank you to Gail Winston at HarperCollins for being such a tremendous editor and advocate. And many thanks to Doug Jones, Alicia Tan,

Kyle O'Brien, Milan Bozic, and the rest of the wonderful team at Harper-Collins who worked so hard on this book.

For their help with certain elements of the book, I'd like to thank Gabe Paul of the Penobscot Nation and Conor Quinn of the Department of Linguistics at the University of Southern Maine for their generous assistance in helping me better understand the Penobscot language; Randall Williams, who patiently helped me understand all things aviation-related; and Donald Soctomah of the Passamaquoddy tribe. I'd also like to thank the Iowa Writers' Workshop and the MacDowell Colony for the gifts of space, time, and funding. And Kelsey Sullivan for his generosity in letting me occasionally escape to his cabin at Stone Meadow.

Thank you to my teachers and mentors: Marilynne Robinson, Michelle Huneven, Lan Samantha Chang, Alexander Chee, and Kevin Brockmeier. And especially to Dog Wallace and Ellen McQuiston, who changed my world many years ago at a tiny college in Waterville, Maine, by showing me just how powerful writing could be.

Thank you to Bryan Castille, Ashley Davidson, and Christa Fraser for being such amazing readers of my work through the years, and even better friends. To Gary Polhemus and Amos Hausman-Rogers, for the music, the joy, and the faith in continuing to create. And to Mark Brandhorst and Sarah Shepley for always feeling like home. Your friendship helped keep many seeds of this story alive for many years.

To my sister, Jennifer Brown, thank you for being there through it all, from our little years to the not-so-little years. Thank you to Sue Newton, Susan Hooper, and David Stark for bringing your wisdom, humor, and love into my life. Finally, I'd like to thank my parents for teaching me when to be patient and when to fight, two unsung traits in life and novel writing, and for the steady love that never ends.

About the Author

GREGORY BROWN grew up along Penobscot Bay. A graduate of the Iowa Writers' Workshop, he is the recipient of scholarships and fellowships from MacDowell and the Bread Loaf Writers' Conference. He lives in Maine with his family. *The Lowering Days* is his first novel.